Hide and SEEK

INTERNATIONAL BESTSELLING AUTHOR
NICOLE S. GOODIN

HIDE AND SEEK

NICOLE S. GOODIN

Hide and Seek (second edition)
Published by Nicole S. Goodin

ISBN: 978-0-473-58777-2

First published March 2018
Cover design by Nicole Goodin
Images purchased from Deposit Photos
Editing by Spell Bound

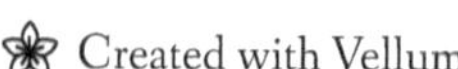 Created with Vellum

I would like to dedicate this book to Chloe Walsh.

For those of you who haven't heard of Chloe, she is an amazing, kind, generous Irish soul. She is a wife, a mother and a valued friend. She is also an incredibly talented author.

She is the author who inspired me to write in the first place and continues to inspire me to write with every book she releases. She is the first author I ever felt the need to 'stalk' on Facebook, the only author whose book I would buy without even having read the blurb and the author I always recommend when someone asks for a new read.

Chloe, thank you for being an inspiration, a role model and a friend.

FOREWORD

This book has been written using UK English and may contain euphemisms and slang words that form part of the New Zealand spoken word.
Please remember that the words are not misspelled. They are slang terms and form part of everyday, New Zealand vernacular.
I.e: I'm from New Zealand and sometimes we say weird things down here... please try and be cool about it.

CHAPTER 1

Hannah
Present day

I *STILL* COULDN'T GET over how god damn hot
the guy was.

He was the only man that had ever set a fire in
my belly like the one that was raging within me right
now. He wasn't what you'd describe as traditionally
'handsome', instead, he was a package of intense, raw
masculinity.

I was sure he could have been the classic, clean-
cut, beautiful boy-next-door type if he'd wanted to be,
but he'd kissed that vision goodbye when he'd
covered his body in ink and grew hair in all the right
places.

Watching him, up there on that stage... it was

everything I had ever fantasised about.

I'd dreamed, for longer than I could even remember, about bagging myself a celebrity.

I was *obsessed*.

Fame, fortune, status... it had been everything to me.

I couldn't explain why I'd cared so much about all that shit in the past, or why I'd thought that that was what love was...

I couldn't have been more wrong.

I knew what real love was now.

I'd changed. *He'd* changed me.

It was ironic really, that I'd changed my priorities just in time to get everything I'd thought I ever wanted.

I had no idea what I really wanted...

Him.

I glanced over at him and my heart thumped at super speed in my chest.

God, he looks good.

He was out there doing what he did best.

Correction... *second* best.

There was nothing Jasper Jones did better than make magic between the sheets.

Absolutely nothing.

The man was skilled like nothing I'd ever encountered.

I sighed as he strummed the guitar in his hands and sang into the mic.

Heaven.

Some crass bitch in the front row screamed out something about wanting to bang my man, and I cringed.

I had to give myself a pep talk to stop from going down there and kicking her ass.

That was the worst bit about this. He was public property now. *Everyone* wanted a piece of him these days.

I loved him long before he'd become 'big time' famous, and I still loved him now, undeniably so, but it was a difficult pill to swallow.

It was my own fault I'd decided, a karma of sorts – he was still exactly the same as he'd always been and I knew he'd never change, but our life... it wasn't the same. Now I had to share him with the whole world.

I'd never been particularly good at sharing – but for him it was worth it.

He caught my eye as he swapped guitars and I blew him a kiss.

He pretended to catch it and blew one back, a cheeky grin on his face.

Oh yeah, so worth it.

Now all I needed to do was get over the lingering terror that was always present in the back of my brain.

That one where I'd wake up one day and it would all be over.

That he'll leave me.

That was the only thing in life I truly feared.

CHAPTER 2

Jasper

"JESUS, man, do you ever get used to this?" I panted as I swigged back a bottle of ice cold water.

I couldn't ever imagine this shit feeling normal.

Nothing about this was 'normal'.

I don't know why I was still so surprised by my new life. I'd watched Parker live like this for years; I'd witnessed firsthand the screaming fans, the shameless women, the relentless hounding from the media... I'd seen it all.

But it's different when it's you.

This was my new normal.

"Nah, J. Not even a little bit," Parker answered honestly as he wiped the sweat off his brow before throwing the towel into the basket in the corner of our dressing room. "Don't get me wrong, I owe a lot to this life, and it's not all bad – but sometimes it'd just be nice to live like a normal dude, ya know? That's what I want one day... but for now, I'm just gonna ride the wave until it ends. You in?"

I was all in.

I nodded and grinned at him. "Hell yeah, wingmen, right?"

He reached his fist out to bump with mine.

That was the best bit about this gig we had going —we had each other. There was no way I would have been able to do this on my own.

I wouldn't have wanted to either. I loved to sing, play guitar too, but I was no solo artist. That stage gave me a thrill that pushed my limits completely, but I had no desire to experience it alone.

It was probably why I'd never pursued a career in music until now.

I knew some people thought I was riding on Parker's coattails, since he had been the biggest thing in music for such a long time... but we both knew they were wrong.

We deserved to have the success we did. *Our* songs were good, *our* voices blended flawlessly... sure, having the head start we did, due to Park being the world's hottest 'it boy' didn't hurt, but it was nothing short of hard work and a crazy fucking life that got us to the top – and kept us there thus far.

Coming clean about the fact that I had music flowing through my veins had been one of the best decisions I'd ever made. I couldn't even remember how I got by without it before.

"How do ya keep your head on straight?" I asked before taking another drink. I was still fairly new to this life, but Park, he was an old hand.

He chuckled darkly. "You know my head never used to be on straight."

That was for damn sure.

"But now..." He looked up at me. "Charlotte," he answered simply.

I should have known that's what he would say. Parker loved his wife something fierce. She kept his cocky ass grounded, made sure he didn't do anything stupid, and she loved him like nothing I'd ever seen.

Nothing... except Hannah.

She loves me like that too.

Right on cue, the door swung open and in they strolled, almost as though they'd been listening against the door – which I wouldn't have put past them.

"Legs," Parker breathed. "How's my beautiful wife?"

I barely even saw her. Charlotte was one of my best friends, but right now I only had eyes for the blonde that was hot on her heels.

"Well hey there, barbie girl," I whispered as she threw herself into my arms, her mouth welding to mine in an instant.

"Damn, you were *smokin'* out there," she

murmured when our lips broke apart. "Hottest rock star I've ever seen."

I chuckled at the familiar conversation. Something similar came out of Hannah's mouth after every show she saw me play – which was every show I did. Charlotte, Hannah, Parker and me, we were a package deal these days.

"You like that, huh?" I teased as I rolled my groin against her hip.

She let out the same breathy moan she always had – right from the very first time I'd touched her.

I could remember that moment as though it was only yesterday.

She nodded quickly, biting down on her lip.

I need to get her out of here.

It was somewhat of a ritual for us to sneak off after a show and sort out some of the pent-up excitement and energy.

Parker liked to run it out. I preferred mine and Hannah's method.

"That was a great show, guys," Lotte praised us. "I liked that arrangement you did for 'Someone New', it was really good."

"I'll tell you what I *didn't* like." Hannah pouted, and I cringed, already knowing where this was heading. "I *really* didn't like that nasty bimbo in the first row throwing her skanky-ass underwear in my man's face," she grumbled.

I held back a laugh, knowing it would do me no favours to get caught being amused at the fact.

Hannah had a lot of great qualities, but level headedness was not one of them.

Jealously, however, was something she possessed in spades. A woman so much as looked at me the wrong way in front of her, which they did, on almost a daily basis, and you could practically see my girl sharpening her claws.

I'd had to hire extra security to keep an eye on her during the shows and public appearances; she would have gotten into a fist fight by now if I hadn't.

That passionate fire inside her was just one of the bat-shit crazy qualities she possessed that I was mad about.

It probably made me sound like a jerk, but her possessive jealously turned me on.

Everything about this firecracker of a woman turned me on.

I knew that probably made me mentally unstable in some way, but I didn't give a shit. I *loved* her crazy.

Hannah Montgomery did it for me, Monday through Sunday – twenty-four-seven.

Every day was like I'd taken a double shot of wild with my coffee, and that was exactly how I liked it.

CHAPTER 3

Hannah

WE STEPPED off the plane and into the waiting, tinted-out SUV, and I breathed a sigh of relief.

It hadn't happened in about eight months, but I was always paranoid about the guys getting bombarded by some crazy-ass fans that had somehow managed to sneak through security.

The last ones had been their own special brand of nuts.

Absolute fruit loops.

And coming from me, that was really saying something; I was fairly wild myself... but I owned it, so I figured it didn't really count.

I was watching the raindrops sliding down the

car window when Jasper's hand gave my leg a gentle squeeze.

"You okay, babe?" His voice pulled me from my thoughts, raspy and seductive. It was like music to my ears even when he wasn't singing.

I turned to face him and gave him a wide smile.

His face broke out in a grin that matched mine and he reached for me, tucking me against his body.

He kissed the top of my head. "You remember my sister is coming today, right?"

I nodded quickly. I was so excited. I'd never met Gypsy, whose real name was actually Florence, because as her nickname suggested, she was a bit of a traveller. She'd been all over the world these past two and a half years, and this was the first time she and Jasper had been in the same place at the same time.

I was also nervous as hell. Gypsy was the only family that Jasper had anything to do with anymore. His dad raised him and his sister, well technically, they raised each other. Gypsy was eight years older than Jasper, and he told me that she was like a mother to him. His dad had disappeared when Jasper turned eighteen, and he had barely seen him since.

This woman's opinion mattered to me.

He kissed my forehead again.

"She'll love you," he reassured me, sensing my unspoken fears. "She already loves you."

"We've only spoken twice, and I was a loud mouth... you know how I get on the phone, and that second time I was a tiny bit drunk, so that never helps."

"Barbie, you were more than a tiny bit drunk. You were totally wasted. The two of you talked for a half hour about mushrooms and whether or not fairies actually lived amongst them like little villages."

"See," I agreed with him. "I told you I'm a loud mouth on the phone!"

"You're a loud mouth in real life too, just so you know," Parker added helpfully.

I flipped him off while Lotte watched on in amusement.

"But she owns it, so it's okay," she told him, a shit-eating grin on her face.

She was taking the piss out of me now too. I flipped her off as well.

"She might not like me. What if she doesn't like me? You didn't like me when you first met me... ugghhh she's gonna hate me," I whined. "Girls do not like me. Tell them, Lotte."

"Girls like you just fine," she argued.

Jasper cut in. "What the hell do you mean 'I didn't like you when I first met you'? Where the fuck did you get that from?" he demanded.

"It's fair enough," I carried on. "I *was* wearing the hooker dress."

"And the hooker heels," Lotte chimed in.

"*And* the hooker heels," I confirmed.

"Don't forget the three inches of my makeup you had caked on your face," she added with a grumble.

I regretted that one to this very day. I still wasn't allowed to play with her beauty products.

One bad call and you're banned for life.

"Alright, alright, the picture has been painted. I looked like a total hooker package."

Jasper chuckled.

"And I was obsessed with this mug over here." I gestured to Parker, shamelessly admitting that I'd gone there dressed like that, in some feeble attempt to appeal to a rock star.

Jasper clasped his chest. "You wound me, baby, my own woman after my best friend."

"Spare me the dramatics, you already knew that." I rolled my eyes.

He laughed again and grabbed my hand. He kissed the top of it.

"Doesn't bother me, I got the girl I wanted anyway."

"But that's the point, you didn't want me then. It wasn't until that night of the gig. I know you wanted me then."

He looked down at me in amusement, his eyes twinkling. "Oh, naïve, little Hannah... you wanna tell her, Park?" he asked, not breaking eye contact with me.

Parker launched into his story almost instantly, as though this was a perfectly choreographed routine they'd practised a hundred times.

"Now don't get me wrong, Han, I wasn't paying a shit tonne of attention for a while there... there were other things on my mind." He smirked down at Lotte, and she beamed back up at him.

Those two were so damn cute it made me want to puke most of the time.

"Now let me just think about it for a minute, it's been a few years since I was a crazy-as-shit guy in a club, carting a red head around and stealing a cell phone..."

Charlotte and I both had to laugh at that.

"But after we dropped you girls off – reluctantly, I might add, for the rest of the drive home, this guy right here," he tipped his head towards Jasper, "he just sat there, a stupid grin plastered on his face."

"You had one to match," Jasper added with a chuckle.

"I was going to get a date with my dream girl," Parker stated, his eyes bright with the memory.

"I knew you were," Jasper replied.

"Excuse me! I think you'll find that I told your stalking ass a great big 'NO'," Charlotte butted in.

That caused me, Park and J to burst into laughter and Lotte to pout.

We all knew she was screwed in the exact same way Parker was. They met by chance, but everything from there on out was fate.

"Anyway, I knew Park was going to get his date with the pretty girl, and that just left me to do what I do best."

"What's that?" I asked curiously.

"Wait patiently. I knew it wouldn't be long until I saw you again, and I knew I wouldn't be letting you walk away from me again once I did. I decided against stalking you and forcing myself on you," he tipped his head in Parker's direction, "not really my style... so I went with the patient method."

My heart swelled. "You really liked me when I looked like a hooker?"

"It wouldn't have mattered if you were wearing a rubbish bag. I saw *you*. I *still* see you."

The intensity in his voice caused my skin to break out in goosebumps.

I buried my face in his shoulder. "Thank you," I whispered.

He always saw me.

"You're forgetting there's one part of you that you can't hide under bad clothes and too much makeup."

I waited for him to explain.

"Those eyes." He stared into them as he spoke. "One look into your eyes and you had me, Hannah. I can see everything in those eyes of yours."

Oh melt...

I leaned forward and kissed his lips softly.

"Then you tried pulling that 'just one time' shit on me, and I knew I was going to have to wait again."

I let out a giggle. "Sorry."

"Don't be. Shit, I'd have waited forever if I had to."

―――――

Jasper had been right. I was freaking out for nothing.

She *loved* me.

Hell, *I* loved *her*. Gypsy was the coolest. I should have known, being related to Jasper that she would be super chilled and relaxed.

I was beginning to think there was nothing in the world that could rattle these two.

Prior to meeting Gypsy, I couldn't understand how a person could travel the world for years on end, never coming home... but now I did. She really was a gypsy; the road was her only home now.

She didn't own a house, or a car. Shit, she barely owned a bag full of clothes.

She had friends on every continent, and people all over the world that were willing to take her in at the drop of a hat.

She'd worked in every country doing just about everything there was to do.

When Jasper had gone to get some more beers, she'd whispered to me that she'd even tried her hand at dancing in a strip club. And while it made her a tonne of cash, it wasn't really 'her thing'.

It wasn't hard to see how she'd made a lot of money doing it. She was a stunning woman. Her long golden hair had small braids through it, and her pretty face housed the same hazel eyes as her brother. Her body was absolutely bangin' – she had curves in all the right places.

It wasn't even so much how she looked, but the way she carried herself. Gypsy had this vibe that drew you in. She was confident and carefree, and you could sense it, just from being in the same room as her.

I took lots of deep breaths around her and silently commanded my pores to absorb some of her awesomeness.

Jasper had caught me doing it and laughed when I'd explained.

Apparently in his mind, Gypsy and I were most similar in the way that we both possessed that 'quality'.

"Woman want to be you, men want to bang you."

I didn't agree with his assessment, but he never let me turn down a compliment these days.

"So... future sister-in-law, tell me how you two met," Gypsy pried.

"Yeah, baby, tell her about our first night together," Jasper taunted.

I poked him in the ribs and shushed him. There was no way I was giving his sister those juicy details, no matter how chilled she was.

I told her the condensed, PG version, but long after she'd left, I was still sitting there, smiling like a fool and thinking about the night that eventually changed my whole life.

CHAPTER 4

Jasper
Two and half years earlier

I'D NEVER SEEN a woman more intriguing.

My eyes tracked her as she followed along behind my crazy-ass best mate as he lugged the girl he'd had his eye on across the dancefloor.

Charlotte – the chick that had turned Parker into an absolute sociopath, had said she was waiting for her friend Hannah.

Hannah...

I tossed the name around in my brain before deciding I liked the sound of it.

To look at her now, she wasn't exactly what you'd describe as beautiful.

She had a shit load of makeup covering what I

was willing to bet was a seriously pretty face... and you couldn't exactly miss the fact that she was dressed like a stripper.

But that wasn't what I saw.

I saw the vulnerable look in her eye when she walked in the door.

I saw the fake confidence she was rocking.

I saw the uncertainty in the way she walked.

She wanted the world to think of her a particular way, when really, she was something else entirely underneath it all.

I didn't know for sure, obviously, but if someone were to make a bet, I would have gone all in.

Whoever she was – I wanted to know everything about her.

I'm going to find out more.

Parker was back over here now, making an ass of himself yet again, but I wasn't paying enough attention to hear what soul-destroying nonsense he was spouting this time.

This Charlotte chick could handle herself; that much was clear.

I chuckled at the thought of her shutting him down.

His ego could do with taking down a peg or two anyway.

Hannah stepped forward in what I guessed was an attempt to intervene in the fiasco that was happening before our eyes.

I leant in, catching her arm gently and spoke to her before she got the chance to move.

"I wouldn't just now."

She froze, and her eyes widened in shock as she slowly raked her gaze up my body until she got to my face. If I had to guess, I would say that she hadn't even noticed me standing right here.

She had been so focused on the little to-and-fro happening between Parker and her friend.

The absolute shell-shocked look on her face when she looked at Parker assured me that she was a fan of my main man.

Who the hell wasn't...

"He's not himself right now, and if there's one thing I know about rock stars, it's that they're unpredictable when they're trying to mate," I joked.

Her mouth dropped open.

"You're Hannah?" I asked her gently.

She nodded, dumbfounded, her mouth opening and shutting as she looked between me and Park.

She knows who I am too.

I gave myself an internal high five.

Lotte reached around blindly for Hannah's hand, but she was so busy looking into my eyes that she didn't even notice.

"I think you're being summoned... *Hannah*." Her name rolled off my tongue like honey and I knew I was going to have to find a way to make it happen again.

I didn't have to wait long.

"Hannah," I called to her. "I need you to come with me, okay?"

"Oh my god, this is *awesome*," she replied excitedly.

I had another word in mind for describing what had just gone down.

I could have kicked Parker's ass.

He'd apparently lost his mind and decided that it was a good idea to steal this Charlotte chick's phone... then come all the way back here to return it to her... and then finally, kiss the poor girl senseless in front of a tonne of photographers, fans and paparazzi...

So now I had a totally unnecessary drama to handle.

"Kelv!" I called to Parker's driver. "Get him the fuck out of here."

"On it." He shoved some idiot with a camera out of the way and tried to barge his way through to where Parker had Charlotte held hostage.

I looked back over at Hannah and suddenly she looked like she didn't think it was so awesome after all. She looked worried.

I grabbed her arm and pulled her flush against me. "I need you to trust me. Can you do that?"

Her eyes were wide again as she nodded.

I swept one of my arms under her knees and hoisted her off the ground, carrying her in my arms.

"Holy shit," she breathed.

"Tuck in close, Hannah, okay?"

She curled into me, one of her arms was wrapped around my neck and her other hand was pressed against my chest.

This might have been turning dangerous real friggin' quickly, but all I could think about in that moment was the feel of her hands on my body and the smell of her hair in my nose.

"Jasper! Who's the red head with Sloan?" some twat yelled out to me, destroying the little fantasy I was creating in my head.

"Her name is... oh what was it again? Oh that's right... FUCK OFF!" I hollered back as I shouldered my way through the mass of people that were gathering around, in an attempt to keep Hannah safe.

"Mr. Jones, can you comment on the girl?" Some pain-in-the-ass reporter appeared in front of me.

"Sure." I flipped her the bird. "And you can put that on record."

She sneered at me and I couldn't help but chuckle. I knew I wasn't exactly doing my job like a professional, but I was sick of this shit.

These assholes all needed to learn that there was a time and a place. Parker gave a shit load of interviews, he had a lot of time for fans, but this, right now, wasn't cool.

There were two innocent girls involved that probably knew nothing about this life and now they were being dragged right into the middle of the circus.

If something happened to the woman in my arms because my best friend happened to be a rock star, I was going to lose my shit good and proper and sue every last one of these bastards.

I need a bloody cigarette.

"Get out of the fuckin' way!" I roared.

There must have been an edge to my voice that let the men standing in my way know that I meant business because the path cleared enough that I could finally see the limo.

"Nearly there, baby," I murmured in Hannah's ear.

I hadn't meant to call her 'baby', the term of endearment had slipped out of my mouth without me even thinking.

I got the door open and slid her into the back seat without too much trouble.

"Don't open the door unless you hear my voice, okay? I sat her down on one of the bench seats. "You're safe in here, just wait for me to come back, alright?"

She nodded and looked up at me with her big green eyes.

I turned to climb out – Parker and Charlotte still weren't here, and I knew I was going to have to retrieve them myself.

"Jasper?" Hannah's hand landed on my forearm.

"Yeah?" I turned back to look at her and she gave me a dazzling smile.

"Thank you for taking care of me."

I swallowed the lump in my throat and nodded once at her.

One smile...

If I hadn't already been completely and utterly done for, I was now.

I took a deep breath as I got out of the car, my hands were shaking, and my heart was racing.

Maybe Parker isn't the only one who lost his mind tonight.

CHAPTER 5

Hannah
Two weeks later

WATCHING HIM INTRODUCE PARKER, the lights shining down on him, he looked like a star in his own right.

He also looked sexy as hell.

"I'm gonna get me a piece of that fine ass, if it's the last thing I do," I announced loudly.

I could see my best friend, Charlotte's, face out the corner of my eye, and even though she didn't say a word, I knew she didn't doubt me for a second.

I wanted Jasper Jones, and I was gonna get him.

I was practically drooling as I watched him stroll away back stage, all sex and swag.

It was fascinating to watch the man move. He

was the master of that body of his – he owned it completely.

God, he's something else.

I couldn't ever remember being this attracted to anyone in my whole life.

He wasn't what I would have classed as 'my type', but that was possibly because he wasn't the kind of man that could be confined within any boundaries or limitations.

He was indefinable.

Masculine, raw, primal...

The weirdest part of this attraction was that I really wasn't a beard kinda girl.

Not at all.

But oh dear lord, did he wear a beard well. He had some kind of sexy lumberjack thing happening that made my insides quiver.

And right now, he was rocking a man bun of all things...

What is happening to me?

Long hair was not a quality I looked for in a man. Short, dark hair was my thing, yet here I was, fantasising about a man with golden blond locks on the top of his head.

Just call me a convert.

I had a feeling Jasper could have been out in the jungle like Tarzan, wearing nothing but a loin cloth and swinging from a rope, and I'd still have wanted to jump his bones.

In fact, now that I'd thought of it, I was sure that

particular fantasy was going to have to be fulfilled one day soon.

If I get my way that is...

I knew I should have been watching Parker perform – I was obsessed with his music, and being side of stage at one of his shows was another fantasy all on its own... but instead I found myself distracted, trying to catch glimpses of the rock star's best friend.

I couldn't think straight when he was near; it was bringing a new meaning to the word obsessed... I was drawn to him in a way that defied logic.

I felt myself burn up as he caught my eye from where he was lurking backstage.

His hazel eyes stared into mine and he winked knowingly before finally turning away.

I stared after him. I could almost still feel his gaze on my skin.

Oh, this is going to be good.

There was something about that man that screamed sex, and I had every intention of finding out if it was an accurate representation.

CHAPTER 6

Jasper

PARKER SHOT me a look across the room and gestured to the stunning blonde woman who was tucked in close against my side.

I wasn't sure when we'd become attached at the hip, but hell, I certainly wasn't complaining.

I met his look with one of my own.

With that look, I took on responsibility for Hannah for the night. I knew his intention was that I would get her home safe and sound, and if it was the way she wanted it – then I would... but if she was willing, the only place she'd be going was back to my house.

He could depend on me to keep her safe either

way; there was no way in hell I was letting anything bad happen to her.

She's mine to protect now.

Parker would have trusted me with his life, but even if he didn't, it wasn't like he had a lot of options right now, from what I could see, he had his hands full with Charlotte. She was *wasted.*

I chuckled to myself as I watched her get hold of Sammy and stumble along towards the exit on his arm, Parker trailing behind, a giant grin plastered across his face.

My man's in love.

That woman was going to be good for him, I already knew it. She was his endgame – he just had to keep his life under control and not fuck it up for himself again.

Hannah looked up at me with her beautiful green eyes. "What's so funny?" she asked with a pretty smile.

"Your BFF over there." I pointed to where the happy couple was now being ushered out the door by a flustered-looking Sammy.

She giggled and rolled her eyes. "She's white-girl wasted."

I took the opportunity of having an outstretched arm to slip it in behind her back, I managed it with the same tact a teenage boy at his first movie date did.

Real smooth, Jones.

She had me so nervous I'd lost all chill.

She raised her brows at me and deliberately

turned herself towards me, wrapping one of her arms around my middle.

So that's how it's done.

I looked down at her, her lips in particular capturing my attention, her top teeth grazing ever so slightly over her bottom lip...

Shit...

"That sounds mildly racist," I murmured, as I desperately tried to keep my cool.

"I'm a white girl. *I* can say white-girl wasted."

Can't argue with that.

She could say anything she wanted with those soft pink lips for all I cared.

Preferably my name, over and over again...

I tugged her free hand into mine. "You wanna get out of here or what?"

"I was starting to think you'd never ask." She winked and turned on her heel, towing me along behind her.

I'm so done for.

CHAPTER 7

Hannah

IT WAS LIKE DÉJÀ VU. I was sitting next to Jasper in the back of a car, driven by someone I didn't know, going god knows where... and just the same as two weeks ago, I didn't give a shit. I was sitting next to *him* – that was all I cared about.

This time there was no Charlotte and Parker, and there was no one to slam on the brakes and put a halt to my fun.

Not this time.

His arm was draped over my shoulders, his fingers trailing lightly up and down my bare arm, sending shivers through me.

We hadn't spoken a word to one another since we got in the car, and if anything, the anticipation was building even quicker because of the silence between us.

There was something about the way he made eye contact with me, most people shied away from it, but not Jasper, he'd been looking at me with such a strong, wanting stare, it was making me weak in the knees.

I'd been dying to get him alone the entire night.

We hadn't even kissed yet and I couldn't wait to experience the feel of his lips on mine.

I rubbed one of my thighs against the other as I imagined just how good his mouth would feel on my body.

"Your thoughts are loud," he whispered in my ear.

His course beard lightly brushed against my ear and I shivered.

"What am I thinking about?" I breathed.

He growled and roughly grabbed me around my middle, hoisting me into his lap so I was straddling him. His hand moved to the back of my neck and dragged my face to his.

I gasped as his mouth crashed against mine.

It was so much better than I could've imagined.

My hands reached for his neck, and I held on for dear life as he kissed me like a man never had before.

I let out a breathy moan and it only seemed to spur him on further.

His hands were all over my body and my legs

were clamped tightly around him, holding him as close as I possibly could.

He sucked my bottom lip into his mouth and dragged it between his teeth.

"Jasper," I groaned as I fisted my hands in his hair.

He sucked in a heavy breath. "You are one frightening little woman."

I looked into his hazel eyes that were swimming with desire.

"Then you're the only one of us that's afraid, because you don't scare me," I whispered.

His eyes burned with intensity. "You *terrify* me," he confessed.

I was about to ask him why, or what he meant by that when I felt the car slow down.

"C'mon." He tugged on my hand and pulled me from the door before the car had even come to a complete halt.

"In a rush, Jones?" a voice called as he dragged me up the path.

"Night's a wasting, Rich," he called over his shoulder.

I glanced back and caught sight of the driver's amused face, he was halfway around the car, presumably on his way to open the door for us.

I gave him a thumbs up.

I was getting some tonight, and I didn't care who knew it.

———

"Nice place."

He winked at me and opened the fridge. "You wanna drink?" he called over his shoulder.

I slipped my jacket off and threw it over the back of the couch. My heels were the next thing to go.

"Hannah?" he called when I didn't answer.

I was undoing the button on my jeans when he spun around.

"Do you... ah..." he stuttered, his train of thought interrupted at the sight of me undressing in his living room. He shook his head to clear his thoughts. "Drink! Want a drink?"

I shook my head slowly, my eyes never leaving his as I slipped the straps of my white camisole down around my shoulders, it fell to my middle and then to the floor around my ankles.

He watched every deliberate movement with absolute focus, like he didn't want to miss a single thing.

I was standing before him in only a white lace strapless bra, and my black skinny jeans. There was no sexy way of getting those off, so for now this was it.

He sat the drink he was holding down on the kitchen counter and prowled towards me, tugging his shirt over his head as he went.

Holy shit.

The body the guy was rocking was freakin' incredible.

I didn't know what the hell his exercise regime consisted of – but whatever he was doing, it was working.

It was working damn well.

He was covered in brightly coloured tattoos, they adorned most of his chest and arms and they fascinated me already, with just one look.

His strong arms came around me and my nose filled with the raw scent of him, he smelt the way a man should.

I inhaled deeply, committing it to memory.

If I could have bottled that smell, I would have.

I couldn't remember reaching for his neck, but all of a sudden, my hands were fisted in his hair, tugging on the blond strands.

His mouth came down on mine with an urgency I mirrored.

I just couldn't get enough.

His tongue slipped into my mouth and I groaned.

If he was this good at kissing, I was going to explode from the pleasure he was bound to be able to give me.

"Bedroom?" he moaned in between kisses along my jaw.

"Hell yes."

I gripped his broad shoulders as he hoisted me up under my ass and carried me out of the kitchen and down the hallway, up the stairs and down another hallway.

I kissed his neck as he strode, carrying me as though I weighed nothing.

He stopped and threw open a door before moving into the room and kicking it shut behind him.

He lowered me down and dropped me on his bed with a soft thud.

He sauntered over and pulled the blind down, giving me a perfect view of the muscles in his back bunching and relaxing.

He turned around and smirked at me in a way that wasn't at all cocky, but instead secure and knowing.

I didn't know how he did it, but he moved so confidently, he was so sure of himself. It was one of the most attractive qualities I'd ever seen in a man.

"On a scale of one to ten, how hard is it gonna be to get those jeans off?"

I bit down on my lip, I was cursing myself for wearing the damn things.

"Eight."

"I can work with eight," he murmured as he reached for the zip I'd neglected to undo, "they make your ass look like an eleven, so I figure it's worth it."

I blushed and laughed nervously. "Hardly..."

Compliments were something I didn't deal well with, it was as though my mind rejected them instantly.

"Don't do that," he warned, his voice suddenly serious.

My eyes widened. "Do what?"

"Brush off praise. I can see it in your eyes that you don't believe what I said."

I shrugged, unsure what to say. No one had ever called me on it before now.

"If I say your ass is an eleven, then it's an eleven, you got it?"

I nodded, my heart filling with warmth.

"Say it."

I stared at him. "What?"

"Tell me your ass is an eleven."

I laughed, but the look in his eye told me he wasn't joking.

"I'm serious, baby, say it. Trust me, it'll feel good..."

This was stupid, and my ass was *not* an eleven out of ten, but I could see he wasn't going to back down, and if I had to guess, he was going to hold out on me until I said it too.

"My ass is an eleven," I whispered.

"Louder."

"My ass is an eleven," I replied with more volume.

"Louder," he insisted.

"My ass is an eleven!" I yelled as loud as I could.

He was right – It did feel good.

He grinned in triumph. "Calm down, you don't have to yell," he teased.

"You're impossible." I laughed.

"God, you're beautiful when you laugh." There was an intensity in his voice that took the air right out of my lungs. My laughter died off and goosebumps broke out on my skin.

He reached slowly for me and tugged my jeans down, shimmying them down my legs and off.

His eyes raked over my nearly naked body. "You know what they say about a girl wearing matching underwear, right?"

He began taking off his jeans as he spoke, and my attention was totally fixed on the way his big hands undid his belt and fly.

"Wh...what?" I stuttered.

He tugged his jeans off and stood before me in only a pair of dark grey boxer briefs.

I swallowed deeply as I took in the large bulge in the front.

"They say that if a woman has on matching underwear, then *she's* the one who decided to have sex." He moved up the bed, his body hovering over mine as he spoke.

I didn't know where to look, each eyeful I caught was better than the last.

"Mine match every day," I replied, my voice husky.

"Well, lucky me," he growled as he claimed my mouth again.

My head was swimming, my senses were totally overloaded by this man. I couldn't think of anything but him, I didn't *care* about anything but *him* in that moment.

I should have had a witty reply on hand to convey

the message that it didn't matter if I had on matching underwear every day or not, because he wouldn't be seeing them, but I couldn't get my brain to send the message to my mouth.

I *wanted* him, and I had a feeling that I was going to want him a hell of a lot more than just once.

"Jasper," I breathed.

"I've got you," he murmured as he trailed kisses down my neck and onto my breasts.

He dragged the cups of my bra down, exposing me to him.

He sucked one of my nipples into his mouth and I moaned loudly. "Oh god that feels good."

My legs wrapped around his hips, pulling him down against me.

He was so firm and lean; everything I touched was toned and tight.

His body was built to fuck, and I was going to give it a run for its money.

"Jesus, you're beautiful."

He ground his hips against mine and I let out a whimper.

His hand skimmed my belly, leaving behind a path of heat as he reached for my underwear.

He tugged them to the side and rubbed his thumb against my most sensitive spot.

My hips bucked up off the bed at the same time a groan escaped my lips.

He rolled off me so he could get better access.

I tugged his face down to mine and pressed my

lips against his. He swallowed my next moan as he pushed his fingers inside me.

I'd never been this close to the edge during foreplay before.

Jasper had me so wound up I couldn't even think straight.

I kissed him firm and fast as I ground myself against his hand shamelessly.

"Come for me," he whispered against my lips.

My whole body was tense as my orgasm built within me, I had his neck in a death grip, our faces only a fraction of an inch apart, our lips barely touching.

"Hannah," he breathed as his fingers pushed me over the edge.

I fell apart staring into his eyes, pleasure rolling over me in waves.

"Oh god.... Jasper, oh.... God," I moaned as he took every last bit from me.

I was so high on the euphoria within my body I could barely even remember where I was.

It wasn't until he slid off the bed and strolled over to the closet that I came back down to earth.

"Get back here, I want more."

He chuckled as he reached inside the door.

He came back with a box of condoms.

"The whole box?" I raised my brows at him.

He winked at me. "I haven't got anywhere to be."

"I like the way you think, Jasper Jones."

He took a deep breath, his eyes caressing my exposed body.

"Lose the underwear," he commanded.

"Right back at you."

I reached behind my back and undid the clasp on my bra, it came loose in my hands and I threw it to him.

He caught it with a smirk.

I slid the underwear down my legs and off my feet in the most seductive manner I could manage.

I threw those at him too.

He groaned. "Hell, woman, I'm not sure I can handle you."

"So, ditch the boxers and I'll see if I can handle *you*."

He did exactly as I asked.

Using both hands, he hooked his thumbs into the waistband of his boxer briefs and slid them down his thighs, his hard dick springing free.

Well shit.

I might have talked a big game, but now that I was looking that thing in the eye, I wasn't so sure.

He was so rock-hard it must have been painful.

He kicked the boxers off and reached for the condoms.

I watched his every move as he ripped open the foil packet and pinched the rubber between his fingers.

"You in a rush?"

"I need you, Hannah."

"I haven't even touched you yet."

"Unless you feel like seeing an early finale, you better keep those hands to yourself."

Well then...

Jasper made me feel powerful. He made me feel like I was enough.

I shoved those feelings down as I watched him roll on the condom.

I rolled onto my back and closed my eyes for a moment. I felt the bed dip and his weight pressing against my body.

His fingers linked with mine and he raised our joined hands up above my head.

His rough mouth kissed down my neck and along my shoulder blade.

"God, Hannah," he groaned.

His hands let go of mine, instead reaching for my hips.

He settled between my open legs, and I could feel the tip of him pressing against me.

"Please, Jasper," I begged, suddenly overcome with want all over again.

He lifted my hips and pushed inside.

"Oh holy shit," I breathed as he filled me.

He was hard as a rock, and it felt as though every part of me was being stretched to the limit.

He gave me no time to adjust before the relentless thrusting began.

I wrapped my legs around him and gripped his broad shoulders.

"Fuck... baby, fuck that's good," he choked out between thrusts.

When the man was right, he was right.

The way he rolled his hips when he pushed in deep had me squirming.

I could already feel another orgasm building... one touch in the right place and I'd be falling apart again.

Almost as if he could sense where I needed him, he shifted his weight and the most delicious pressure came down on my clit.

"Oh yes, like that," I cried.

"Hannah." My name falling from his lips was his only reply.

He pressed again, and I fell over the edge. Wave after wave of pleasure rolled through my whole body, from the top of my head to the tips of my toes.

Oh wow...

This was more than I could take, it was too much, my body couldn't cope.

His pace quickened for a few strokes before he tensed, his own orgasm tearing through him.

He moved slowly in and out of me, milking the last of both of our pleasure.

"Stop," I whimpered. "Jasper, god, stop... I can't take any more," I moaned.

He thrust once more before stilling and collapsing on top of me.

"Holy shit," he muttered. "I can literally see stars."

I laughed, and he lifted his head up to look at me.

He was so ruggedly gorgeous. His eyes were like windows to his soul. Warm hazel pools, swimming with emotion and expression.

He lightly brushed his lips against mine. "You're so beautiful," he told me again.

"That was, ummm... *wow*."

"It was incredible, Hannah. *You* are incredible." He was looking right into my eyes, his look so intense I nearly shuddered.

What is happening here?

He kissed me once more, causing my pulse to race yet again, before slipping out of me and lying down next to me.

His arm came around me and he tugged me into his side.

He covered us both with a blanket, not even worrying about the condom.

He kissed the top of my head, once, twice... three times.

He's so sweet.

He's perfect.

I tried to swallow deeply, my mouth suddenly dry.

This wasn't a one-night stand.

Not even close.

I'd had my fair share of one-night stands, but this was something different.

The way he was holding me... the connection we

shared... the intensity between us was something deeper than just sex.

It scared me.

I'd never been a girl that scared particularly easily, but I was scared now.

I'd been telling the truth earlier when I'd told him I wasn't afraid, but if he were to ask me that same question again now, I wouldn't be able to give the same answer.

I was developing feelings for him after only one time together.

That wasn't how I did things.

I didn't want a relationship, and I certainly didn't want to have feelings.

I'd decided a long time ago that I was single and on a mission.

I'd made myself a list of celebrities and I was going to bed one of them if it killed me.

This was the *fun* stage of my life and I didn't want to find myself tied down.

I ran my finger lightly over the ink on his arm and wracked my brain to try and figure out why all I could think of was him.

In an instant he'd replaced every other face in my fantasies.

His name had replaced every other on the list.

He's become my fantasy.

I didn't know what to do with that information. I couldn't process it.

My brain couldn't make the simple connection

that everything about him *was* fun. That I *was* living my fantasy right now… instead I was just getting a message that told me to panic.

I couldn't see that everything I'd ever wanted was staring right back at me. Instead, I just felt fear. Fear that it would all be ripped away from me if I let it in.

"I need to pee."

I rolled away from him and swung my legs over the side of the bed so I was sitting on the edge.

He leant up and placed a kiss to the bare skin on my lower back.

Seriously… so sweet.

"Toilet's through there," he murmured. I could feel his beard tickling me, and I liked it far more than was safe.

I turned my gaze in the direction he pointed. I tugged the sheet in an attempt to take it with me.

He chuckled and helped free it for me.

"Don't get shy on me now, Hannah, I've seen every inch of that gorgeous body."

I managed a flirty smile in an attempt to conceal my impending freak out.

I wrapped the white sheet around my body and slipped into the bathroom, closing the door behind me.

I ran the cold tap and splashed some water over my face.

What do I do?

I stared at my reflection in the mirror.

All the places he'd kissed me were slightly pink –
from the beard on his face, no doubt.

Much to my dismay, I liked it. I liked the way it
looked on me, as though he'd left his mark.

I'm so screwed.

I liked him.

I could feel the connection between us. I
would've had to be blind not to see it. It hummed like
a live wire. It was an intensity I'd never come face to
face with until now.

I'd shared chemistry with men before, but it was
nothing more than sex. I'd had feelings for boyfriends
before, but I'd never felt drawn to someone in
this way.

I sat down on the toilet and tried to take a few
deep breaths.

Calm the hell down.

I needed to think this through.

I've got options.

I could go back out there and ignore my fears, act
normal – well, as normal as I would ever be, and see
what happened next.

I could go out there and be honest with him, tell
him I was afraid, but that I liked him and wanted to
see him again.

Or I could bullshit my way out of there. Tell him
it was fun, but it wasn't going to happen again.

Just nip it in the bud.

That was my safest option. If I didn't get
involved, then I didn't get hurt.

Un-hurt me was my favourite me.

I stood up off the toilet.

You can do this, you can do this...

I chanted to myself internally.

Just don't look at his bangin' body or his gorgeous eyes and you'll be golden.

I opened the door, and the first thing I saw was that sexy body, sprawled out on the bed, a blanket low on his hips, barely covering him at all.

Shit. Step one: fail.

"Are you hungry?" he asked. He was doing something on his cell phone.

"Ummmm... I guess I could eat?"

"I'm ordering takeout. Come choose what you want."

"I'll eat anything."

I glanced around the room trying to figure out where my clothes had gone.

Ah crap.

Half of my stuff was up here; the other half was in the living room.

"The chicken chow mien is really good."

"Uh huh, whatever you think." I glanced around again and spotted a shirt of Jasper's lying on the ground.

I grabbed it and shrugged it on.

So much for making a quick exit.

Here I was with intentions to tell Jasper I was leaving, and now I was ordering food.

Shit, shit, shit.

I was so busy internally fretting that I didn't notice he'd put down the phone and was staring at me.

"Come here."

I froze.

"What for?" I squeaked.

"You're freaking out. So come here."

How does he know that?

"Come on."

Here goes nothing.

He patted the space next to him on the bed.

I sat.

His shirt was covering everything that needed to be covered, but I still felt totally exposed to him.

I could still feel where his fingers had touched me... where his mouth had been... I could still feel the weight of his body on mine.

"I'm fine," I lied. "I just, um, I just wanted to tell you that this was fun, and I had a really good time."

His eyes narrowed slightly as he studied me. "Are you brushing me off?"

Well hell. Straight to the point then.

"It's not like that, Jasper, it's just... you know, this is just a one-time thing..."

"A one-time thing," he deadpanned, disappointment flashing across his face.

"Yeah?" I shrugged. "That's what this is, right?"

He stared at me for a few beats, and I could have sworn he was deep inside me, flicking through my instruction manual.

"Sure, baby. One night."

"One *time*," I clarified.

He chuckled and shook his head. "Nuh uh. Now *that* I'm not agreeing to."

"You're holding me hostage for the night?" I giggled nervously.

"I'll tie you to the bed if I have to."

One night couldn't hurt, right?

Spending the night with him sounded a hell of a lot better than going home right now, alone and pissed off at myself.

I held my wrists out to him. "What are you tying me up with?"

He smirked, and my insides flipped.

One night definitely can't hurt.

CHAPTER 8

Jasper

WELL FUCK ME.

That was not how I was expecting that to go.

Well, the first hour or so was *exactly* how I was expecting that to go, but the ten minutes that followed... that could piss right off.

A one-time thing...

I ran my hand through my hair and groaned.

Is she serious?

How on earth I was supposed to do *that* with her and then go about my life as per usual, I had no idea.

My mind had felt like it was filled with fog ever since I'd driven her home earlier today.

I needed to get my head on straight before Parker

came home and caught me looking like someone had kicked my puppy.

I headed for his studio, making sure to set the feature on the alarm system that would let me know when he arrived home. I knew I was pushing the boundaries by singing and playing in his home. It's not that he would have cared about me using his stuff, but I didn't want him to know – and doing it right under his nose was probably looking for trouble.

I wasn't great at singing or playing like Parker was, but I loved it. I always had. Doing what Parker did – being a musician and sharing my music with the world had been something I'd dreamed about when I was younger.

When Park had got signed, I'd let the dream die away. I could have resented him, or turned into a jealous bastard, but that wasn't my style. I'd rather be happy for a friend and give up a dream rather than chase a dream that might never happen and not have my best mate in my life.

It had been the easiest choice I'd ever made.

So now I just played for myself.

I grabbed an acoustic guitar off the rack and strummed the strings, checking it was tuned.

A few slight tweaks of the tuning pegs and I was ready.

I took up my usual spot and plucked at the strings, the first few chords of Jason Mraz's 'I won't Give Up' filling the space around me. This room had some seriously good acoustics.

I was feeling this song hard right now, it reflected the way I felt – that Hannah was something that I wasn't about to give up on.

Keeping my voice low and raspy, I crooned the verse and then belted out the chorus.

I *would* be here patiently waiting. That was something I could do.

It wouldn't be easy, but I had seen the deliberation in her eyes and I knew that she wasn't convincing even herself with what she'd said.

If I had to guess, I would say she wanted me... and that scared her.

But I was a patient man. I could pass the time.

There was one thing I was one hundred percent certain about, even after only just one night; I already knew she was well worth the wait.

I strummed the final chord and sucked in a deep breath.

I'd totally lost myself in that song, so much so that I'd missed the notification on my cell phone to say that the gate at the front of Park's property had been opened.

"Shit," I muttered under my breath.

I hurriedly put the guitar back where I'd found it and jogged out of the studio, heading for the living room. I didn't have time to delete the recording that would have been made, but I knew that Parker wouldn't find it anyway. He only ever listened back to his recordings right after he made them.

"You here, J?" he yelled out from the front of the house.

I flicked the TV on and started channel surfing. "In here," I hollered back.

One look at Parker's mug and I knew he'd had a good night – well day, at least. I had to hope that he at least had enough self control not to have done anything more than fall asleep with Charlotte last night, given the state she'd been in.

"You're looking awfully pleased with yourself."

"That's because I am." He smirked.

"Your little lady can't be feeling so great... I'm surprised she's not still drunk now," I drawled.

I flicked through a few more channels as he opened the fridge.

He chuckled. "Nah... excessive vomiting works well like that. She was more than fine this morning."

I grimaced. "That's gross, man."

He laughed again. "I know. How fucked up is it that she literally threw up all over me and I still wouldn't have wanted to be anywhere else."

I chuckled and shook my head in mock disgust. "That's love, bro."

"Drink?" he asked, holding up a couple of cans of coke.

I lifted my chin in response.

"I took her home earlier... hung out for a bit... Hannah turned up still wearing last night's clothes."

"Huh," I mused, suddenly interested in what was happening on the TV.

"So, what did *you* get up to last night?" He sank down to the couch and tossed me the can.

I could feel his eyes on me, probing for answers.

"Oh, you know, a bit of this, a bit of that."

"That all?"

He knew exactly what I'd been up to. It was pretty bloody obvious. Park was no idiot, he knew I'd been keen on Hannah since that first night, and he'd seen for himself the chemistry between us last night. That, and the fact that he'd left me responsible for her when he'd left, coupled with him witnessing her arriving back home today, didn't leave much to the imagination.

I didn't answer.

"Sharing is caring, man." He smirked.

I glanced at him, my eyebrow raised. "You're not going to let this go, are you?"

"God no," he deadpanned, snagging the remote from my hand.

For someone who was always moaning about having no privacy in his own life, he sure as hell didn't seem to have a problem getting all up in my business.

"Hannah came home with me, mind-blowing sex ensued, we talked, more mind-blowing sex and then I drove her home earlier."

"Home, home?" He tilted his head in the direction of my place.

"Yup." I popped the p.

"And here you were telling me off for that not so long ago."

He was right. I never brought women home; it just wasn't a good idea.

I had plenty of money, thanks to Parker, so it wasn't like I couldn't afford a hotel room when one was required.

But Hannah was different.

I'd never expected to have her shut us down before we'd even got started, but even if I'd known in advance I still would have brought her home with me.

Hannah wasn't the kind of woman you took to a hotel.

I wanted her in my bed.

I wanted the vision of her in my bedroom.

I wanted her scent on my sheets.

"It's Hannah, Park... I might not know her that well yet, but she's your girl's best friend, she's going to be around either way, and besides, I trust her – I couldn't take her to some seedy hotel."

"Sounds like you two had a good night." He sipped from his can, still eyeballing me carefully.

"We did."

And then I got tapped and gapped.

"You seeing her again?"

"I'm sure I'll see her around."

"Oh burn... was she not into it?"

He was trying to goad me into running my mouth.

I shrugged. "We're friends, we had a fun night. Not all of us need to fall in love." I covered my nervous energy with a cocky smirk and stood up.

"I'm out. Later, man."

"Catch you tomorrow, lover boy," he called as I walked out the door.

———

"Hello?" her sweet voice answered.

"Hey... it's... ah, Jasper."

She giggled. "I know who it is."

"I didn't know if I was meant to call... or not." I winced at myself.

I needed to get my shit together and stop freaking out over this chick. Even if she meant what she said, and I never had her again, I was still going to be seeing plenty of her.

Our best friends were together now – possibly forever.

Hannah was going to be in my life whether she wanted to be or not.

"Jasper, we're friends, you can call anytime you want."

Friends...

"So, if I call you every night, you won't think I'm a stalker?"

"Oh no, I'll definitely think you're a stalker, but I'll answer anyway." She giggled.

Note to self. Call TWICE a day.

"So how was Parker when he got home?" She giggled.

"Like a pig in shit."

"Sounds about right. They were here when you dropped me off... I'm pretty sure they'd been bumping uglies, if you know what I mean."

I held back a laugh.

"I resent that. I can't speak for Charlotte's hoo-ha, but I'll have you know that Parker has a very nice penis."

I was messing with her, I mean, for all I knew, he did have a nice penis, but I hadn't exactly inspected it myself.

"You did not just say that."

I grinned. "We both heard it."

"And hoo-ha? What are you, twelve?"

"I've got other options, what do you prefer? V-jay-jay, schniny, pink taco, fan-dango, penis fly trap, meat curtains, cooch... any of these catching your fancy?"

"You're a bit of a weirdo, you know that, right?"

"I like to think so."

"Please don't let me hear you refer to it as 'meat curtains' ever again." She shuddered.

"Noted."

She laughed, and I took a moment to just listen to the sound.

"He noticed you were doing the walk of shame," I informed her.

"I'll have you know there was not one ounce of shame in my walk, thank you very much."

"I told him we'd spent the night together."

"I told Lotte too..."

"What else did you tell her?" I probed. I was digging for information as much as anything else. I didn't actually care what she'd shared with her best friend – that was up to her.

"Just that we'd decided to leave it as one night, and that we're friends."

We'd decided....

I almost laughed out loud at that.

She had decided, I'd just gone along with it, taking whatever I could get.

"Then we're all on the same page."

"We are."

"You busy?" I asked, hoping the answer would be no. I wasn't ready to let her go yet.

"Not even a little bit."

"You wanna play a game?"

"Strip poker doesn't really have the same effect over the phone, you know that, right?"

I chuckled. For someone who just wanted to be my friend, she sure wasn't against flirting.

"I was thinking more along the lines of turn for turn, but hell, there's always video chat..."

She giggled. "Alright, hit me with it, what's this turn for turn?"

"You ask me something, I answer, then it's my turn to ask you something – turn for turn."

"Oh, I'm so in... I've got *so* many questions."

I lay down on the couch and swung my feet up to get comfortable. I had a feeling I was going to be here a while.

————

"What pisses you off?"

I shrugged even though she couldn't see me. "Nothing really."

We'd been asking each other questions for the past hour, and I'd learnt a lot about this woman... I now knew her favourite food, what music she liked, how she preferred her eggs, her favourite sex position...

It was valuable stuff.

"Oh c'mon, there must be something that just gets you wound up," she insisted.

"I mean... trying to manage Parker's career isn't fantastic for my stress levels, but I wouldn't say it pisses me off."

"Nah, that's not what I mean... hang on, I'll just put you on speaker while I put on my PJ's."

My throat turned dry. I had the most perfect vision of her undressing and right now it was front and centre, taunting me.

"J? You still there?"

"Yip, sorry... yeah... I'm here."

"Good, so like seriously, I *need* to know."

"Why do I feel like if there *was* something, that you'd use it against me one day..."

She laughed. "I'm not willing to promise that wouldn't happen."

"Are we talking world peace situations or like leaving the toilet seat up kinda shit?"

"Hmmmm." She deliberated for a minute. "Toilet seat, I'm talking pet peeves here..."

"Okay then... nothing worth mentioning."

"Oh for fuck's sake, Jasper, you can't be laid back all the time; it's just ridiculous, there has to be something."

"You know what? You're right. You're actually doing a pretty good job of pissing me off right now."

I could have sworn I heard her rolling her eyes through the phone. "Oh. Ha. Ha. Ha," she replied sarcastically. "You're impossible."

"Yeah, I totally agree, out of the two of us, *I'm* the impossible one," I deadpanned.

She laughed, and I could hear her rustling around.

"You wanna know what pisses me off?"

"I'm gonna take a wild stab in the dark and say... me."

She giggled. "Well you might be infuriating, Jasper Jones, but at least we know you're not stupid."

We talked for hours and hours until the battery on my cell went flat.

I could talk to Hannah about anything, she was so easy to open up to, and everything that came out of her mouth fascinated me, even though it was complete nonsense half the time.

I was in a world of trouble here.

If she didn't wake up to the fact that we were great together, I was going to have to figure out a way to not think about her every five seconds.

I shook my head at my own stupidity.

There was no way I was forgetting about Hannah Montgomery anytime soon.

CHAPTER 9

Hannah

THANK GOD FOR PARKER SLOAN.

If it weren't for the fact that my best friend was so busy falling in love, Charlotte would have one hundred percent noticed how off my game I was.

I'd mucked up two colours this morning alone – one had turned out looking like a genius executive decision, the other just a flat-out royal fuck-up.

Could have been worse I guess.

My mind wasn't with me today.

It was with *him.*

In his bed, underneath his body, tangled up with him.

I couldn't think of anything but the way he felt... the way he smelt... how good he looked...

All I wanted to hear was his voice, up against my ear... through the phone... however I could get it.

I was so screwed.

This was not what I wanted to happen.

The intention was to get him out of my system and move on with my life.

That was not my reality right now. It was more like the one night of him all up in my business had hit some kind of reset button, or maybe the needy bitch button... because, shit, I couldn't remember ever feeling this needy where a man was concerned.

I wasn't stupid. I might have pretended I didn't catch his expression when I'd told him our night wouldn't be having a repeat session, but I saw it alright.

He looked how I felt.

He was good, I had to give him that, the disappointment was only on his face for a fraction of a second before he became the composed Jasper he seemed to be most of the time.

I knew I was being a flaky cow.

I wanted him. He wanted me.

It should have been simple.

There shouldn't have been a problem, but where I was concerned, there was *always* a problem. I was a problem magnet. Sure, I created ninety-nine percent of them all by myself, but still.

Nothing ever seemed to go smoothly or without incident when I was part of it.

This would be no different.

I knew I could have gone back for seconds, thirds or fourths maybe even... but I knew that one day, Jasper would wake up and want something I didn't have to give, and then it'd be all over and the only person hurt would be me.

As Julia Michaels would say, 'I got issues'.

I pulled up the messages he'd sent me earlier today.

To: Hannah
From: Jasper Jones
I found something that pisses me off...

Next message...

To: Hannah
From: Jasper Jones
Not seeing you for 2 days... that really grinds my gears.

I couldn't help the silly grin that spread across my face.

To: Jasper Jones
From: Hannah

Well you're in luck, double J, I've just been told we're all going out for dinner tonight. You in?

To: Hannah

From: Jasper Jones

'Double J'? that sounds like a bra size. And yeah, I'm in, if you're going, I'm going.

I laughed and slipped my phone back into my pocket.

I felt calmer instantly. Knowing that I was going to be seeing him in only a few hours was like a soothing balm for my nerves.

"So, let me get this straight..." I giggled again. "You got locked outside, stark naked... in front of about fifty or so paparazzi?"

"Essentially... yes."

"Oh my god, that's so good." I cackled. "How does that even happen?"

"Yeah, J, how does that even happen?" Parker chuckled as he took a sip of his beer.

"Just bad luck was all." Jasper smirked.

I had a feeling that there was more to this story, and I'd never been one to let things go, but my pending interrogation was halted by the sight of

Charlotte hurriedly rushing across the restaurant, a panicked look on her face.

Parker was out of his seat before I could even speak.

"What's wrong?" he demanded, reaching for her.

"I'm fine," she babbled. "Seriously, I'm fine."

He ushered her into her seat and she turned her gaze on me.

"So... you remember Bryce, right?"

Oh no... not again...

"My ex-boyfriend, Bryce?" I squeaked.

She nodded furiously. "Yeah... he's here."

This was not good news. Bryce and I hadn't been together long, but he'd made a fool out of me when we'd gone our separate ways. The guy was a womaniser, and I had an unfortunate habit of bumping into him and looking desperate and alone. He always had a new model on his arm, and he always made me feel like shit.

I relayed this information to Parker and Jasper in hushed tones, my eyes darting around, keeping an eye out for him.

He was a cocky bastard, and if he'd seen Charlotte, he would probably come looking to see if I was with her.

"Show me what he looks like," Jasper demanded.

Lotte pulled up his Facebook profile on her cell. "That's him."

He snorted. "I think we can handle him, right,

baby?" He looked down at me adoringly and wrapped his arm around me, tugging me in close.

"What are you doing?" I murmured.

He tipped my chin up using his thumb. "I'm finishing this losing streak you've been on."

He was staring at me with an intensity that made me shudder.

This wasn't for show in the slightest.

"Jasper," I whispered.

"I've got you, Hannah."

"I know you do."

I had a feeling Jasper would always have my back.

He lowered his lips to mine and I forgot all about Bryce. I forgot all about Parker and Charlotte watching us... I forgot that we were even out in public.

One of my hands found his bicep and gripped it tightly, the feel of his tense muscle only spurring me on.

His tongue slipped into my mouth and I could think of nothing but him.

"Hannah!" I heard Charlotte hiss.

I pulled back, only slightly, so our lips were an inch apart, our foreheads resting against each other.

Holy hell, what a kiss...

Someone kicked me under the table.

"What?" I breathed.

"Hey, Hannah."

I cringed.

Bryce.

I took a deep breath and pulled away from Jasper, looking to where I'd heard his voice.

"Bryce... hey."

He was dressed in his usual formal attire, I could have sworn the man wore a suit to the gym, and he also had his usual accessory – a wafer-thin model draped around his body.

"You look well."

Jasper took my hand and intertwined his fingers in mine. I could feel his gaze on my face; he hadn't even looked at Bryce once.

"Bryce, this is Jasper," I introduced them. "And you remember Charlotte... and you might recognise Parker Sloan?"

Bryce's jaw dropped for a fraction of a second at the mention of Parker's name.

I could feel Jasper burning holes into me with his eyes.

I met his gaze and goosebumps broke out on my skin.

Power, strength and intensity radiated from him and I would have been willing to bet that everyone else in the room could feel it too.

Jasper raised our joined hands to his lips and kissed my skin.

"This is Mindy," Bryce replied.

I didn't even glance her way; I couldn't pull myself away from the all-consuming look in Jasper's eyes.

"Hate to be rude," Jasper finally spoke, "but we're sort of in the middle of something here." He didn't take his eyes off me, but there was no mistaking that he was speaking to my ex-boyfriend.

Bryce mumbled something about having to get going too, and when I finally managed to pull my eyes from the hazel pools in front of me, he was already gone.

"Well that was intense." Lotte laughed. "You sure you weren't born to be an actor, J?"

Jasper chuckled, his hold still on my hand.

I tugged on it but he only gripped it tighter.

"In case he comes back." He smirked.

"Seriously, that was so deep it was hard to watch, that poor bastard didn't know what to do with himself." Parker chuckled.

I giggled nervously.

"I think you won that round, Han." Lotte held her hand out for a high five and I awkwardly gave her one with my left hand since Jasper still had my right held hostage.

What had just happened finally sunk in. I'd just had an encounter with the dreaded ex-boyfriend and felt absolutely zilch towards him.

"Oh god, that was like the perfect cliché moment." I laughed. "You're a talented fake boyfriend, J."

He leaned in and whispered in my ear. "I'll take the compliment, but there was *nothing* fake about that kiss."

I knew that too. That kiss was real.

———

I looked at the screen of my phone again and smiled.

To: Hannah
From: Jasper Jones
I had fun with you tonight, you ever want a fake boyfriend again, you let me know.

I so badly wanted to text back and tell him that what I really wanted was a real boyfriend.
Him.
But as per usual, when it came to things that actually mattered to my heart, I was too chicken-shit.

To: Jasper Jones
From: Hannah
You're the best fake boyfriend a girl could ask for. Thanks for being there for me... Goodnight J x

CHAPTER 10

Jasper

STILL IN THE god damn friend zone.

Unbelievable.

I was falling head over heels for the woman, and she was convinced she just wanted to be my friend.

There was no way I was buying what she was selling. She undressed me with her eyes every five seconds and her heart raced so often I was worried she was going to go into some kind of cardiac arrest.

She flirted with me over the phone and via text, every single day... but that didn't change the current situation.

I was still friend-zoned as hell and it was *killing* me.

Apart from kissing her in the restaurant, I hadn't touched her since that night.

It had been five days, twelve hours and about thirty-six minutes since I'd touched her the way I wanted to.

I'd been inside that woman for hours on end and here I was, about to spend the afternoon with her and I wasn't even allowed to hold her hand.

I didn't even know where the hell we were going. She'd come up with the ridiculous idea that we should take turns planning something 'fun' for us to do together... 'friends hang out' she'd said.

Today was her turn.

Fuck my life.

I was essentially dating the woman now, but I couldn't lay a finger on her.

I wasn't so much of an unreasonable bastard that I couldn't be happy about spending time with her, because I was, I was fucking ecstatic to be getting the chance to be in her company. But I was a guy, and she was the sexiest damn woman I'd ever laid eyes on – so naturally, it was a struggle.

I constantly had to remind myself to be patient, to bide my time.

I was getting her alone, and while she was with me, she wasn't with anyone else.

That was a win, albeit a small one, but still a win in my book.

I knew this dance couldn't go on forever – eventually I'd make her see that we were too good together to be apart.

I leant against the wall and waited for her to pick me up.

I wasn't thrilled with this part of the deal either, but she'd insisted, and if there was one thing I was quickly learning about Hannah, it was that you didn't often win an argument against her.

Woman was mad as hell.

My hands shook thinking about the effect she had on me. This wasn't something I was familiar with. Plenty of women had had an effect on me over the years, but it was nothing more than physical.

I craved Hannah's body like an addict did hard drugs, but judging by the fact that I was here, and had agreed to her stupid 'friend' bullshit, I was even more hooked on the kooky mind inside that pretty head of hers than I was with her bangin' body.

I reached into the back pocket of my jeans and pulled out the pack of cigarettes I kept in there for emergencies.

This was a motherfucking emergency if I ever had one.

I was freaking the hell out over this girl.

I was full of advice when it came to Park and his constant stream of fuck-ups with Charlotte, but I couldn't even ask him to return the favour. He thought Hannah and I were a one-night stand with no feelings involved – that's what we'd told both him and Charlotte.

Her idea – not mine.

My blood boiled as I thought about her as nothing more than a random fuck.

There's no god damn way.

If I'd known the words 'one-time thing' were going to come out of her mouth, I never would have brought her into my bed so soon.

I would have waited.

Courted her like a gentleman should.

I would have done us both the favour and done things the right way.

Now, one whiff of her perfume and it took every ounce of my self control not to rip her clothes off and take her hard and fast.

Fuck my life.

I lit the cigarette and took a drag.

I only allowed myself three puffs on the death stick before throwing it to the ground and stubbing it out with the heel of my boot.

I didn't get emotional often, but when I did, my calm mask always threatened to slip right off. Relaxed was a part of who I was – I was the composed one, Parker was the hot head.

I needed to get my shit under wraps.

A sure fire way to get my game face back was to stick a smoke between my lips. I was just a bad ass, little teenage punk without a care in the world when I had one of those things burning away into my lungs.

I was a pack-a-day kinda guy back in the day. I'd

given it up when my sister had bet me I couldn't, but every now and then I just needed the feel of one.

I had a feeling that I was going to smoke more of these fucking things than I had in the past eight years if this woman was going to be in my life.

Which she is.

And it'll be worth every damn one of them.

A loud honk startled me.

I looked up and muttered a string of curse words under my breath.

Oh hell no.

You have got to be kidding me.

I shook my head at her.

There's no fucking way.

She wound down her passenger window. "Jasper, what are you doing? Get in."

"Hell fuckin' no, woman." I crossed my arms over my chest. "You look like a god damn Barbie doll in there."

She rolled her eyes from where she sat in her hot-pink VW beetle.

She has got to be shittin' me.

"Get in, douche bag."

"That looks like something a kid gets in a happy meal."

"What's the matter, Jones? Worried someone will take the piss out of you?" she taunted me.

I sized the thing up. "I'm worried about a lot of things... I won't even fit in that car."

"Only one way to find out. C'mon, in you come..." She patted the passenger seat encouragingly.

Nuh uh.

I didn't move an inch.

There was no way in hell I was getting into that car.

I might have been the most laid-back bastard I knew, but even I had my limits.

"Nope."

She sighed and climbed out of the car.

Oh shit.

I backed up, as though having a foot more space was going to protect me from her charms.

The woman was cunning. She knew exactly the kind of power she was wielding.

"Jasper," she cooed as she rounded the hood of the 'car'. "Please?"

Shit, shit, shit.

She was standing in front of me now and I didn't know where the fuck we were going, but I would have followed her just about anywhere in those skin-tight black jeans.

I groaned.

Literally.

Out loud.

They were the same jeans she was wearing *that* night and I couldn't help the visual I had of me peeling them from her body.

She looked me up and down like I was a lollipop

she wanted a taste of, and I realised I was fighting a losing battle.

"I *need* you to get in the car, Jasper." Her soft pink lips caressed my name and I just about gave in right there and then.

Stay tough, man, you're stronger than this.

"That seat's saved for Ken," I murmured as she tucked a strand of blonde hair behind her ear.

Now I could see her bare neck and, Jesus... the things I wanted to do to that neck.

Kiss that sweet spot below her jaw...

Nibble on her ear...

"You're going to get in the car, J... you know it..." She took another step towards me. "I know it... we *all* know it, Jasper Jones."

She was right in front of me now. She slowly slipped her hand around mine and leaned forward to whisper in my ear. "I *want* you in my car, Jasper."

Shit.

———

She looked over at me and laughed as she weaved through traffic.

"Oh c'mon, it's not *that* bad."

"If you say so, barbie."

I chuckled at the evil eye she gave me. That was the only positive to come from this little excursion so far. Hannah had earnt herself a new nickname.

She was putting on a show of hating it, but if I had to bet, I'd say she liked the idea of a pet name.

She was my barbie now.

"So, where we headed, BG?"

She looked at me out the corner of her eye.

Ask... c'mon... you know you want to...

I waited for it.

"Alright, I'll bite... what's 'BG' mean?" she finally asked.

I smirked at her and let her stew for a few moments.

She raised her brows.

"Barbie girl." I chuckled.

She flipped me the bird, but I didn't miss the smile curving up the corners of her mouth.

I glanced out the window again. "Seriously though, where are you taking me?"

She'd driven us right out of town; we were on the very outskirts now.

I'd been out here to play paintball with a few mates a while back, there were all kinds of BMX tracks and a few swimming holes in the river, but I couldn't think of anything out here that Hannah would deem a good time.

"We're just going for a ride," she answered vaguely.

"Alright then." I attempted to sit my feet up on her dash but failed miserably, because, as predicted, a guy my height just didn't fit in a car like this.

I look like a freakin' clown.

Her laugh rang out through the enclosed space and the magical sound took my mind off our mystery destination for long enough that I didn't notice we'd finally pulled over.

She pointed out the windscreen at a motocross track. "You see that?" A bike flew over a jump and down into a valley as she asked.

Excitement thrummed through my veins. I was an adrenaline junkie. I'd seen magazines publish articles stating that it was Parker that had petrol in his veins, but in reality, he was just along for the ride ninety percent of the time.

I was the real addict.

I sat forward in anticipation. "Yeah, I see that alright."

Surely we're not here for this?

She grinned like a loon. "Well then, let's go for a little ride, Ken."

———

"I'm running the risk of sounding like a real prick right now, but do you know how to handle one of those things?" I gestured to the bike that came flying into the open area in front of us before screeching to a stop.

"Oh, sweet, innocent, little Jasper." She shook her head with a grin. "You're in for a treat, my friend."

She strolled away from me, her walk all sass and

attitude... those friggin' jeans clinging to her ass like a second skin.

God damn.

Might have to upgrade that ass to a twelve.

The dude on the bike pulled off his helmet when he saw Hannah approaching him and grinned at her like she was his favourite person in the world.

She probably was.

The woman was like a magnet.

"Vin!" she yelled out as her walk sped up to a run.

He leapt off his bike and flicked down the stand – I had to give props to the guy, he looked like a total badass doing it.

I glanced around, I looked like a loser standing here on my own – so I followed.

"Where the hell have you been, girl?" He held his arms out and Hannah threw herself into them and squeezed him tight.

"Ugh, you stink," she complained as she let go of him. "How long you been out here?"

"Lost count after the first couple of hours." He grinned.

Hannah turned and smiled at me as I came to stand next to her.

"Jasper, right? I'm Vin." He held out his hand to me.

No introduction necessary apparently.

I took his hand in mine and shook it. "Nice bike."

It was more than a nice bike – it was a dream

ride.

Yamaha WR250F.

"Thanks. It's good to meet you. I've heard *all* about you." He winked at Hannah.

She blushed.

Interesting.

"Well I've heard nothing about you; this little fruit cake here kidnapped me in that ridiculous car of hers and wouldn't tell me where we were going."

"You made the man ride in that cupcake on wheels?" he groaned.

I like this guy.

"Took the words out of my mouth." I glared at her.

Hannah shrugged unapologetically.

He held his hands up in gesture to our surroundings. "So what do you think of the place?"

I smirked. "I gotta tell ya, it's not what I was expecting, that's for damn sure." I looked at Hannah in question, still not entirely sure what we were doing here.

"I think Hannah here gets that exact reaction an awful lot." He raised his brows at her.

She waved away his comment. "Enough chit-chat, you got my shit ready or what, Vin?"

He turned on his heel and we both followed. "Good to know you're as demanding as ever," he drawled as he headed for a big shed along the perimeter.

Hannah looked up at me and smiled the biggest

I'd ever seen. "This is going to be so much fun." She clapped her hands together in excitement.

Vin reached the shed he was after and hoisted up the roller door. "Your noble steed awaits, madam." He gestured inside the shed.

"Do you ride, man?" I heard him ask me.

I couldn't even answer; I was too busy staring at the hot-as-fuck bike in front of me.

"Holy shit, is that a KTM EXC 250?" I asked no one in particular. I don't know why I was even asking, I already *knew* it was. The orange and black bike stood proudly on its stand in the middle of the space.

"Oh, he rides," Hannah answered Vin before turning to me. "And yeah, he sure is... best one on the market."

I glanced over my shoulder at her as she strolled in and ran her hand over the bike lovingly.

I picked my jaw up off the floor long enough to ask, "*He?*"

"Hell yeah, 'he', if I'm going to have a something between my thighs you better believe it's gonna be a male. And I know, I know, it's a little big for a girl, but I don't give a shit. You know I can handle it."

That's her bike?

I chuckled loudly at her unexpected innuendo. "It's yours?" I nodded in the direction of the grunty machine.

This was the first I was hearing about her riding, but it was becoming pretty obvious that she fit in this world one way or another.

"It's mine," she confirmed. "So... surprise..."

God damn.

I groaned. "Jesus Christ, woman, you should have come with a warning label."

She stared at me with smouldering eyes and I knew I was affecting her too.

"Why didn't you tell me you liked to ride?"

She shrugged. "It's not something I share with just anyone."

My lips turned up into a slow grin. I wasn't *just anyone* to her. She'd made a slip, a small one, but a slip nonetheless, and judging by the blush covering her cheeks, she knew it.

A throat being cleared broke the moment.

"I hate to break up this little... whatever this is..." Vin chuckled, gesturing between the two of us. "But I gotta go out, you'll be alright for a couple of hours?"

"Yeah, yeah, you take off," Hannah called back from where she was now tinkering around with some spare parts on the work bench down the back.

I thought she was attractive beyond belief before this moment, but now... now she was on a whole new level.

A girl that knew engines... knew bikes...

Shit... she might be my dream girl.

"You're on my ride, Jasper."

"No shit?"

"No shit." He nodded. "Don't break it."

Oh hell yeah.

A smirk and the toss of his keys into my waiting

hands and he was gone.

Hannah grabbed a handful of pink and black motocross gear and a chest protector from a box in the corner of the room.

I swallowed slowly. She was going to put that getup on and I was going to lose my shit big time.

"See if that fits." She grabbed another jersey from the bench and tossed it to me. "Vin's got more shit you can borrow in his shed."

"How'd you know I knew how to ride?" I asked as I slipped it on. It didn't fit like my old favourite, but it'd do.

"Parker told me. He said, and I quote, that you were a 'crazy-ass mofo on a bike', does that sound about right?"

I shrugged. "Well it certainly doesn't sound wrong."

She climbed onto the bike and started it up before revving the engine hard. "I really hope you're not all talk." She smirked before tearing out of the shed.

I rubbed my hand over my chest where my heart was thumping like crazy.

Hannah was so unexpected, so spontaneous and fun...

Dream girl alright...

I had to have her. That girl was made for me.

She was *going* to give up this stupid idea of hers; there was no way in hell that her and I were destined to be a one-time thing.

CHAPTER 11

Hannah

I WAS DRESSED head to toe in motocross gear, and it was so hot I was absolutely covered in sweat, and I still couldn't remember having this much fun, ever.

I pulled off my helmet and shook my hair out as I watched Jasper fly around the corner and skid to a stop on the loose gravel.

I'd just pulled out my show-stopper trick and I could have sworn I'd seen his jaw drop from inside his helmet.

I was *that* good.

Vin had dubbed it the 'H-bomb'. He'd named it after me since I was the only girl that had been able to not only contribute to it when we were playing around creating it, but because I was the only one who could actually nail the whole thing without eating shit.

I knew J hadn't been expecting any of this, but that was me...

Full of surprises.

And I wasn't the only one.

Parker was right; Jasper *was* a crazy bastard on a bike. If it wasn't for the fact that I knew he could afford to replace it, I would have been worried as hell about him smashing up Vin's bike.

That Yamaha was his baby.

I shouldn't have wasted my time worrying. Jasper might have been wild on two wheels, but he gave the bike and the track the respect it deserved.

He was actually pretty good too – he could throw a whip like a boss.... he was no Eli Tomac, but I wouldn't have swapped my afternoon riding partner for anyone in the world.

Jasper Jones was something else.

We were the same person in so many ways, but at the same time we were complete opposites.

We both craved a rush, that much was clear, but when he wasn't chasing that high, Jasper was chill.

Like, super chill.

I, on the other hand, was not.

'Chill' was not one of my defining qualities.

I was more known for being hyperactive and for losing my mind over shit that didn't actually matter in the slightest.

I talked too much, and I *always* talked too loud.

I was the crazy girl, and he was the laid-back boy.

But when all that was said and done, I could vouch the shit out of the saying 'opposites attract', because, Christ... I'd never been more attracted to a man in my entire life.

I watched like a hawk as he shed the helmet from his head and whipped off the jersey he was wearing, revealing his bare, tattoo-covered torso.

I could just about feel the dribble rolling down my chin.

His body was lean and defined, his muscles tight and strong.

He reminded me of a puma or some other type of lithe, agile cat.

"Holy shit, biker barbie, what the fuck was that last trick you pulled?" he chuckled as he strolled towards me.

Holy shit is it hot in here?

I couldn't think straight with him looking like that.

I did the only thing I could think of and followed his lead by stripping off my jersey and standing in front of him in only my sports bra, riding pants and boots.

He looked like sex on a stick, and I was going to do my damn best to make him feel as off kilter as I did right now.

His step faltered, and his eyes took a slow appraisal of my body.

I heard him mumble something under his breath that sounded a hell of a lot like 'motherfucker', and I grinned in triumph.

I kicked down my stand and waited for him, excitement thrumming through my veins at the prospect of what might go down next.

I'd tried to convince him that what went on between the two of us shouldn't happen again, but I knew I was kidding myself. One roll in the hay with him was never going to cut it.

He was an itch I needed to scratch.

I knew it – and I was pretty sure he knew it too.

Hell, I was pretty sure Parker and Charlotte would have known it as well if they weren't so caught up falling in love with each other.

"Your thoughts are loud again," he murmured as he reached me.

His arms wound around my middle, almost as though it was without thought, the same way mine went around his neck.

My heart was beating so fast I was sure he could hear it.

He ran his nose up and down mine for what felt like forever. It was like he was just drinking in the moment.

"You're so damn addictive," he breathed.

I deliberately tipped my face up to meet his, our mouths only brushing lightly.

"You sure?" he whispered, his voice uncertain.

The fact that he was willing to stop this, to check

that it was what I really wanted only made me want him more.

"Couldn't be surer."

His lips crashed against mine and the thrill I felt made the moves I'd thrown only minutes before on my bike feel like child's play.

Our slick skin met with a soft thud as he dropped his hands under my ass and hoisted me up onto the seat of my bike.

I threaded my fingers into his damp hair and pulled him closer.

How I ever thought I was going to resist this man was beyond me.

"You wanna get out of here or what?" his husky voice asked.

It was not lost on me that it was the same question he asked me before taking me to his bed last week.

I smirked. "I was starting to think you'd never ask."

CHAPTER 12

Jasper

"I SWEAR TO GOD, barbie girl, if you even try and feed me some bullshit line about this not happening again, I'm gonna be pissed..."

I'd been joking with the comment, I was so sure this was her way of giving in... but the way she froze sent chills through me.

I turned, ever so slowly, so I could see her face, hoping the entire time that I was reading her reaction wrong.

She shot me a sheepish look.

Oh hell no.

"Hannah, you can't keep doing this to us," I groaned as I scrubbed my hands over my face.

"Can't we just admit that it was good and then go

back to being friends? I really like what we've got going on and I don't want to lose it," she pleaded.

"*Good?*" I plucked the word from her sentence and threw it back at her in outrage.

"Seriously?" she snapped, "*that's* what you heard from all that?"

I shook my head; I was beyond exasperated with this.

"No, we damn well can't, Hannah. I know that this isn't 'just sex'. I've had plenty of 'just sex' before and this *isn't* that. It's not even fuckin' close."

"How much is *plenty?*" She narrowed her eyes at me, her flaring jealously only enforcing the point I was trying to make.

"Seriously?" I repeated her own words back to her. "*That's* what you heard from all that?"

I grabbed her and held her close.

I didn't want to keep doing this, but I couldn't lose her either.

She groaned in frustration. "Why is this so hard?" she whispered as she buried her face in my chest.

I pulled her in even tighter. "It's not." I ran my fingertips up and down the bare skin of her arm. "It just feels that way because you're fighting a losing battle."

"What's that meant to mean?" she demanded.

"You know what it means, Hannah, you know where this is going."

"It's not going anywhere." She pulled herself from my arms and sat up on the bed.

"You're scared."

"I am *not* scared." She got to her feet and sat her hands on her hips dramatically.

She was exuding a pissed off energy that almost had me fooled... if it weren't for the fear in her eyes.

This was her fight or flight moment, and I could tell that she was hell bent on choosing the latter.

I can't lose her.

If she ran now, I was going to have a hell of a time getting her back.

There was only one thing for it.

I sighed. "I want you, Hannah, in any way I can get you, okay?" I reached for her hand and she let me take it. "If that means we just hang out, or we're friends with benefits, or we're together... I don't care... I'll take *anything* I can get when it comes to you."

She breathed a sigh of relief, and I tugged on her hand until she was back on the bed next to me.

"Thank you," she whispered. "I'm just not in a good place for a relationship right now..."

This wasn't what I wanted. I didn't want to have sex with her and not get to call her mine, but right now...this was all I could get.

We were spending more time with each other than anyone else, neither of us were seeing other people, and we were having the most mind-blowing sex I'd ever experienced.

It wasn't entirely a bad deal.

For now.

"Just promise me that you'll talk to me, okay? If you're freaking out, you have to talk to me."

She looked into my eyes for a moment, revealing the vulnerability there.

I kissed her forehead. "Okay?" I asked again.

She reached over and snagged the bag of lollies off the end of the bed. "Fine... now have some sugar and shut your trap."

"Oh, baby, I'm already sweet enough," I quipped, happy to fall back into our usual light banter.

"Oh you *didn't*..." She laughed at me. "That might be your worst one yet."

I shrugged and snatched the lollipop I knew she'd been saving out of the bag in her hands.

"Jasper, that's not funny." She gave me a death glare as I unwrapped it from its packet.

I watched her as I brought it up slowly to my mouth.

"Jasper..." she warned. "Don't do it."

I shoved it in my mouth at the same moment that I dodged the hands that came flying towards my face.

"You're a dead man!" she shrieked.

I fended off her arms and legs as they came for me. "But I'm a dead man with a lollipop." I chuckled.

"Ugh!!" she screamed as she threw her entire body in my direction.

I caught her and rolled her over so she was pinned under my weight.

"Mmmm this is a *good* lollipop."

She thumped her fists against my chest.

"What's the matter, BG?"

She didn't reply, just grunted and groaned until she had an arm free enough to reach my face.

I had to give it to her, the girl knew how to persevere.

She got hold of the stick and pulled.

I couldn't help but laugh at the look of utter determination on her face.

I bit half of it off as she tugged it from my mouth, putting the final nail in my coffin.

I crunched it up between my teeth as I grinned at her.

"I hate you."

"It's not all bad, baby, you still have half, and if it makes you feel better I'll let you suck on my lollipop."

"You put that thing anywhere near my mouth right now and I really can't guarantee it'll be coming back in one piece," she hissed without missing a beat.

I burst into laughter.

I rolled off her and watched her pouting at her half-chewed treat.

"Oh god," I wiped the tears from my eyes, "you really are crazy."

"You'd do well to remember that, Lollipop." She popped it into her mouth, looking every inch the sex kitten as she did it.

"What are you going to do about it, huh?"

She pushed herself up and swung her leg over so she was straddling me.

She seductively pulled the lollipop through her lips.

I could feel myself getting hard again, she was so damn sexy.

"You're going to pay for this."

I skimmed my hands up and down her bare sides.

Her eyes were fixed on mine and I could see nothing but desire in them.

I thrust up only a little with my hips, letting her know the reaction she was invoking in me.

She let out what I was learning was her signature breathy moan and pushed back against me.

"I think I'm ready to pay now."

CHAPTER 13

Hannah

WELL SHIT.

I didn't know how it had happened again, but it had.

Here I was, at his place again, absolutely sated right down to my bones.

I'd told him I couldn't do a relationship and he *still* wanted me. He'd wanted me another two times to be exact.

"I'm hungry." I nudged him in the ribs.

"Eat some more lollies," he mumbled in his sleepy state.

"Those are long gone."

"I need a nap," he groaned.

"I need food."

"Kitchen's downstairs, mi casa es su casa."

I didn't need to be told twice.

"You want anything?"

"Get me whatever you're having." He rolled over and buried his face into the pillows.

"Permission to snoop around your house granted or denied?"

"Fill your boots, you little weirdo," he answered lazily.

I grabbed my cell and headed off downstairs. I was only wearing his t-shirt and nothing else, and I was regretting not asking if he had a maid or any type of security in this place. If he did, they were about to get a real good view of my ass.

I flicked the light on in the kitchen; I wasn't sure when it had got dark out, but that explained why I was so hungry.

I wasn't one of those girls that ate a crouton for breakfast and a salad for dinner. I needed to be fed and watered at least every two hours.

I rummaged around in his fridge and pantry until I found what I needed to make pancakes. He even had bacon to go with them.

I turned on the stereo and danced around as I cooked the pancakes and bacon in the frying pan.

I found some maple syrup and some frozen berries that I defrosted, and I was ready to go.

I stacked the food on a plate and laughed to myself as I thought about hiding them and making him think I'd eaten them all.

Better yet, I'll hide entirely.

I grabbed my phone off the counter.

To: Jasper Jones
From: Hannah

I have pancakes. This is not a drill. Come find me.

I flicked off the lights and the music, grabbed the stack of pancakes and hid in the first place I found.

I listened hard, trying to tell if he was moving around upstairs, but I heard nothing. I was about to pull my phone out again when I heard him call out.

"Hannah?"

I stifled a giggle.

I'm such a little kid.

"Why are all the lights out?" he called again.

I stood quietly in my hiding place.

"Hannah what the hell? Are you even still here?"

The light flicked on in the kitchen.

I took out my phone and text him again.

To: Jasper Jones
From: Hannah

Don't you know how hide and seek works?

· · ·

I heard the ding of his phone and then him chuckle.

"You're a real fruit loop sometimes," he called.

I grinned to myself.

Yes I am...

"Alright then," he called. "Ready or not, here I come..."

My heart thumped in my chest at the anticipation of him finding me.

I could see the glow of him flicking on lights as he moved around the house, but I couldn't hear a sound from him.

Where is he?

I leaned forward, really trying to figure out where he was.

The door in front of me swung open so fast I nearly dropped the stack of pancakes I was holding.

Jasper's grinning face came into view.

"Found ya."

"Scared me half to death you mean?"

He took the plate from me and chuckled. "I can't believe you took the pancakes with you."

"If I didn't, you wouldn't have bothered looking for me now, would you?" I explained as I scrambled out of the closet under the stairs.

He didn't answer, just laughed again as he swaggered off towards the kitchen.

I took a moment to appreciate just how much of a god he really was.

He had on nothing but a pair of gym shorts, slung

low on his hips, and his bare, tattooed body was seriously drool-worthy.

He'd tied up his unruly hair in a bun on the top of his head. He had the sides of his head shaved shorter, but he had left the top section longer. It was grown out and needed some serious attention.

A job for another day.

Even with the scruffy look he had going on, he was undeniably sexy.

He turned back around to face me.

"You coming outta there or what?"

"I guess so... I'm just admiring the view."

He rolled his body around, gyrating his hips. "What? This old thing?"

"Oh... my... god." I choked out between my laughter. "Did you just shake your dick at me?"

He shrugged. "I don't know... did you *see* my dick shaking?"

Smartass.

I strolled over to where he was now munching on a rolled-up pancake. "Damn, barbie, these are good."

"You sound surprised."

"I am."

I grabbed a pancake and a couple of slices of bacon. "You wound me."

"I'm starting to think I should be suspicious of you, you're hot as hell, you're funny, you ride a bike like a total badass *and* you can cook...? I smell a rat."

As much as I knew he was giving me a hard time, I still blushed, and my heart raced at his praise.

His hazel eyes were dancing with mischief and his smile was wide and easy.

He was seriously gorgeous when he smiled. Teeth weren't something I could ever say I'd paid a lot of attention to, but I could safely say that Jasper had a really great set of teeth.

"What can I say, I can do it all," I bragged.

He snagged a piece of bacon off my plate. "I'm not buying it, you've gotta suck at something."

I swatted at his hand half-heartedly.

God, he is gorgeous.

His whole body was toned and strong, his muscles tensing and bunching with every movement he made.

"Seriously, what kind of working out have you been doing? Because damn..."

A sly smile spread across his face. "Don't change the subject."

I sighed dramatically. "Fine, I can't sing to save my life, I can't bake anything worth eating and I'm messy as hell."

He nodded, apparently taking stock of my answers.

"So spill... I know you didn't get a body that fine from running around being Parker's drama extinguisher."

He chuckled. "I run, I lift weights... I use the rower... I jump rope." He shrugged. "Nothing crazy, I just mix it up... and I don't usually eat pancakes for dinner."

"Ugh." I rolled my eyes. "I could run for an hour every day and still not look like that."

"Like a twenty-eight-year-old dude?" he quizzed, tilting his head to the side as he studied me.

I narrowed my eyes at him. "You know damn well that's not what I meant."

"But do I?"

"Stop talking me around in circles."

He chuckled as he took another bite.

"Is this how this is going to go?" I sat my hands on my hips. "You trying to get a rise out of me twenty-four-seven?"

"Twenty-four-seven, huh?" He winked. "Sounds like you're planning on seeing a lot of me, BG."

Deep breaths....

In and out...

"I'm going to take that as a yes," I ground out the words.

He smirked, clearly enjoying himself. "Whatever floats your boat."

The man was impossible.

Getting a straight answer out of him was like pulling teeth sometimes. He seemed to know exactly how to push my buttons already and he was forever trying to wind me up.

It was only a matter of time before I lost the plot with him – it was brewing, that was for sure.

"Stop tryna piss me off and eat your damn pancakes."

He saluted me and took another bite. "With plea-sure... these were worth playing hide and seek for."

"You mean *I'm* worth playing hide and seek for, right?"

He grinned at me. "Hell yes, BG, I'd look for you forever."

CHAPTER 14

Jasper

"OH C'MON, just one peek in their dressing room?" she begged me.

"Hell no, woman, you tryna get me fired?"

She strolled off not so subtly in the direction of the room I'd just insisted she stay away from. "Live a little, Lollipop."

She'd been at it with that nickname all week.

I jogged after her and wrapped my arms around her middle.

"You can't just walk into DNCE's private room; Joe Jonas' security will kick your ass."

"It'd probably be worth it." She giggled as I lifted her feet off the ground and carted her off in the opposite direction.

"You're such a party pooper," she complained as I carried her.

I set her back down next to where Ricky and the other boys from the band were hanging out, shooting the shit.

"Goldilocks!" Ricky boomed. "What's new with you, girl?"

"Nothing." She pouted. "Absolutely *nothing* is new with me because Lollipop here won't let me have any fun."

He raised a brow at me, a shit-eating grin on his face. "Lollipop, huh?"

I smirked at him but didn't reply.

"Yeah, you know, because he's got such a sweet-tasting candy stick." Hannah winked at him.

Pete and Jim both burst into laughter. Ricky blinked at her a couple of times, unsure if she was joking or not, before joining them, his howling laugh exploding out of him.

She thinks she's so funny...

"That's it, you're out of here." I picked her up again and tossed her over my shoulder before carting her off down the narrow corridor that ran around the side of the stage.

"And seriously, Rick, Little Red... Goldilocks... what's with the friggin' fairytale quips?" She yelled back at him.

I laughed.

"Good luck with that one, Jasp, I think you're

gonna need it." He called after me as we disappeared around the corner.

"Put me down, I promise I'll be good," Hannah pleaded through her giggles.

"Nice try, you don't even know the meaning of the word."

I waved away a few concerned looks from some of the stage crew.

This wasn't the first time we'd had a mad woman backstage, but she *was* the first one who was actually allowed to be here.

"You're making a scene," I scolded her with a smack on her ass.

"Me?!" she screeched, "You're the one making a scene. Put me down!"

I glanced up and down to check we were alone before opening the door to what I knew was a storage room.

It had been full with stage equipment earlier, but it was bound to be emptied out now that we were only a couple of hours from getting started.

I had a shit load of things I should have been doing right now – screwing around in what was essentially a dark closet certainly wasn't one of them, but hell if it wasn't on the top of my list.

"What are we doing in here?" she whispered as I stood her back on her feet.

"We're just gonna wear you out a little bit, you know... calm you down."

She glanced around; taking in her surroundings

before lifting herself up to sit on one of the speakers that still remained.

"Quick screw in the storage room, huh? Saucy." She smirked.

I stepped in between her legs. "Who said anything about quick?"

She bit down on her bottom lip and rolled her head back as I trailed kisses up her neck.

"What if I'm not interested?" she murmured.

"Its sex or sedation, barbie girl, you go ahead and make your choice."

Her laughter cut off as I slid my hand up the inside of her thighs.

She gasped as I made contact with her soft skin.

The simplest of touches got the best reactions from her.

I slid my hand painfully slow towards its destination.

"What's it gonna be?" I murmured to her.

"Sex," she answered quickly, "I'll go with the sex."

"Good answer."

I reached up the rest of the way.

Oh hell, she's so ready.

"You like all this secret sex, don't you, my dirty little barbie..."

I pushed two fingers inside her and she moaned loudly, causing my already-hard dick to pulse.

I couldn't get enough of her.

Her hands found their way to my belt and tugged

on the buckle before undoing my button and sliding down the zip.

Her hands were working so fast, like she was in a frenzy already.

"Fuck, Hannah."

She felt so good around my fingers; I was dying to get inside her already.

She tugged my jeans and boxer briefs down enough to free my dick.

I grunted with pleasure as she took me in her hands and started working me up and down.

Our foreheads were resting together, both of our ragged breaths mingling in the space between us.

"Let me down," she whispered.

I pulled my fingers out of her wet centre and she slid herself off the speaker.

She dropped to her knees in front of me before I even realised what she was doing.

I hissed as she took me into her mouth and sucked hard.

"Holy fuck, Hannah, that feels so good, baby."

She bobbed her head back and forward as her hands worked what she couldn't take into her mouth.

I didn't know how she wasn't gagging right now; the woman obviously had the gag reflex of a total champion.

I threaded my fingers into her hair and thrust into her mouth gently, testing the waters to see if she would fight me on it.

She didn't.

She hummed in appreciation and took me even further into her hot little mouth.

Well fuck me.

I thrust into her again, speeding up as I went.

"If you carry on with this, I'll be coming down your throat pretty soon," I warned her, my voice gravelly and hoarse.

She looked up at me through hooded lids and gave me a thumbs up.

"You're... so... fuckin' good... at... this," I choked out between thrusts.

I was so close.

I felt my balls tighten and pull up at the same moment that the door behind me swung open and light pooled into the room.

"Oh, fuck yes," I groaned as I spilled my come down Hannah's throat.

"Shit," a voice came from behind me. "I'll come back soon."

"Good idea," I choked out as she sucked me dry, milking every last bit I had to give her.

I couldn't find it in me to care that we'd just been snapped; I was riding the wave.

The door shut, and we were enveloped in the dim light again.

Jesus...

Hannah released my still-hard dick with a pop and looked up at me.

"Christ, Hannah," I choked out when I could remember how to speak again.

"Well shit... I just got caught sucking your dick." She giggled.

"Nah, I just got caught getting my dick sucked." I chuckled. "They couldn't see you, baby." I pulled her up to her feet.

She smirked. "Is it wrong that I kinda wish they had?"

I growled and claimed her mouth. "You really are a dirty girl."

She was turning me on so much I hadn't even gone soft. She'd just sucked one of the most intense orgasms I'd ever had from within me and I already felt like I could go again.

"Turn around," I told her.

She did exactly as I asked, spinning around so her ass was pushed up against my crotch.

I ran my hand over her lower back and up to the bare skin between her shoulder blades.

I pressed down so she would bend, only stopping when she was draped over the same speaker that had just protected her modesty.

If that guy were to come back right now, she was not going to be afforded the same courtesy.

"This dress was a good choice," I praised as I slipped it up, revealing her bare ass in the g-string she was wearing.

I ran my palm over the smooth skin of her ass cheek, fighting hard not to spank it.

I hooked my thumbs into the sides of her underwear and slid them slowly down her legs, trailing my breath on her sensitive skin as I went.

Toying with her, I slid my fingers all the way up from her ankle to the apex of her thighs.

She shuddered as I made contact with her wet folds.

"Jasper," she moaned.

Hearing my name on her lips spurred me on further.

I leant over her and spoke in her ear. "I don't have a condom," I told her. "So I need you to decide. I can make you come however you want."

"I don't care," she moaned as she pushed herself back against me.

"I need you to tell me, BG."

"I don't care if you don't have a condom, I want all of you."

I didn't need to be told twice. I also didn't need to quiz her about birth control or STD checks. Hannah was no idiot, she knew the risk of unprotected sex as well as I did, and she wouldn't have agreed if she had any reason not to.

I stood, lined myself up and pushed inside her with one firm stroke.

Oh Jesus.

I literally saw stars.

I couldn't remember anything ever feeling this good.

"Oh fuck, Hannah." I ground the words out.

She pushed back against me and I nearly lost my mind.

"You... feel so... good," she whispered.

I leant down over her, tugging her ear lobe into my mouth and fisting her hair in my hand as I pushed into her, fast and hard.

She was making a hell of a racket, moaning and whimpering, but I didn't give a shit.

Everyone in the place could probably hear us by now.

She was pushing back, meeting me thrust for thrust.

I stood up straight, one hand still fisted in her hair, the other gripping her hip.

"Are you coming with me, baby?"

I reached around her and rubbed her clit with my thumb.

That was all it took for her to lose control.

"Yes, oh god...yes," she moaned as her walls tightened around me.

I followed right behind her, light flashing behind my eyes with the overwhelming sensation of being inside her with nothing between us.

She came calling my name, over and over again.

"Jesus Christ." I shook my head, trying to clear my thoughts.

"Yup... just... yup."

"Are you okay?"

"Just give me a minute to find my way back down." She giggled.

"You up in the stars too, BG?"

"That would be an understatement."

I gently eased out of her and bent down to pull her underwear back into place.

She turned around and returned the favour by tucking me back into my boxes and redoing my jeans and belt.

"That was fuckin' wow," I breathed as I pulled her into me.

"Agreed… I'll never be able to look a storage room in the eye again."

"Neither will that dude that walked in on us earlier."

She giggled. "I need the bathroom."

"You're insatiable; surely we don't need to defile the bathroom too?"

She rolled her eyes. "Oh be quiet, you dirty bastard." She kissed me briefly on the lips. "But seriously, I can feel this shit dripping down my thighs."

I must have been a dirty bastard after all, because the mere thought of that had my dick twitching in my pants.

"Let's go do the walk of shame." I smirked.

"How many times do I have to tell you? There's *no* shame in my walk." She winked.

CHAPTER 15

Hannah

"I HEARD that Jasper got caught getting a blow job backstage," Charlotte whispered to me from the booth we were sitting in.

I nearly spat out the mouthful of rum and coke I'd just taken.

"Seriously?" I choked out.

"That's what Brent told Levi, who told Ricky, who told *everyone*. They're saying that Mikey walked in on them right as he was blowing his load."

Sweet baby Jesus...

I laughed. "Trust Rick to spread the gossip."

"He's literally telling *anyone* that will listen." She laughed.

"Who was the chick?" I took another sip and tried to act blasé about it.

I had a feeling that Charlotte was gauging my reaction. She knew Jasper and I had slept together once and I got the vibe that she thought there was more going on. Jasper and I openly spent quite a lot of time together, and even more time behind closed doors.

People were bound to notice eventually.

"Apparently he didn't see."

Turns out I'm happy about that after all.

"That's hilarious; I'm definitely going to ask him about it."

"So, you're okay with it?"

I was more than okay with it, actually...

"Okay with what?" I feigned confusion.

"Jasper and... other women."

I was having a hard time keeping myself in check right now. It was too funny. I didn't like to bullshit my best friend, but I *really* liked having a dirty little secret.

I glanced over to where Jasper and Parker had been talking. It didn't seem to matter where he was in a room, I was always aware.

They were looking over in our direction. Parker clapped Jasper on the shoulder and headed our way.

"To tell you the truth, I'd be more worried if he wasn't getting any action." I squeezed her arm and stood up. "I'm off to interrogate him."

"Give him a high five for me." She smirked.

I strolled across the room, heading for Jasper, a sly grin on my face due to the fact that my thighs were still sticky from our earlier fun.

Ricky appeared out of nowhere in front of me, a shit-eating grin on his face. "So, you weren't kidding about my man's 'sweet-tasting candy stick' then, huh?" he waggled his brows at me.

I could have denied it black and blue, but I was pretty sure Ricky already knew exactly what was going on. That, and the fact that I didn't actually care if he knew about us. He could have told everyone that he thought it was me down on my knees, but he hadn't.

I licked my lips and winked at him.

"Seriously....?" He whistled low. "Damn... Jasper is one lucky son of a bitch."

"You tell anyone about this and you'll be the exact opposite," I warned him.

He looked me up and down. "You're kinda a scary chick."

"I'm glad you think so," I called to him over my shoulder with a laugh.

I had my sights set on Jasper Jones now.

He had his sights firmly on me too.

"Hey there, Lollipop," I breathed as I brushed past him.

"Barbie girl," he replied with a nod.

"Half the room is talking about your junk," I stage whispered as we both turned to face the bar, our backs to everyone.

"Only half? That's a little disappointing."

"If it makes you feel any better, it's the only thing I can think about."

He glanced behind him to check who was looking before running his thumb down my arm.

"I can't even think straight, I'm still back in that storage room, balls-deep, bare back inside you."

Goosebumps prickled my skin and my heart thumped in my chest.

It might have been the least romantic thing he could have said, but that was why I liked it so much.

It was dirty and raw and primal, and I couldn't wait to do it again.

"I don't want to give you a big ego, but that was possibly the hottest sex of my life," I confessed.

"Don't lie to me," he replied quickly. "That was the hottest sex of *both* our lives and you know it."

I blushed. There was no way in hell that *I* was the hottest sex of his life. The guy was super skilled, and no one got that good without *a lot* of practice, but I knew he wouldn't hear of me arguing with him – so I didn't bother.

"You're coming home with me tonight," he stated.

I shook my head in amusement. "No, I'm not."

He turned inwards, resting his back against the bar, and to anybody in the room, it would have looked like nothing at all.

I however, didn't miss the brush of his lips against my jaw, and I certainly didn't miss the hand that he slipped under the front of my dress.

I tried to hide my gasp as his fingers skimmed up the inside of my thighs.

"Shouldn't you buy me a drink before you feel me up?" I whispered as I leaned into him.

"Zeke!" he called over his shoulder to the bartender without missing a beat.

He appeared almost immediately. "What'll it be, Jones?"

"A rum and coke for the lady – no ice, and I'll take another beer."

I didn't have a clue how he knew my drink of choice for the evening, but somehow, he'd gotten it exactly right.

The bartender turned away to make our drinks.

"How'd you know that's what I was drinking?"

He glanced at me and chuckled. "I could smell it on your breath."

"You could smell the no ice, could you?"

He chuckled louder, his hand lightly gripping my thigh as he did. "If you think I haven't been watching every move you've made tonight, then you'd be mistaken."

Excitement raced through me.

This man drove me crazy; he made me want like no one ever had.

The thought of his eyes on me, when I hadn't been aware gave me goosebumps.

Zeke placed a glass in front of me and I thanked him.

"Drink your drink," Jasper instructed as his fingers continued their trip up my thigh.

I picked up the glass and at the same moment the amber liquid hit my lips, his hand made contact with my underwear.

"Jasper," I whispered.

We were in a room full of people and his thumb was caressing me in a way that should have been illegal.

If anyone was looking hard enough, they would see the way his arm was snaked under my dress – and the blow job saga would be long forgotten.

"You've got a choice to make, BG, either I can make you come now," he flicked my most sensitive spot for emphasis and I shuddered, "or I can make you come at my place."

"Asshole," I muttered as he stroked me again.

"Come home with me." His eyes blazed with intensity.

I didn't know what he was doing down there, but it felt good – too good.

I could feel myself sagging against the bar, my legs seeming as though they might give way.

He took a slow, appraising sweep of the room at the same time as he moved aside my underwear and pushed his fingers inside me.

Oh sweet Jesus...

"Okay," I blurted out. "Let's go."

He nodded, a satisfied smirk on his face. He

turned back towards me, slipping his hand out of my dress as he did.

"So needy."

"Shut up."

He was right; I was beyond needy right now. He'd worked me into a state with his fingers and now he was acting like we had all the time in the world.

He laughed. "You know I can't leave without saying goodbye."

"Like hell you can't... if you're not outside in five minutes, we're going to have problems, you hear me?"

I pulled my phone out of my bag.

To: Lotte

From: Hannah

I'm getting a ride home with Jasper, don't do anything I wouldn't do x

He watched over my shoulder as I tapped out the text.

"There... goodbyes done, let's go."

"Yes, ma'am." He chuckled.

CHAPTER 16

Hannah
Present day

I TAPPED OUT THE MESSAGE, a shit-eating grin on my face.

To: God of Sex
From: Hannah
There's a situation backstage, I need your help, and don't tell Park... he'll freak out.

I rolled my eyes at the name he'd given himself in my phone. It was something new every month or so – this one had appeared yesterday.

.   .   .

To: Hannah
    From: God of Sex
    Where?

I knew he was out on the stage, testing out the sound equipment. The show was scheduled for just over three hours' time. I could hear the fans outside the venue already, itching to get inside.

I had about thirty minutes with him before he needed to start his usual pre-show ritual, and I had to actually do something that was part of my job description.

I typed out a quick message telling him where to meet me.

This venue was the first place I'd ever had sex backstage and I was dying for a re-run. Some of the hottest sex of my life had been in dingy closets and arena storage areas, but the time in this very room, over two years ago was still the one that took the cake.

My anticipation grew as I looked around. I could still recall being on my knees a mere foot from where I stood waiting for him now.

I heard voices in the hallway and then the door handle turned.

He walked in silently, his eyes trained directly on me.

I didn't say a word as he shut the door behind

him. I didn't miss the fact that he flicked the lock. I didn't know when an interior lock had been installed, but I didn't doubt the fact that it was his doing.

He watched me. "There's no problem here."

I shook my head. "Not one you can't fix anyway."

He sauntered over to where I stood, circling me until he was standing behind me, his front to my back. "You liked it so much the first time you had to come back for seconds, huh?"

"I'm sentimental like that."

He chuckled. "You're something alright."

His fingers skimmed my neck as his hand swept the hair out of his way.

His lips followed, the rough hair from his beard providing a delicious contrast to the soft touch before it.

"On your knees," he told me, his voice soft but commanding. "Let's see how sentimental you really are."

———

Holy hell...

If I'd thought the first time back here was phenomenal then I had absolutely no words for whatever the hell that just was.

Off the charts.

I had to admit, I did miss the additional layer of excitement that having someone from the crew bursting in had created, but I was happy to let Jasper retain his modesty this time.

And besides, the things he had done to me in that room were better left behind closed doors.

I held back a moan as I thought about the way he'd just brought me to climax over and over again.

I was in such an orgasm bubble I didn't notice the stressed look on my best friend's face.

"Where the hell have you been?" Charlotte yelled at me as I approached her.

"Ummmm...." I wracked my brain trying to come up with something useful.

"The lighting guy fucked up and brought the wrong stuff with him, he's gone to get what we need now, but it's gonna be cutting it fine."

"Shit," I muttered.

"Where's Jasper? Park needs him."

I shrugged and tried to appear interested in the stage crew's set-up.

I saw her out the corner of my eye, she looked up from her clipboard and narrowed her eyes at me.

"Oh you dirty little shits," she cried. "You've been out back getting busy, haven't you?"

I tried to stifle a giggle, but it didn't work.

"You're like a couple of horned-up teenagers." She shook her head in mock outrage.

"You can't talk! I've shared a hotel suite with you and Parker, remember?" I grabbed the clipboard from her hands and looked over what we still had left to get done.

She blushed furiously.

"And besides," I shrugged, "It's not the first time I've had sex in that particular storage closet anyway... so no big deal."

"Oh my god!" Lotte shrieked. "It was *you!*"

"Probably," I drawled. "But if you want me to know what the hell you're talking about, you might have to be more specific."

I glanced over at the microphones, checking they were set up exactly how the guys like them.

"You're the mysterious blow job girl from two years ago." She pointed her finger at me accusingly, her mouth dropping open in shock. "You were the one that got caught sucking Jasper's dick!"

I laughed long and hard. "Oh god, are you just realising this now?"

Ricky appeared out of nowhere, a shit-eating grin on his face. Apparently, he'd been listening to our not so private conversation.

"Get up to speed, Little Red." He chuckled. "You should know by now that there's just something about a live concert that brings Hannah here to her knees." He winked at me.

I laughed. "You know what, that one wasn't half bad."

I held out my fist to bump knuckles with him.

"Alright, that's enough you two," Charlotte announced. "Ricky, your drums are a hot mess and they're not going to fix themselves... and you..." she pointed at me again, "go and do something that doesn't involve you taking your pants off, alright?"

I blew her a kiss and headed off to check on how the security was going outside.

"One problem with that request, Little Red," I heard Ricky's booming voice say. "She's wearing a skirt."

I cracked up laughing.

Touché.

CHAPTER 17

Jasper
Two and a half years earlier

"C'MON, Jasper, don't you trust me?" She snipped her scissors at me.

"You literally just threatened my manhood; of course I don't trust you."

I was lying, I trusted her with everything I had. I just liked to mess with her.

I still hadn't figured out why I did this. Hannah always got her way when it came to me. We both knew it, and yet I still dug my toes in and fought her every step of the way.

It usually resulted in her chucking a fit, me laughing and then her getting her way.

It was our thing.

She got wound up and I got turned on.

She acted like I pissed her off to no end, but judging by the fact that she was always here when she wasn't working or with Lotte, I'd decided she enjoyed my company as much as I did hers.

"It needs a cut. This mop is *not* sexy... the sides are all grown out... for God's sake, just let me fix it."

She was plugging in a set of clippers now, setting herself up a little salon in the middle of my friggin' kitchen.

She sat a stool down in the middle of the space. "Sit."

"What are you going to give me if I do?"

"A haircut, Lollipop, a fuckin' haircut is what I'll give you," she snapped.

I grinned. Her patience was wearing thin.

I'd become surprisingly well schooled in knowing just how far I could push her, and more than that, I'd figured out exactly what it took to bring her back from the brink.

It was like a perfectly balanced circus act that I was one hundred percent hooked on performing.

She was sexy as hell when she was mad.

"You know that's not what I meant, barbie girl."

She clenched her fists together and closed her eyes while she took a deep breath.

I laughed into my hand while she wasn't looking.

"Jasper Jones, I swear to the mother of all things holy, if you don't get over here right now, I'm leaving."

Her eyes were still closed in frustration.

I sauntered over to where she stood, steam practically coming out her ears.

She didn't hear me coming; she never did, so when I touched her arm she jumped, her eyes flying open.

"Do you have any idea how pissed off you make me?" she demanded.

"Do you have any idea how much it turns me on when you let rip at me?" I stroked the back of my fingers down the side of her face and she turned into my touch, her lips rubbing against my skin.

"You're infuriating," she murmured.

"You're irresistible."

"J..." she warned, her voice wavering with uncertainty.

"Cut my hair." I cupped her chin gently. "Because as soon as that's done, I'm taking you out."

"Where to?"

"None of your business."

She nipped at my finger with her teeth and I pulled my hand back.

"Feisty." I winked at her.

"You're such a long day sometimes." She rolled her eyes and shoved me down onto the stool.

Next thing I knew I had a cape on and she was working away at the sides of my head with a set of clippers.

I'd tried to talk to her, but she shushed me. Apparently, Hannah took haircuts pretty seriously.

"How's it look?" I probed after about twenty minutes. She'd been working away with a pair of scissors at the longer hair on the top of my head.

I was pretty sure I should have been alarmed by the amount of blond locks I'd witnessed dropping to the ground, but I couldn't *not* trust her.

She stood back for a moment, taking stock of her work, her long fingers working through the strands in a way that made my spine tingle.

"It looks *really* good." Her voice was husky – she meant what she said.

"Great, book me in for another in six weeks' time then."

"Don't you wanna see for yourself first?"

I shrugged. "Nah... if you like it, then I like it."

It's all for you anyway.

———

"Just tell me where we're going?" she begged for the hundredth time.

"Not happening, barbie, just be grateful that we didn't have to drive in a toy car to get there."

"Asshole," she muttered under her breath.

I raised a brow at her and she batted her eyelashes innocently.

"Stop whining and tell me about your week."

She smiled. "I had a great week actually... we had a music video shoot and they filmed about ten different looks within the one clip, it was so much fun."

"Whose shoot?" I prompted.

"Echo in the Bone, you know that girl band?"

I nodded casually. I'd slept with one of those girls once, but I sure as hell wasn't going to bring that up now.

"I wasn't the only stylist on set, thank god, but the director pulled me aside at the end and personally asked me to work the next shoot. He was really impressed with my work."

My chest swelled with pride. My barbie girl had skills.

"Congratulations, babe."

"Thank you." She beamed before narrowing her eyes at me. "At least some people appreciate my efforts."

I grinned wide. She was still salty with me after the haircut theatrics today. I was just messing with her, the haircut I was rocking was the best one I'd ever had.

"You know I appreciate you."

"Wouldn't kill you to say it every once in a while." She tsked.

I knew she wasn't being serious. I could see the smile playing at the corner of her lips.

"This is the best god damn hair cut I've ever had. I look fly as hell." I gestured to myself in a sassy, self appreciating gesture.

She laughed and shook her head at me. "Ain't that the truth."

I indicated to turn off, and her focus shifted to what she could see out the window. It wasn't much, it was dark out and this parking lot didn't have even a hint of light in it.

It was all done on purpose.

It was meant to look like no one was here and nothing was going on, when really it was quite the opposite.

"Well this looks dodgy," she deadpanned. "I'm getting an 'I'm about to get mugged' kinda vibe from the place."

I smirked as I pulled the car to a stop. "Let's go find out."

I rounded the car and took her hand in mine when I found her in the darkness. "Just stay close and follow me."

"So mysterious," she teased.

I couldn't see her, but I could picture the cheeky expression she'd be wearing.

"They don't call me 'the mystifying Jasper' for nothing."

"Literally not one single person calls you that."

I chuckled as I towed her along. She was so fun to be around. This was what we did best...

Talk shit and have fun.

Being with her was as easy as breathing.

I knocked on the door three times.

"If this is a d-low BDSM club or something, I'm going to be seriously impressed."

"You into that kinky shit, BG?" I asked with an eyebrow raised.

"Wouldn't knock it until I'd tried it."

Good to know.

We waited for a moment before the door swung open. "Well god damn... they told me Jasper Jones would be in tonight, but I swore back and blue that you were a grumpy old bastard that stayed home these days."

"I wish, Bunter, I wish." I grinned at the man standing in the lit-up entryway.

He ushered us in and shut the door behind us.

"Damn, J... how the hell'd you convince a hotty like this to come out with you?" He held his hand out to Hannah. "Name's Bunter."

Hannah shook his hand, "Hannah, and he kidnapped me and brought me here in the boot of his car."

She said it with such a straight face I think Bunter actually believed her for a minute.

"We're gonna head in." I placed my hand on the small of Hannah's back and led her towards the door that I knew would take us into the main room.

"There's some serious heat in there tonight," Bunter called after us.

"Is there ever not?" I chuckled.

I looked down at Han. "You ready for this?"

"If I'm about to get a whole lot of cock and balls

in my face then I might go wait in the car... if it's literally anything else, then sure, why not."

"Trust me, no cock and balls."

She gestured for me to go ahead.

I swung the door open and ushered her in. the dimly lit room was humming with energy and the tunes were pumping. The huge room was entirely soundproofed; nothing could be heard from the outside.

"Holy. Shit. Is... is this 'The Backwards Virtue?'" She gaped as she took in the scene in front of us.

I was shocked she knew the place by name. It was obvious she hadn't been here before, and usually the only people who knew about it were the people who frequented it.

It was the most exclusive scene in town.

"How'd you know that?"

"Oh my god, that's Miley and Liam," she hissed. "And, sweet Jesus, is that Jennifer Lawrence?"

She was dancing around on the spot now – her excitement levels were through the roof.

I laughed at her. "You work with celebs every day, babe, calm down."

"I only get the models most of the time, and no offence, but I don't rate them the way Leo DiCaprio does... these are like legit celebs... oh my god, I think I'm gonna pass out."

"Can you handle this, or should we go?" I baited her.

She bit. *Hard.*

"If you even so much as mention leaving again, so help me God, Jasper Jones, I will end you."

"You can't ask for selfies," I warned her.

She gaped at me in horror. "I would *never*... I am *not* an animal."

I chuckled and pulled her into my side before kissing the top of her head. "You're such a little fruit cake."

"I know, right." She grinned up at me. "I've heard whispers about this place, but I'm in no way important enough to know what we're meant to do here, so you might have to give me a heads up..."

"Well, I'm no Channing Tatum, but I'll see what I can do."

"Channing Tatum is here?" she squeaked excitedly.

"Wouldn't have a clue."

She rolled her eyes dramatically, and I realised that even though she was super pumped to be here and she was dying to do some famous-people spotting, her eyes had been on nothing but me for the past few minutes, and that was the best feeling I'd had all week.

"You're looking at me," I murmured as I brushed her hair behind her ear.

"I like looking at you."

"More than Miley and Liam?" I leant in closer so our lips were almost touching.

"More than Miley and Liam."

"More than Magic Mike?" I chuckled.

"More than *anyone*," she breathed in a rare moment of unfiltered honesty.

She pushed up on her toes and our lips pressed together.

Hannah had never kissed me in public before.

I knew the reason she was doing it now was probably because she could sense the freedom in the air here more than the fact that our relationship was taking a leap into the next stage, but a guy could dream.

She didn't know it, but every person in here signed a non-disclosure agreement when they walked out the door and you were only allowed in here in the first place by being on the arm of someone who had full access.

There were all kinds of people that spent time in this room. Models, singers, actors and actresses, businessmen, millionaires, billionaires... this place was an escape for most of these people.

There was only one bona fide rule. No adultery.

This was not a place that people could come to cheat on their spouse.

That one rule was what I respected the most about it.

I slung my arm over her shoulders and kissed her temple. "Come on, let me show you around."

———

"Oh my god, I feel like that chick off *Mean Girls*," Hannah gushed.

"You're going to have to be more specific," I drawled.

"You know, 'that's why her hair's so big, because it's full of secrets'...?" She shot me a look that let me know I should have known what she was talking about.

"I can safely say that I do *not* know."

She stopped in her tracks and gaped at me. "That is totally unacceptable. You're lucky I don't terminate this," she gestured back and forth between us, "right now."

"I'm a dude, BG, wouldn't you be more concerned if I *did* know what the hell you were talking about."

She giggled. "Valid point, well made."

I tugged her along to keep us moving.

"Do I have to keep this a secret from Lotte?"

I shrugged. "I'll ask Park. He's got full access, *obviously*. So he could take her anytime he wanted, but I'm not sure it's really her scene."

Han giggled and looped her arm through mine as we strolled back to my car.

"It's not her scene at all."

"Did you have a good time?"

"Are you kidding me?" She squeezed my arm. "That food we ate was incredible, and the dancing... the drinks... I had a great time with you, Jasper."

"We could have done all that anywhere."

"You're right." She rested her head on my shoulder. "And don't get me wrong, having dinner with Chris Pratt was like a dream come true... and then Rihanna going up to sing... O. M. G."

I chuckled.

"But it was *you* that made my night, Lollipop."

Well damn...

CHAPTER 18

Hannah

FIFTEEN TIMES...

I still wasn't exactly sure how the heck you slept with someone by accident *fifteen* times, but I'd done it.

I guess it wasn't exactly an 'accident' per se, but I'd sure as hell told myself after each time that it wouldn't happen again, but every single time, it damn well happened again.

Half of my brain was telling me to stop being so bloody stubborn and to just give into it. I liked Jasper; I liked him a lot if I was being honest with myself.

I liked him too much. That was the problem.

That was where the other half of my brain came in – the half telling me that it was a terrible idea, that he'd realise I wasn't worth the hassle and then he'd leave... and I'd be left hurt and alone.

I glanced at my reflection in the mirror and cursed myself for not having a higher sense of self worth.

I never went anywhere without my hair done and my face made up, Lotte was the only person that had seen me without it all since I first started doing it – and that was mainly because she had mad skills and I preferred her to do it for me, but also because I trusted her. I'd never once felt judged by my best friend. I knew she thought I was a nutter sometimes, but she loved me for it and she was always there for me, no matter what.

Even when I'd put on that ridiculous skanky outfit and plastered far too much makeup over my face, I knew she thought I looked like a hooker, but I could still remember what she'd told me when we'd got back home.

It was when I'd put on my pyjamas and washed off my mask.

"See... that is the real Hannah, this girl right here. I know you feel like you're not enough, but you're so much more than enough. You are kind, honest, caring and beautiful, babe. Any man who wants you any way other than this is not going to be the right man for you, I can guarantee you that, okay? And just in case you don't believe me, you're banned from my makeup, indefinitely."

I'd almost been able to believe her. I'd *wanted* to

believe her, but the part of my brain that told me it couldn't be true had flared up again and shut me down.

That's why I was so afraid of trying for something real with Jasper.

That little voice would always be there in the back of my head, whispering lies and giving me doubts.

"What's up with you today, girl?"

I glanced over at Jess, one of the other stylists who was in the salon today.

Once a fortnight I hired a chair in one of the most upmarket salons in not only the town, but the whole country.

I had my most high-end clients come in on these days.

The day was packed with cuts, colours, up-dos, and styling.

I didn't retain too many clients down here. It was too much admin. But I had a group of about twenty that I was comfortable with. I had a few models, some business men and women, and quite a few famous men's wives.

This was the group that I could add another zero to the final price and they wouldn't even blink before handing over their credit cards.

I wasn't one to brag, but I had earnt myself a damn good reputation in this business and I was turning people away on the daily.

"Hello... earth to Hannah?" Jess called.

I blinked at my own reflection still staring back at me.

"Sorry, I was away with the fairies."

"I noticed." She giggled. "You've been doing it all day."

"Have I?" I replied absently as I swept up the area around my chair.

"I mean, you're totally on your game when you've got a client in the chair, but in between... you look kinda lost."

She wasn't wrong.

I was like a lost puppy wandering around, no clue where I was going.

"Are you okay?"

I liked Jess. She was a sweet girl and she seemed to have her shit together. Her husband was a lovely man, and she had a gorgeous two-year-old at home.

She was the perfect person to ask for advice when I couldn't talk to Lotte.

"Actually, no... have you got time to go for a drink and a chat?"

She smiled at me. "Of course, I've always got time for my favourite stylist."

I smiled gratefully at her. I did her hair for her every six weeks and she returned the favour by doing mine.

"Let me just call Matt and let him know I'll be late."

———

"So... who is he?" Jess asked as she picked up her glass of red.

I eyed her suspiciously. "I never said it was about a guy."

She laughed. "Oh, honey, it's *always* about a guy."

I rolled my eyes.

Ain't that the truth.

"So, who is he and what's he done wrong?"

She sipped her wine and waited for me to answer her.

I sighed. "He's done *nothing* wrong. In fact, if anything, he's done everything right."

"I don't get it."

"Neither do I," I groaned. "He's incredible... he's patient and kind, he's sexy as hell, he's an absolute god in the sack... he's funny and sweet..."

"I'm not really seeing a problem here... he sounds like a keeper."

"That's the problem... I'm scared if I decide to keep him, that one day he'll decide he doesn't want to keep me."

"Oh I see." She nodded her head. "This is one of those, it's not you, it's me, problems then..."

I nodded my head as I swallowed a mouthful of my red. "Totally me."

She nodded, and I could tell she was thinking it through.

"How often do you see him?"

"Ummmm..." I thought back over the past few weeks. "Nearly every day actually."

Huh.

I hadn't realised it was quite so frequent. Jasper had become a part of my everyday life without me even realising it.

"And when you're not together, do you talk?"

"We text back and forth all day... and if we're not together in the evening, we talk on the phone until we're both tired."

"Okay... and judging by the 'god in the sack' comment, I take it that you're sleeping together?"

I grinned sheepishly. "It was just meant to be one night; a bit of fun and move on... but I guess it just hasn't worked out that way..."

She laughed. "Yeah, it rarely does..."

"If he wasn't so freakin' good at it, it would have been fine," I grumbled. "We could have been friends."

She glanced around the room as though she was checking to see if anyone was listening. She leaned in closer to me. "I'll let you in on a little secret," she whispered. "A single man and a single woman, who have already had sex and obviously find each other attractive, are *never* going to be able to be just friends."

"But—"

"No buts," she interrupted me. "You can't tell me that you'd be happy if he called you up and told you that he'd met someone great, can you?"

My eyes widened. "God no," I blurted out. "That would not be good news."

She shot me a look that said 'I told you so'.

Shit.

I groaned and lay my head down on the table.

"Where is he now?" she asked.

"Away for a few days. He's with Parker on a show."

I cringed, only realising after I'd spoken that I'd accidently revealed more about my mystery man than I'd intended to.

She grabbed my hand and squeezed. "Please tell me you're talking about Jasper Jones."

Dammit.

"No comment." I grabbed my glass and slugged back the last of my drink.

"Oh yes, girl, yes! He is seriously gorgeous."

"You are not wrong about that."

"How do you feel about him being gone?"

I scrunched up my nose. "Honestly... I miss him like crazy."

"Oh, honey, I don't know why you're stressing out about getting into a relationship with this guy – you're already in one." She giggled.

Oh shit, she might be right...

"I'll tell you what I think you should do."

I sat forward, listening intently.

"Take some time to think about it while he's away. You need to decide if you think he's worth the risk of getting hurt, because in a relationship you have to be willing to trust the other person... and the other thing you need to do is look in the damn mirror and see how stunning you are, you need to think about how fabulous you are at your job, what a lovely person you are and how Jasper would be lucky to have you, okay?"

I blushed. "I don't know about that..."

"Well I do." She patted my hand. "You're a total catch, Hannah, you just need to see yourself for what you really are."

I didn't have anything to say to that.

"I think I need another wine," I joked.

"Oh hell..." Jess whispered. "Incoming..."

I frowned at her, not understanding what she meant when a tall, dark, handsome stranger appeared at the table next to me.

He flashed me a charming smile.

"Do you think I could I buy you ladies a drink?" he asked.

He was a cute guy, and normally the answer would have been yes, but that was before Jasper.

I groaned again in frustration, setting my head back down on the table.

"Thank you, but no thank you, I'm married, and she's just figured out that she's in a relationship." Jess laughed.

Ah crap.

CHAPTER 19

Jasper

I WAS in love with her.

I wasn't one of those guys that went around denying the truth.

I love her.

I knew she was feeling something for me too. She may not have been in love with me yet, but I knew she felt something.

I caught her looking at me often enough and she always had a smile on her face when I was around.

She was calmer when I was near and when we were alone, and really together, I felt like I was seeing the version of herself that she kept hidden under that layer of false confidence she wore like a second skin.

The same way I wore my cool, composed armour

to face the world, Hannah wore a loud laugh and a smart mouth. It was her shield, her way of being fearless.

I could see right through it. I always had.

I saw the beautiful, down-to-earth woman that she was under her makeup... I saw the fragile heart she held close... I saw the insecure mind she kept hidden... I saw it *all*.

I saw *her*.

And I loved *everything* I saw.

I knew damn well I could never walk away from her – not unless she didn't want me there, but I couldn't carry on like this. I didn't want to have her once and then have her ripped out from underneath me again.

I couldn't watch her battle with herself any longer.

I could see it in her eyes that she didn't believe the words coming out of her mouth anymore than I did.

She wanted more than this, but she was scared.

I could almost smell her fear from across the room; it was so obvious she may as well have had it tattooed across her forehead.

I was going to ease those fears, even if it took me the rest of my life.

If she was there with me then it would be a life well spent.

The minute I got back from this trip, I was going

to tell her how I felt, and she was going to hear it whether she liked it or not.

I tapped out a text to her as I waited for Parker to finish his interviews.

To: Barbie Girl
From: Jasper
I miss you. My day's all fucked up without you here to give me grief.

Her instant reply made me smile.

To: Jasper
From: Barbie Girl
I miss you too, but I'm totally prepared to give you grief via text message if it's required?

To: Barbie Girl
From: Jasper
There's a lot of things that are required right now, BG, not one of which you do via text message...

I was chuckling to myself and scrolling through my Facebook, waiting for her reply when I saw it.

Holy fuck.

This was not good.

This was bad – epic proportions kind of bad.

Shit, shit, shit...

I knew Hannah would see it. She had an addiction to gossip and one too many subscriptions to those stupid celebrity apps.

I had about three minutes if I had to guess, before she laid her eyes on what was taking over the internet.

I was wrong.

My phone dinged with an incoming message.

To: Jasper

From: Barbie Girl

If that shit is true you better bring that little son of a bitch back here so I can knock his teeth out. Lotte is going to DIE when she sees this.

Jesus Christ.

It was worse than I thought.

The image of Parker and his ex-girlfriend, Katie, stared back at me from the screen of my phone. That silly bitch, Shelley Corbett's words making a mockery of everything I knew to be true.

'When the baby momma is away, Parker will play'

It was complete bullshit – and 'baby momma'... for fuck's sake.

Friggin' Lotte.

She thought she was so damn funny, but that fake pregnancy stunt she'd pulled a little while back had turned into a total logistical nightmare for me.

I had reporters contacting me at all hours of the day and night trying to get the scoop on the 'pregnancy'.

As if my day wasn't busy enough already.

This Facebook post was going to make everything a thousand times worse.

Hannah could *not* tell Little Red about this. It would break her heart. Even if she had the sense to realise that it wasn't true – that Parker would never do that to her, she was still going to be crushed.

I hit the green phone button and hoped to God that Han would pick up.

It rang and rang.

"Hey, you've got Hannah, if you think I'd want to call you back, leave me a line, if I won't – then don't bother."

"Fuck!" I hissed. "Hannah, if you get this, keep that shit to yourself. You know Parker would never do that. Just let me fix this."

I knew I was too late. Hannah was loyal to a fault when it came to Charlotte and she wouldn't have even considered keeping this from her.

I would have been the same way if the roles were reversed and it was Parker that might have been getting screwed over.

I tried calling three more times and I even tried

Charlotte too, but to no avail. It was obvious that the girls were in crisis mode now.

I was just going to have to do my best to manage this shit storm from here.

This might have technically been my job, but I didn't have much of a clue about what to do when it came down to it. I didn't have any experience in damage control... Park and me, we were just figuring this all out as we went along.

We could really use a publicist right now...

I had to think like Parker. I had to decide what action he'd want to take...

I knew that the moment he got wind of this, he would want to talk to Lotte. If he couldn't get her on the phone, then he would do anything in his power to get to her.

He'll want to go home.

That wasn't exactly going to be an easy task, since the private jet wasn't due back until tomorrow, but one thing we did have on our side was celebrity status.

Fortunately for him, rock stars had a lot of power.

I pulled up the number for the airline and prepared myself to do some serious name dropping.

———

I'd left it as long as I possibly could. The flight was boarding in an hour and a half and we still had to get over there.

I'd had no luck getting hold of Shelley fuckin' Corbett or anyone else that might have been helpful.

I was out of ideas other than going to talk to Park.

The douches in suits weren't going to be happy, but they could kiss my ass.

It wasn't like Parker needed to brown nose anyway.

I decided to give Hannah one more call before I hunted him down.

It rang three, four, five times and I was just about to hang up when she answered.

"Shit, Jasper, you're persistent, I'll give you that. I'm kinda busy right now, but you can tell Parker that if this shit with this *Katie* chick," she sneered the name, " turns out to be true, I'm going to cut off his balls with a knife then feed them to him on a fork, piece by piece, you understand me?"

I was about to answer when I heard Little Red's voice in the background, yelling for Hannah to get off the phone.

"I gotta go," she hissed before hanging up.

I didn't even get a word in.

"Shit," I muttered.

I dialled again, and it went straight to voicemail.

She's gone.

We were on our own now.

I jogged around until I got to where Parker had been doing his meet and greets and was currently schmoozing the label execs.

"Park, man, we need to talk," I whispered in his ear.

His whole body tensed. He knew this wasn't going to be good news. I never interrupted him when he was doing his thing.

He nodded stiffly at me and turned back to the suits. "I just need a minute with my manager, something's come up."

Something came up alright.

I tipped my head towards the dressing room. There was no way I was breaking this to him out here where anyone could see or hear.

"What the hell is it, J?" he demanded as soon as I heard the click of the door shutting behind us.

"It's bad news, man. You're not gonna like it," I warned.

"Just fucking give it to me, I can't take this suspense bullshit... you know that."

I sighed and reached into my pocket for my phone. I pushed a few buttons and found the post I was looking for. I shot him a sympathetic look as I handed it over.

He shook his head at the photo in front of him and frowned. "Katie?" he asked in confusion. "What the hell has this got to do with anything?"

"Look at when it was posted, and check out the caption."

I watched as he read the thing word for word.

"That fuckin' bitch!" he bellowed. "I'm gonna end her for this."

He was pacing the room now, his go-to move when he was freaking out.

"I think you've got bigger problems right now," I told him quietly.

He froze and went white as a ghost.

"She doesn't think it's true, does she?" He stalked across the room and got right in my face. "Holy shit, man, have you talked to her, or to Han?"

I clamped my hands down on his shoulders. "Calm the fuck down," I instructed. "I spoke to Hannah."

He let out a relieved breath.

Not such good news...

My expression must have been telling the story because his face paled.

"It wasn't good. She told me to tell you she was going to cut your balls off and feed them to you with a knife and fork, and then I heard Charlotte yelling at her in the background to get off the phone."

He stared blankly at me.

"I didn't get a word in before she hung up, and now I can't get hold of either of them."

"Get me on the next plane home, J, please." His voice was broken, and I could tell he was barely holding it together right now. Charlotte weas more important to him than anything... I couldn't imagine him being able to function if he lost her over this.

"Already booked," I told him. "Get your shit, Park, these suits will have to manage without you... we gotta go, right now."

I took a piss and headed back out to find Parker.

I couldn't wait until we got back and he sorted this shit out with Lotte.

He'd been a jumpy bastard the whole flight, and I wasn't sure I could handle sitting next to him and his twitching leg for much longer.

I pulled my cell from my pocket and powered it up.

I reasoned with myself that I should try and call Han again, but in reality, I just needed a little more time away from Mr. highly strung.

I pulled up Han's number, but changed my mind. She wouldn't answer me earlier so there was no reason she would answer now.

I pulled up Facebook, intent on checking out just how far this garbage had spread now.

Social media might have been Parker's best friend most of the time, but it certainly wasn't doing him too many favours right now.

I skimmed past a picture of Charlotte and Parker before freezing and back tracking.

A smile spread across my face as I read the caption.

"Missing this guy right now, but at least I know he's taking a piece of me with him wherever he goes. Shelley Corbett, let's play a game of spot the difference, shall we? (And I'm not talking about the blonde piece of ancient history) #Don'tLetTheTruthGetInTheWay-

OfAGoodStory   #FreshInk   #LookingForTrouble #NiceTry #PSI'mNotActuallyPregnant"

Charlotte didn't take any shit from anybody.

Parker was going to be stoked beyond belief with this. His woman had his back one hundred and ten percent.

I headed back over to where Park was sitting, his obvious agitation still rising.

He jumped as I sat down and made some comment about me taking a shit.

I wasn't listening, I was too busy being in awe of Charlotte Watson. I laughed loudly, the whole situation was suddenly incredibly funny now that my best friend's relationship was no longer at risk.

"Park, man, I think I just might love that girl of yours," I told him, still staring at my screen.

"What the hell are you talking about?" he demanded, grabbing the phone from my hands.

A huge grin spread across his face as he took in the post on the screen in front of him.

"It's a shame she couldn't tag Katie." I chuckled. "She's got sass that girl, and hell... I like it."

This was how a relationship should work.

She had his back and he had hers. They were a team.

This was exactly what I wanted with Hannah. I wanted it all.

"Well damn," Park stated, still smiling like a fool.

"Yeah, man," I agreed. "That's epic."

———

"We're going to scare the shit outta them, you know that, right?"

"They'll be asleep." Park shrugged.

"Exactly, man... don't you know how creepy it is to sneak into a woman's apartment in the middle of the night when she's asleep?"

"I've got a key."

I shook my head and chuckled. "Yeah, too bad she doesn't know that."

"Technicality." He smirked.

Parker was still a total sociopath when it came to Charlotte. The sneaky bastard had had me take her keys and make a copy one day.

I knew I probably should have said no, but hell, I'd always been more of a yes man and it was bound to give me some type of entertainment at some point anyway, I'd reasoned.

Apparently, that time was now.

"Hannah's liable to beat our asses with a frying pan or something, you realise that, right?"

His step faltered. "You're right, that chick is crazy, but I'm going in anyway."

"I'll walk behind you."

He flipped me the bird and slid the key into the lock.

CHAPTER 20

Hannah

MY BEST FRIEND was one badass bitch.

That post that she'd cooked up had absolutely slayed that giant drama queen, Shelley.

And those hash tags...

Don't even get me started...

Parker was one lucky bastard having a woman as dedicated to him as my best friend was.

She'd been scared, but she'd kept her cool. She hadn't flown off the handle like I would have.

I was the woman who reacted first and thought it through second.

If someone had shown me a picture of Jasper and another woman and claimed it was current, I would have flipped my lid.

Just the thought of the fictional scenario made my blood boil.

I took a deep breath and reality hit me like a slap in the face.

Jasper *could* be with other women if he wanted to be. He could be with another woman right now for all I knew... and he wouldn't be doing a thing wrong.

This was the point Jess had been trying to make the other night.

He wasn't going to be mine if I couldn't sort my shit out.

I was the one who was forcing this stupid friends bullshit on him.

What the hell am I doing?

I wanted him to be mine. Officially.

I didn't want to fight my feelings anymore.

He was a truly incredible man, he was patient, kind, and sexy as hell.

He liked to wind me up, but he always found a way to calm me down again afterwards.

So worth it.

The man was an absolute god, and I wanted him to be all mine.

I can't go on like this.

I had to tell him that I wanted more, before it was too late.

I knew I was taking a risk, and that I might end up with my heart broken, but I couldn't ignore the truth any longer.

If he were to leave me now, I'd still be broken.

I knew I needed to work on myself, and the issues I had – but right now it wasn't my main priority.

He is.

There was no sense at keeping him at arm's length – I was already invested.

I may as well enjoy the whole package.

I looked at my phone again and considered calling him, but decided against it.

This wasn't a conversation we could have over the phone.

We both had our hands full right now anyway.

Charlotte was fretting like an old woman, and I doubted Parker was going to be much better.

I had a feeling that he would be on his way home, but I didn't want to get Charlotte's hopes up.

I'd done my best to placate her, but she was still so far from being relaxed.

I was over here having a mega revelation and borderline melt down and she was so distracted, she hadn't even noticed.

"Why don't we watch a movie in bed? There's no point in just sitting around waiting for a call that probably isn't coming," I suggested.

She glanced longingly at the screen of her phone again and sighed.

"Fine."

I rushed over to the DVD cabinet and grabbed the first action thriller I saw. There was no way in hell I was getting caught in the rom-com trap, she would have been bawling within minutes.

I flicked the lights off and we headed towards my room.

We both froze as we heard a key turning in a lock.

What the hell...

"Did you just hear—"

"Shhhh," I interrupted her whisper.

Shit, shit, shit... someone's here.

"Grab a weapon," I hissed.

"I don't have a fucking weapon," she hissed back. "I'm a makeup artist, not a ninja."

"We're both going to die," I whispered. I knew I was being dramatic, but I was starting to panic.

Where the hell is Jasper when I need him?

"The bathroom," she whispered back. "Get to the bathroom, right now!"

The sound of the door handle turning spurred us into action and we dashed for the hallway.

"They've got a key... we're gonna die!" I cried, in full hysteria mode now.

We were the only people that were supposed to have keys to this place. But clearly someone else had one too.

Charlotte shoved me into the bathroom and locked the door behind us.

I started babbling, I pointed to the phone in her hands, but I wasn't sure what the words coming out of my mouth were.

I'm gonna die.

This is how it ends.

Charlotte had the phone to her ear, but I didn't have even the faintest clue who she was calling.

I was going to get murdered in my own home and I never even had the chance to tell Jasper that I was in love with him.

Wait, what?

The realisation that I was in love with him hit me like a pickup truck.

Holy shit.

I love him.

God, I've been an idiot.

I was busy floating around on cloud nine when I saw Lotte reaching for the lock.

"What the hell are you doing?" I hissed, swatting her hand away from the door handle.

"It's Parker."

"You are bat-shit crazy, woman, he's not even in town... are you trying to get us killed?"

"It's Parker for fuck's sake," she repeated more loudly this time.

"Shhhhhh," I shushed her.

She may have been my best friend, but right now the silly bitch was going to get us killed.

"I bet you two grand that it's Parker," she told me, as she held my arm back and turned the lock with her free hand.

I attempted fruitlessly to grab for the lock, but it was too late.

"I can't use two grand if I'm dead," I cried dramatically.

She slipped out the door and I slammed it shut behind her, re-fixing the lock.

It was every man for himself now.

"Parker?" I heard her call.

I pressed my ear up against the door. I heard a lot of muffled voices and then crying from Lotte.

"I hear crying!" I yelled. "Are you being killed?"

I heard a half-laugh half-cry.

"I told you it was Parker, you fool."

"How'd he get a key?" I demanded.

I was no sucker.

I wasn't coming out of this hiding spot until I was good and convinced that I wasn't about to be murdered.

There was more muffled talking I couldn't make out.

"*Forced* Jasper to make a copy you mean," I heard his voice and my whole body relaxed.

"Jasper?" I called timidly from inside the still-locked bathroom.

"Yeah, barbie?" he called back.

Oh thank god.

They really are here.

I slowly unlocked the door and peeked around the frame.

Sure enough, Parker was there, his arms wrapped around an exhausted-looking Lotte.

And then there was *him*.

My knight in shining armour.

"I'm not giving you two grand," I told Charlotte as I breezed past, heading towards Jasper.

She laughed, and I could tell that she and Parker were going to be just fine.

"I think I need a hug too," I told Jasper as I reached him. I was trying to play it cool, but between the threat of an intruder and the realisation that I was in love with him, I was well and truly on edge.

"Bring it in, you little fruit cake."

I could hear Parker and Charlotte talking behind me, but I took no notice.

I was exactly where I needed to be. I could feel his head resting on top of mine as he breathed me in.

"She's exhausted," Parker spoke to Jasper. "I'll be staying the night, you wanna head home or crash here?"

"He can stay here," I answered quickly. "I don't really want to be alone right now either."

Parker nodded and carried Lotte off to her room.

"C'mon." I tugged him in the direction of my bedroom. "We need to talk."

―――――

"I lied," I blurted out the second we were alone.

His eyes shot up to meet mine in question.

"I lied to you… when I told you that you didn't scare me… I lied." I felt my bottom lip trembling. "You frighten the hell out of me, Jasper… I've tried to keep my distance emotionally from you and protect myself, but I can't do it anymore. I'm not only hurting myself, I'm hurting you too and that's the last thing I *ever* wanted to do."

He stood tall as he moved his incredible body into my personal space. He brushed my hair back from my face and cupped my chin in his rough hand. "What are you saying?"

"I'm saying I was wrong to keep you at arm's length... I want you. I want all of you; I can't have another night with you and not know if it was my last."

He chuckled darkly and leaned in so close I could feel his breath against my cheek. "I lied too. I told you I could do this 'friends' bullshit.... I told you I could do it... I fuckin' lied."

I gasped.

"You're my woman, not my god damn friend... and if you think that I'd ever let one of these nights be our last, then you don't know me as well as you think."

His words sent a bolt of hope ricocheting through my body.

"What are *you* saying?" I whispered.

"I'm saying you're *mine,* Hannah, you have been since the first moment I laid a finger on that soft skin of yours. One look in those green eyes and I was totally screwed."

"But you said—"

"Forget what I said," he interrupted me. "I said what you wanted to hear, because I knew you'd get there eventually... I'm a patient man, BG, but you've pushed me to my limits these past few weeks."

"You were humouring me?" I whispered.

"Hell yes I was. I've wanted this, you and me, from that first night, Hannah. I've just been waiting for you to catch up."

"I'm sorry it took me so long."

He wrapped his arms around me, his smile wider than I'd ever seen it.

"You look so happy."

"You've got no idea," he growled before welding his mouth to mine.

His lips were firm, but soft, tender but passionate.

He nipped at my bottom lip and I moaned.

"I've missed that sound." He chuckled as he rested his forehead against mine.

"I've missed *you*." I kissed his lips again.

"It probably makes me a terrible person, but I'm stoked we're back early."

"Then I'm a terrible person too."

We stood there, holding onto each other, just soaking up the feeling of being together.

I thought about Lotte and Parker and the nonsense that had just threatened to tear them apart.

I didn't want my life to be like that. I knew we couldn't hide forever, but for now, maybe we could.

"Do you hate the idea of keeping this to ourselves for a little bit?"

"As long as you've finally got the memo, I

couldn't care less," he answered without even taking a minute to think about it.

"Even if we didn't tell Park and Lotte just yet...?"

His eyes narrowed slightly as he opened his mouth to speak.

"I just need a minute to adjust and enjoy this, once we come out, then everyone will know, and it won't be just ours anymore... I know you're not the rock star, but trust me, you've got your own fan club, and you being off the market is going to be news," I blurted out before he could give me an answer.

"I've been off the market for a while now and hell hasn't frozen over." He smirked.

Butterflies fluttered in my stomach. "You could have filled me in on that piece of information..."

I crawled over to him and swung my leg over his hips so I was straddling him.

"You weren't ready to hear it."

He was right. He was always right when it came to knowing what I needed.

"So, you're my boyfriend now?" My heart was beating so fast at the very idea of it, I was seriously worried about having a heart attack.

"Nope," he replied seriously. "*Boyfriend* isn't going to cut it. That shit's for kids. You're my future, baby, you're the most important part of it and there's no way I'm walking around being called a 'bf'."

Relief flooded through me and I laughed. I laughed so long my sides hurt.

Jasper Jones didn't do anything by the book.

He was right; if he could put up with me, then I was his future... that type of crazy dedication deserved something more than the term 'boyfriend'.

"Then how am I meant to introduce you when we go public with this thing?" I ran my hands through the longer strands of hair on the top of his head.

His eyes sparkled, and I knew I'd opened myself up to a bunch of smartass suggestions.

"How about you just call me... 'god of sex'?"

I shook my head.

"Maybe... 'big dick Jasper'?"

I giggled and shook my head again.

"What about, 'the best I've ever had'?"

"True, but no."

He grinned triumphantly.

"You know I don't actually give a rat's ass what you call me, as long as I get to be the best you've ever had.... *right now*. Preferably several times and then just throw that on rinse and repeat every day."

"You've got yourself a deal."

"And if you want to keep this quiet I can do that, but only for now, I'm not hiding you forever."

I nodded in agreement as I lay down on the bed.

He toed off his shoes and stripped off his shirt. "You know what, there's one more thing I need to say."

I sat up and looked at him. I knew this was important; Jasper's face was never this serious.

"I've discovered something over this past week or

so… all this time we've spent together…" He seemed at a loss for words, like he wasn't sure how he was meant to tell me what he wanted to.

I caught his eye and he stared at me with so much emotion it took my breath away.

"I love you, Hannah, *that's* what I wanted to tell you."

He loves me?

Thank fuck for that.

I crawled across the bed and threw myself into his arms.

"I love you too."

CHAPTER 21

Jasper

"SO, are you going to tell me what the hell is up, or are you just gonna keep strolling around like some kinda pompous prick same as you have been for the past two weeks?" Parker demanded from where he was sitting, watching me.

"Tough choice, but I think I'll go with door number two."

I carried on mixing the eggs I was making for breakfast, whistling an upbeat tune.

I couldn't think of anything but her telling me she loved me. She said it every single day and there were seriously no better words in the world.

"Seriously? Whistling? You have *got* to be getting laid."

"Maybe I am," I mused.

"Holy shit, you are! I fuckin' knew it! I told Charlotte you were getting your end away."

"And what did she have to say about that?"

He chuckled. "She told me to mind my own damn business."

"Smart girl that one, you should listen to her." I tipped the eggs into the pan and busied myself with finding a spatula.

I hated lying to Park. I never lied to him... *ever*. But I was now. For *her*.

It wasn't so much lying as it was avoiding the truth, but essentially that was the same thing, and I didn't feel any better for it.

I had to admit though, all the sneaking around was actually kinda fun. My excitement levels were through the roof, and having to play it cool when we were in company added another level of anticipation for the time we did have together.

Being in a room full of people and being the only two in on a secret was oddly arousing.

I was tired as shit though – sneaking around meant if I wanted to have guaranteed uninterrupted time with my girl, I had to stay up half the night. Not that I was exactly complaining, it was a hell of a way to spend a night, but I was starting to think it would be a lot easier to just come clean.

"You really not gonna tell me who this chick is?"

I didn't answer.

"Fine... but whoever this girl is, or guy... sorry, I shouldn't just assume..."

He was trying to provoke me; I knew that as well as he did.

I'd never been one to bite.

I chuckled and shrugged. "You know my motto, Park, always try everything once."

Parker wasn't quite as controlled when it came to not taking the bait.

"Seriously? A dude?" He gaped. "I mean... that's cool man... I just... I... didn't know." He rubbed the back of his neck awkwardly, clearly lost for words.

He was just too easy; fucking with him wasn't even a challenge these days.

I couldn't help it; I burst into a fit of laughter.

"Holy shit... the look on your face is the best thing I've seen all week."

I wiped the tears from my eyes and scooped the eggs out of the pan and onto the two plates on the counter.

"Fuck's sake, J, can you just give me a proper answer for once?"

I snorted. "Unlikely." I shoved a plate at him. "Your breakfast is ready."

He snagged his phone and typed out a quick message.

I smirked. "You just text Little Red to see if she thinks I'm into dudes, didn't you?"

"How the hell do you know that?" he demanded.

I chuckled. "I can read you like a book, man. Always could."

"Would be great if that worked both ways," he grumbled as his phone dinged.

"Gotta have a bit of mystery, keep the spark alive and all that." I winked at him, my laughter barely restrained again.

He read her reply and laughed.

"What'd she say?"

He glanced at the message again and grinned. "She said... 'Hell to the freakin' no, fool, that man is all about the titties and the girl bitties'."

I nearly spat out the mouthful of orange juice I'd just drank.

Charlotte was hilarious. And she didn't beat around the bush either.

"If you don't marry that girl one day I'm gonna have to kick your ass."

"If I don't marry that girl one day I'll have to kick my own ass." He shot me a shit-eating grin and shovelled a mouthful of food into his mouth, apparently now satisfied that I hadn't turned bisexual overnight.

I smirked to myself at my successful attempt to distract my best mate from the love life I actually *was* hiding.

Too easy.

CHAPTER 22

Hannah
Present day

I WAS FREAKING OUT. Like, big time freaking out.

He has a ring.

Jasper was hiding a ring. And not just any ring, the biggest god damn pink diamond ring I'd ever seen in my entire life.

I'd known instantly it was for me, I *loved* pink. I was a tall, skinny, blonde girl who was so into the colour pink it wasn't even funny.

God damn it, I really did earn the nickname 'Barbie'.

He was going to give me this ring. He was going to ask me to be his wife.

I could already picture it.

He wouldn't get down on one knee. That wasn't Jasper's style – or mine. We weren't known for being traditional, not in the slightest. That was Charlotte and Parker's thing.

Not that a tattoo-covered rock star and his porcelain-doll-looking wife exactly screamed traditional, but still.

Jasper would be more likely to lob the thing across the room at me and say something like 'so how about it?' or 'Barbie, can I be your Ken?'.

Holy shit.

I shoved the giant rock back into its bright pink satin box and put it back into Jasper's junk drawer, the iPad charger I'd been searching for long forgotten.

My hands were shaking, and I couldn't seem to get enough air.

Breathe, Hannah, breathe.

Charlotte would be here soon, she'd know what to do.

She always knew how to calm me down when I was losing my shit.

I rushed up to the bedroom I shared with J and stripped off, trying to take deep, calming breaths as I went.

I threw on a light, denim, spaghetti-strap dress with my tan-and-white sandals and glanced at myself in the mirror.

My blonde hair was longer than I usually kept it; the bob style had grown down past my shoulders now. I'd thought about cutting it off recently, but Jasper seemed to like it longer. He'd said, and I quote, that he 'liked having something to hold onto', so I'd decided to grow it out, like it was when I was younger.

He'd actually gone on to be really sweet and tell me that he liked me with shorter hair just as much, but he thought the slightly longer, more wild-looking hair suited me and my personality better. He'd told me hundreds of times that I didn't need to wear so much makeup on my face, and I'd eventually learned that he preferred me without it entirely.

Looking at my reflection in the mirror right now, the strands in loose waves and my green eyes bright and wide, I had to agree with him.

"Han?" I heard Charlotte call from downstairs.

"Up here," I hollered back.

I was doing up the buckle on my watch when Lotte appeared in the doorway.

There was silence for a few beats before she spoke.

"What the hell happened?" she demanded.

I gasped in surprise and met her eyes. I'd thought I had been doing a good job of appearing calm.

"You're doing that whole twitchy wild animal thing you do when you're stressed." She narrowed her blue eyes at me.

"He's going to propose," I blurted out the words without a second thought.

It was only once I'd spoken them aloud that I

realised how absolutely thrilled I was about this revelation.

I was freaking the hell out, but I was so excited I could hardly think straight.

I was going to marry the only man that had ever loved me the way a man should love a woman. I was going to marry the man that I truly believed was meant for me.

Charlotte shrieked in excitement and jumped up and down clapping her hands. "Oh my god! How do you know?"

She bounded over to me and pulled me in for a hug, both of us now jumping around like excited little girls.

"I found the ring."

"That bastard bought you a ring and didn't even take his best girlfriend to help? I'm insulted, I really am." She pouted.

I laughed, my tone shrill and nervous.

"Did he do good?" she asked as she glanced around, presumably looking for said ring.

"I freaked out and shoved in back in the drawer," I explained with a giggle. "But he did good, he did *so* good, Lotte."

I took her downstairs and dug around for the box. I pulled it out and she whistled a long, low sound.

"That's one hell of a ring, girl." She brought it up closer to her face. "Jesus, would you even be able to lift your hand with that thing on it?"

"You can't talk." I pointed at the ring she wore on her left hand. "Parker didn't exactly hold back."

She shrugged and grinned. "True."

I tucked the ring back in its hiding spot.

"I'll be your maid of honour, right?"

"I'm not even engaged yet." I rolled my eyes at her.

She rolled hers right back. "As if you'd ever do anything but say yes."

Of course I'll say yes.

The idea was so exciting, but as I thought about saying the word yes to him, panic rose in my chest again.

What if he decides I'm too crazy for him in ten years?

What will happen then?

"We gotta go." Lotte glanced at her watch. "We'll be late, and you don't keep this girl waiting."

Just calm down...

I grabbed a sheet of paper from the kitchen counter and scribbled down a note to Jasper.

I'll find you when I get home, I love you.

Ready or not, here I come.

H x

I sat it where I knew he'd see it.

"You two are so weird." She giggled as she glanced at the note.

"Yup," I agreed shamelessly as I locked the front door behind us. "But we own it, so it doesn't count."

Charlotte just laughed at my usual defence of my

wacky behaviour as we got into the tinted-out black SUV that Parker had bought Charlotte for her twenty-seventh birthday.

"No Sammy today?" I quizzed. Normally the guys insisted that we have Sammy drive us everywhere we went, or at the very least, have a member of the security team with us.

"Nope." She grinned. "This place has been added to the 'safe list'." She shook her head in bewilderment.

Charlotte dealt incredibly well with Parker's life, but any opportunity she got to live a normal life, she took it.

And I don't blame her.

I'd witnessed numerous disagreements between Park and Lotte, usually about things that Lotte insisted on doing for herself – mundane things, like the grocery shopping. Parker wanted them to use a service. He wanted to do *anything* and *everything* that kept Charlotte out of the public eye – safe and protected.

I was beginning to gather that Charlotte was usually the winner of these types of arguments. Not only had she gone to the store herself last time, but Parker and three of his security guards had gone too.

I'd held up the glass of wine I was drinking on my balcony to toast to them when they had arrived back from the store. Charlotte had given me a victorious grin and a double thumbs up. Parker had flipped me the bird.

I glanced over at my best friend as we pulled into a street I'd never visited. I might have been a total fruit loop, but she was sassy as hell – she didn't put up with any shit from anybody these days.

Parker and Jasper might have been two of the most successful recording artists on the planet right now, but Charlotte didn't give them an inch if she didn't want to.

I knew why she did it, Parker did too. She'd been so severely controlled by her last boyfriend that she needed to feel like she still had control over some part of her life.

I knew she didn't feel suffocated or controlled by Parker, it was actually quite the opposite. She almost didn't function quite right when they were apart.

But old habits die hard I guess.

Parker never wanted Lotte to feel that way ever again, and the cunning woman used that to her advantage; that's how she won so many battles.

Jasper wasn't quite as bad as Parker, I'd had a few lectures about keeping myself safe; I had a team of bodyguards I could call on whenever I needed to, and Sammy was always skulking around somewhere, doing his best to follow Parker's orders and keep Charlotte protected.

Truthfully though, I rarely went anywhere without either Jasper, Charlotte or Parker anyway.

In fact, I couldn't remember the last time I was somewhere, other than home, on my own.

The thought actually made me feel kind of claustrophobic.

I decided that when I got home tonight, I was going for a run. Alone.

"Where the hell are you taking me?" I demanded as Charlotte pulled her flash-ass car up and stopped in a dodgy-looking side street.

"You'll see," she replied, her eyes twinkling as she swung her door open.

I climbed out and glanced around sceptically. "*This* place is considered *safe?*"

"You'll see," she repeated, indicating that we were going to go through a grimy-looking door on the side of this shitty little street.

She raised a brow at me, daring me not to follow.

Charlotte had rarely steered me wrong in life, but I had a feeling that that was about to change.

Ninety-five percent of me hoped she was.

"Finally, something exciting is happening around here." I grinned as I followed her through the door and into a dark hallway.

―――――

"You're really going to let me ink up this virgin skin?" Asha, asked Lotte with a grin.

"Just do it already," Charlotte groaned, her free hand covering her eyes.

I still couldn't believe what I was seeing. I'd tried

to get this little wuss to get tattooed with me all three times that I'd visited a studio.

My tattoos were all small. I had a star – I got that when my grandmother passed away. She was an amazing lady and I liked to think that she was up there in the stars watching over me. I had a daisy chain around my ankle – there was no reason for that one other than the fact that I like daisies and tattoos were addictive, and my third one was a tiny pair of scissors that I'd got when I'd become regarded as one of the best hair stylists in the industry.

I may not have been able to hold a flame to the tattoo collection of my boyfriend, but I was no ink virgin.

"Let me see what you're getting."

Charlotte pointed with the hand that Asha didn't have pinned down on the wrap-covered bench. There was a sheet of paper resting on the seat next to her.

It was a small design, a music note and a heart intertwined together.

It was simple, but beautiful.

It suddenly all made sense. Charlotte had organised for Parker and Jasper to go to some interview across town that they'd be at all morning. Since we'd declined that particular request four times previously, I didn't understand why she'd accepted this time... but now I did.

She needed Parker out of the way so she could

get a gorgeous tattoo as a tribute to their love, just like Parker had done when they'd been first starting out.

"I love it... *he's* going to love it, Lotte."

"He better," she grumbled as Asha made a start on the outline on Charlotte's wrist.

The buzzing of the tattoo gun gave me tingles. It really was so damn addictive.

"Asha, babe, you didn't tell me we had beautiful guests," a cheery voice came from behind me.

Asha laughed lightly without taking her eyes off her work. She moved the needle like a pro – I could see why she was the only person that Parker let ink him anymore.

"Charlotte, Hannah, that's Hawke," she offered without breaking stride on her work.

I held my hand out to the forty-something-year-old guy that had appeared from out back. He wore a pair of faded jean shorts and a plain back singlet. And if I thought that Jasper was covered in tattoos, I was wrong. This guy was *covered.*

"Jesus, do you have any bare skin left at all?" I blurted out without thinking as he took my hand in his.

"Han!" Charlotte scolded me like a parent would a rude child.

Hawke just laughed deep and loud.

"Well actually... I'll show you."

He turned around and Asha laughed. "You've done it now, girl."

I didn't know what I was expecting, but it

certainly wasn't for him to drop his pants and show me his bare, totally un-tattooed ass. Even still, it wasn't quite enough to shock a girl like me.

"Touché, sir, touché," I drawled.

He laughed again.

He buckled his belt back up and then rubbed his hands together excitedly. "So, what am I giving you, blondie?"

"Nah." I shook my head. "I'm just here for moral support." I grinned at Charlotte's grimace.

"Oh c'mon... I can't tempt you into anything? On the house? Since you took looking at my hairy ass like a real trooper and all," he offered.

Now that was an offer I couldn't refuse.

I strolled over to look at the wall of tattoo photos and recognised one almost instantly.

"Hey, I know that wolf."

I looked back over my shoulder at him and he came over to see.

"I know that wolf well." I smirked.

Hawke looked at me sideways. "You and Jones, huh?" he asked with eyebrows raised in surprise.

I nodded as I traced my finger over the image that sat low on my boyfriend's hip. "Oooooh yeah."

"You'll be familiar with a lot of my work then." He pointed out a few more images that adorned Jasper's body.

So this is where he comes...

I was familiar alright.

I could tell you exactly where on his body all those images were placed.

I'd spent countless hours studying his art, finding out why he got it, what it meant to him...

Hearing him talk about them was nearly as addictive as getting the tattoos myself.

I turned to the big man next to me. "I know what I want to get."

CHAPTER 23

Jasper

HIDE AND SEEK, baby.

I scrawled the note and placed it over top of the one she'd left for me. I had no idea where her and Charlotte had gone, Parker didn't either. Charlotte's Range Rover was gone, and I swear Sammy knew, but the bastard wasn't talking.

Parker was probably losing his shit good and proper by now. His wife was god knows where, and with no protection to boot.

I wasn't thrilled about it either, but I trusted Hannah's judgement and her ability to keep herself safe.

"Code accepted, access granted," the security system alerted me over the speaker system.

I knew what that meant.

She's home.

My face broke out in a grin as I sprinted for the hiding spot I'd thought of earlier.

This shit is weird.

I knew it was weird, we both did, but that made it all the more fun. I'd bet we were the only adults around here racing around to play hide and seek, and that was what I liked about us.

We weren't like everyone else.

I skidded to a stop and listened for her.

I was hoping she'd come through the front door like she usually did when it wasn't raining, and not through the house.

My plan was to wait until I heard the familiar line, and then slip through the internal access into the garage where she'd just come from.

I heard the front door open and her footsteps as she walked into the kitchen.

Success.

"Ready or not... here I come," she called out, the excitement in her voice evident.

That one line had my pulse racing.

I snuck into the garage, into the storage area and waited.

The anticipation was killing me already. I could still remember being a little kid, hiding just like this, excitement and nervous energy thrumming through my whole body. Trying to be still, making an effort to even breathe quietly...

The prize for winning back then was nothing like the prize I'd receive now, even though I wouldn't win. I already knew that.

She'd find me. She always did.

I could hear her walking around upstairs and I knew it wouldn't be long before she ran out of places to look. She'd come for me then.

I crouched down lower and tried to make my big frame smaller than it was.

Not an easy task.

I could hear her downstairs now, and I knew she was getting closer.

I tried to breathe quieter, my excitement not helping in the least.

She opened the door. "Well, well, Jasper Jones, I know you're in here somewhere," she called.

I peeked out and looked at her; she had her back to me, and my god, what a back it was. Her slim shoulders and toned arms on show, and those damn fine legs were on display too.

Fuck the game. I need her.

I rose quietly from my spot, if there was a skill I did possess, it was creeping around. I could move as quiet as a mouse if I wanted to.

I approached her slowly, not wanting to startle her. I could tell the moment she knew I was behind her.

The side of her face curved up in what I knew would be a satisfied smile.

She loved the game – she was such a little weirdo.

Just like me.

But more than the game, I knew she loved what came next.

I stopped behind her, my body only just touching hers, and I felt her tremble slightly from my breath at her neck.

"I found you," she murmured as I kissed her exposed shoulder, trailing kisses slowly up her neck.

She full-on shuddered. Facial hair might have been a pain in the ass sometimes, but right now, I wouldn't have changed it for the world.

Sensory overload.

It was Hannah's secret spot. Down the back and sides of her neck, the hair on my face tickling and scratching her as I went.

"You always find me," I replied huskily.

"Will you always find me?" she asked, her voice oddly vulnerable.

I spun her around quickly, and gripping each side of her hips, hoisted her onto the bonnet of my BMW.

"In any corner of the earth," I answered. "I'll always find you."

"That's what I was hoping you'd say," she whispered.

I didn't know what that meant, but I'd given up trying to understand the deep and inner workings of this woman's mind a long time ago.

I knew how to make her happy, I understood her better than most people ever could, and she loved me.

I'm doing okay.

I slipped the thin straps of her dress down her shoulders.

"No bra," I mumbled appreciatively.

"No underwear either," she whispered in my ear.

I groaned.

Fuck me, the things this girl does to me.

Hannah Montgomery was the only thing in this world that had the potential to break my cool exterior.

Not even music, as much as I loved it, could get the reaction out of me that she could.

I loved her like nothing else.

I wanted to make her my wife.

She looked up at me with lust-filled green eyes and I nearly said it out loud. The only thing that stopped me was not having that ring in my hand.

I'd spent more than some people made in their entire lives on that damn thing, because I wanted it to be perfect for her – like she was for me.

I contemplated running to get it, but my girl distracted me by unzipping my fly and dropping my jeans around my ankles.

The business I had to attend to here was far too important.

It could wait a while longer; we had forever.

Right now, I was going to fuck the woman of my dreams on the hood of my brand new car, and I was gonna do it right.

CHAPTER 24

Hannah

HE NEARLY DID IT.

I knew he'd been thinking about it, and it would have been perfect – for us at least. Not exactly a story you'd tell your grandchildren, but perfect nonetheless.

But he couldn't ask me. Not yet. There was something I needed to do first.

One final game – for lack of a better word... before I became his wife.

Mrs Jones.

God, I hoped like hell that he'd win this next game because I really liked the sound of that.

I kissed him fiercely as I slid off the bonnet of the car.

I needed to make a call.

He slid my straps back up into place and tugged the hem of my dress down, his thumbs grazing my stomach in the process.

He grinned as I sighed at the contact.

It didn't seem to matter how long we'd been together, how many times we'd had sex, or even how frequently, one touch was always enough to turn me to jelly.

"You ruin me," I whispered.

He smiled up at me the same way he always had, and I melted a little bit more.

"I'd be worried if I didn't."

I could feel his breath on my stomach and I knew it would only be a moment before he saw it.

His breath caught.

He's seen it.

"Han..."

"It's a 'J'," I told him before he could ask. "Which I'm sure you can see."

"Is that..." I heard him swallow deeply.

"A tattoo." I finished for him. "For *you.*"

He made a growling sound that made my stomach flip.

I giggled as he licked his finger and rubbed at the ink, checking to see if it was going to rub off.

"It's real," he breathed, getting to his feet.

"It better be. It wasn't exactly fun."

"I can't believe you did that."

"I wanted to make sure that you knew I was yours."

He pulled me in so our foreheads were touching.

His warm hazel eyes were closed, and I could tell he was having a hard time keeping his emotions in check.

"In this fucked-up world," he finally spoke, "that's one of the few things I know for sure."

"I know I can be crazy..."

"I *love* your crazy," he interrupted, "It's the best thing about you."

The words were so sincere I had a hard time doubting them... but somehow, I still found a way.

———

I heard the water turn on in the shower and the glass door shut as Jasper entered.

I knew I had about ten minutes to make my call, fifteen if he was planning on washing that mop of hair on the top of his head.

The call that could change everything.

He answered on the fourth ring. "Hey, princess... long time no talk..."

I glanced at the bathroom door. "Hey... I need your help."

He paused for a moment before answering simply. "Anything."

I took a deep breath and twirled a strand of my hair around my finger.

I had to trust someone with this thing, and it was going to be him.

It needed to be him.

So I told him my plan... he listened, told me I was nuts, and then agreed to help me.

CHAPTER 25

Jasper

TO: Parker

From: Jasper

She got a fucking tattoo man, a TATTOO. It's a little 'J'.... Fuck me.

A god damn tattoo. Shit I love that woman.

To: Jasper

From: Parker

Little Red got one too. Nearly made it worth blowing a gasket when I couldn't find her earlier. So damn hot.

. . .

To: Parker:

From: Jasper

You need to calm your shit, bro.

We got ourselves a couple of badass bitches.

I chuckled as I sat my phone down on the kitchen counter.

That man really needed to lighten up.

He was going to end up being one of those old dudes on blood pressure medication if he kept flying off the handle the way he did.

Charlotte was a smart girl, our lives were fucking crazy, but she had a good head on her shoulders and she'd been with him a long time now, this wasn't her first rodeo.

My phone chimed on the counter. I unlocked the screen with a lazy swipe.

To: Jasper

From: Parker

I wanna do a demo of the new song tomorrow, come over about 10?

Tell Han to come, Charlotte's not leaving my fucking sight.

I rolled my eyes and chuckled.

"Barbie?!" I yelled down the hall.

"Yeah, babe?" Hannah called back from wherever she was.

"Little Red is grounded, wanna come keep her company tomorrow while we lay down a couple of demos?"

Her laugh rang out through the hall of my house.

A house that wasn't a home without her.

"He sure knows how to overreact, huh?" she yelled back with a giggle.

Understatement of the century.

I responded with a chuckle.

"Sounds like a plan."

"Oh and babe?" I called again.

"Yeeeaaah?" she replied suspiciously.

"Did Lotte send us over the dodgy side of town for that stupid fucking interview just to get us out of her hair?"

I strolled down the hallway quietly as I waited for her reply.

"How *was* that interview?" she yelled back as I followed her voice.

Found you.

I rested my shoulder on the door frame of the studio she'd had installed for me as soon as she'd found out I could sing, and watched her for a moment.

She was so pretty; her brow was furrowed in concentration as she clicked away on the computer in the corner.

"Don't change the subject, barbie girl."

She jumped out of her chair and clutched her chest. "For fuck's sake, Jasper, how many times do I have to tell you not to sneak up on me like that!"

I chuckled and raised a brow at her, waiting for my answer.

She shot me daggers as she sat back down and started clicking at the computer again.

"Well? Did I sit through three hours of fucking torture just so she could get herself a love shrine in permanent ink?"

She smirked. "I'm not saying that she *did* set you guys up, but also I'm not willing to say that she didn't."

I'll take that as a yes.

"I'll be getting that little redheaded she-devil back for this."

"Oh c'mon... you love the tattoo."

Can't argue with that.

"She could have sent Park without me," I grumbled.

"You're a package deal now, baby."

"Yeah, yeah." I strolled towards her. "What are you doing on here anyway?"

"Making a mix tape."

"Of what?"

"Of you... and Parker."

I came up behind her and looked at the screen over her shoulder.

"Like an actual mix tape?"

She grinned. "Well a 2018, USB version."

"What do you want that for?"

"What's with all the questions?" She giggled.

She was playing it cool, but I knew her well enough to know that she was up to something.

Now I just had to figure out what it was.

"You know me," I drawled. "I get curious."

"Curiosity killed the cat."

I chuckled at her comment.

"I just wanted it for my car."

We'd brought her a brand new, white Mercedes sedan about six months ago and while she loved that thing to death, she hardly ever got to drive it.

She did still pout every now and then about me trading in that awful bright pink beetle she used to drive, but I couldn't stand the sight of the thing in the car shed any bloody longer.

I knew she didn't really care, it was hard for her to stay mad when she had a damn fine replacement.

"Alright then." I kissed the top of her head and left her to it.

I knew she was bullshitting me, but I loved myself a good mystery – and Hannah was nothing if not a puzzle to figure out.

CHAPTER 26

Jasper
Two years earlier

"OH C'MON, you're not still mad, are you?" I chuckled as I unlocked the front door.

"Oh, this isn't mad; trust me, when I'm mad you'll know all about it." Hannah shot me a death glare, and I was seriously a little bit afraid.

Ah crap.

I loved pushing her buttons, I really did, but I never wanted to make her doubt the way I felt about her.

I was hoping the surprise I'd had organised might have gone a small way to gaining her forgiveness.

She was still pissed at me for the way I asked her to move in with me. She thought I'd left it until the last minute to be funny – but truth was, it wasn't until I'd walked into the half-empty apartment that she'd been sharing with Lotte that I realised how much I wanted to ask her to move in.

It was as though it hadn't really sunk in that Lotte was moving in with Park until that moment. It wasn't until I'd listened to her talking about how she was going to have to get a new coffee table to replace the one Charlotte took with her that I knew the only place she belonged was at my house with me. She didn't need a new table and washing machine, she needed to pack her shit and get her ass where it belonged.

So I'd told her that.

I wasn't exactly known for being diplomatic, and I knew damn well that Hannah loved a show, so ideally, I would have planned something that would have swept her off her feet, but unfortunately the blurt-out-before-thinking method was far too common of an occurrence for me.

"I'm sorry I messed it up for you, it should have been special."

She sighed and turned back to me. "You haven't even given me a key, Jasper, it makes me think you felt pressured into this... I'm worried you only asked me because you felt sorry for me being on my own."

I laughed loudly at her ludicrous statement, which apparently was the wrong thing to do.

She stamped her foot and grumbled. "I'm serious, dickhead."

I took a couple of slow tentative steps toward her, like I was approaching a wild beast, which essentially, I was. "If I didn't want you here with every god damn last bit of me, you wouldn't be here, Hannah."

I wrapped my hands around her and felt her relax into me.

"Trust me, barbie, there is nothing in the world I want more than to have you living here. I want your ridiculous amount of clothes taking up all the wardrobe space, I want to have to yell at you at least twice a week about clogging up the drain with hair, I want all those stupid beauty products that you don't even need all over the bathroom vanity, I want you next to me every night... I want it all." I kissed her forehead.

I wasn't accustomed to seeing her this vulnerable and exposed.

"What if you get sick of me? Working *and* living together now?"

So this was the real crux of it. She was scared. Hannah came across as a fearless warrior, but when it came down to it, inside she was often still a scared little girl.

I gripped her chin between my thumb and finger and lifted until she was looking me in the eye.

"I could spend every minute of every single day with you, Hannah, and it *still* wouldn't be enough. But since that's the only option there is, that's the one I'll take, okay?"

I could tell she got the message this time. She looked like she might have been going to shed a tear.

"Okay," she whispered simply.

"Okay?"

"Okay... but..."

I braced myself for the 'but'.

"But your hair is nearly as long as mine, and if we have clogging issues, I am *not* taking the rap for that one."

She had me on that.

I chuckled. "Alright, that's fair enough."

She pulled free of my hold and grabbed my hand.

I tugged hard, pulling her back against me. "I meant what I said, I love you more than *anything* and there's no one else I'd rather have sharing my life. I *never* want you to doubt that again."

She shook her head. "I can't promise that... you know how I get."

I sighed dramatically. "I'll just *always* have to be there to make you see sense then, won't I?"

I placed a chaste kiss to her lips and tugged her along behind me into the living room.

"Jasper?" she asked cautiously as she looked around the previously cluttered space. "Where's all the boxes?"

I grinned with my back to her and shrugged. "I put them away."

"Put them away where?" she demanded, panic rising in her tone.

I grinned wider. She was so much fun when her temper was rising.

"Drawers, wardrobes, wine cellar." I marked the locations off on my fingers.

"Oh god," she groaned. "Look... it's not that I don't appreciate it, but I have a process, Jasper, I have a process, alright? And now there is going to be shit all in the wrong places and I'll have to hunt for stuff..."

"Breathe."

"And stop being a smartass, you don't have a bloody wine cellar."

"Have a little faith, barbie."

I swear her eye twitched.

I subtly shifted my arm to cover the crown jewels.

She hadn't stooped to the nut-tapping level just yet, but I was walking a fine line right now and I knew it.

I watched her take a deep breath – her go-to technique when I was grinding her gears.

"You." She pointed at me. "Sit. And don't touch *anything* for five minutes. Got it?"

I saluted her and sat my ass down on the couch.

She came back downstairs about half an hour later, as quiet as a mouse.

I held back a smirk as she slowly approached the couch and sat down next to me.

I didn't say a word, just flicked the channel up one and took a swig of the beer I'd gotten for myself in her absence.

I chuckled at a familiar scene in the movie I was watching.

Happy Gilmore, an oldie but a goodie.

We sat there like that for a solid five minutes, me watching the movie, waiting for her to crack, and her squirming in her seat.

"Alright, I'm sorry," she eventually blurted out. "I should have known you wouldn't stuff it all anywhere."

"Keep talking..."

"It's perfect, thank you. I don't know how you did it."

"I'm a genius."

"You're a genius," she agreed. "And you're gorgeous, and an absolute king in the sack..."

I chuckled. "Anything else while you're kissing ass?"

She smacked my arm and then moved closer to snuggle in. "Seriously though, how the hell did you know where to put everything?"

"I hired a magical unicorn to help guide me."

"Jasper, don't be stupid."

"You're right, unicorns aren't real. I used my crystal ball."

"You're impossible," she groaned.

"C'mon now, barbie, you know a good magician never reveals his tricks. So, stop asking and open your present already."

"Present?" She perked up. If there was one thing that could shift Hannah's mood it was the promise of a present.

It wasn't about the material item, I think it was more about the gesture... about her knowing that I'd seen something and thought of her.

I'd once gotten her a new set of laces for her chucks and I swear she'd acted like all her Christmases had come at once.

I could pick her a bunch of wild flowers and she'd almost well up with tears.

I tilted my head towards the light pink box I'd sat in the middle of the table.

She squealed and leapt to her feet.

She returned with the box clasped in her hands and a sparkle in her eye.

"Open it," I encouraged.

She carefully undid the satin bow on the top and lifted the lid off the box.

She lifted the tissue paper and gasped.

"Jasper..." Her voice was barely above a whisper.

The first thing to come out was her house key. I'd had it cut on the day I'd asked her to move in with me, and when I'd seen that they could make the keys coloured, I couldn't resist.

"It's pink." She giggled.

"Of course it is... keep going." I nudged her knee with mine.

Next was a pink garage door remote control – I'd

ended up having to drop my name to get the rush order on that one. That had been a surreal experience to say the least. I'd gotten quite accustomed to dropping Park's name, but never my own.

"What's this for?" She pulled the plastic card out of the bottom with a puzzled expression.

"That's your all-access pass."

"Is it for the gate?"

I shook my head. "Nah you already have the pin number for that... this is a little more personal."

She looked me up and down. "Please tell me you didn't make me an all-access pass to get into your pants?"

"You can thank me later."

"Oh I will." She winked at me before making a show of tucking the card into her back pocket.

She was so gorgeous. I still couldn't figure out how I'd managed to pull a woman like her. She was so full of light. She made *everything* better.

"What?" she beamed at me.

"Nothing, I just love you."

"I love you too. Thank you for my key."

"This is your home, baby, *our* home, okay? You're not living in *my* house, *we* are living in *our* home, you got it?"

"I've only been here five minutes and you're already bossing me around," she answered with a cheeky grin.

"Oh, baby, if you want me to boss you around, you only have to ask."

"Where do I sign?" She smiled. "Seriously though, thank you." She kissed my cheek. "I'm sorry I went all crazy bitch on you earlier."

"It's all good, I'm used to it... you're an absolute fruit loop."

She smirked. "I know, but I own it."

I'd heard that very line at least a hundred times from her mouth.

She snagged the remote from my hands and changed the channel to some trashy reality show.

"So, this is how it's gonna be, huh?"

"You want me to make myself at home, don't you?" She batted her lashes at me innocently.

Dammit.

She had me wrapped so firmly around her little finger it wasn't even funny.

I glanced between her face and the absolute nonsense she was watching for a few minutes.

"I haven't had a chance to really thank you. What you and Lotte are doing for us is perfect."

She smiled and turned her attention away from the screen. "It's gonna be so fun. And now I'll be able to fend off any skanks trying to get their hooks into my man myself." She smiled wider, her expression turning almost wicked.

My possessive lioness...

"You'll save Sammy a job." I shot her a cheeky grin. "But you're really okay with giving up your business, barbie?"

Hannah was an incredible hairdresser. She'd

taken me on a shoot with her a few months back, and the respect that both her and Lotte had from everyone in the industry was amazing to witness.

I was proud as hell of my woman that day.

I was stoked she was joining us on the team, but I was worried she'd miss her old life and end up regretting her choice.

"Hair is what you're, ya know, passionate about and shit, you're not gonna get pissed with me for taking it away?"

She rolled her eyes. "Okay, number one, *you* didn't 'take it away', Lotte and I restructured. Number two, I'm not giving it up entirely. And number three, *you* are what I'm most passionate about. I can go back to being a full time stylist anytime I want. Right now, I'm exactly where I want to be."

I rubbed my hand over my chest. It got hard to breathe when she said stuff like that to me.

I nodded. "So, do you actually know how to be a manager and run PR?" I asked with a shit-eating grin.

She stood up from the couch. "Not particularly. Do you actually know how to be a rock star?" she quipped.

"Touché..." I chuckled as she walked away with a sassy grin. "Touché."

CHAPTER 27

Jasper
Present day

"THAT WAS HORSE SHIT," I moaned. "Take it from the top."

Hannah opened her mouth to speak – argue with me if I had to guess, but I cut her off.

"I know you're going to tell me it was great, but it wasn't."

She shot me a sheepish look. "I thought it was really good."

"You think everything that comes out of my mouth is good, baby, but I can do better."

She rolled her eyes and mumbled something smart under her breath. She waved her hand in a gesture that indicated we should go ahead and start over.

"Ready?" I asked Park.

We were both perched on stools with our guitars.

This was our process; we wrote on our own a lot of the time and then came together to co-write and iron out the kinks in our lyrics, after that we would work the chords and finally lay down a demo before taking it to the production company to record the final version.

We liked to keep to ourselves as much as possible and this worked for us.

We made the record company enough money that they generally let us do things our way anyway. I think they knew that if push came to shove, we'd walk and start our own company.

It's probably what we should have been doing anyway, but extra admin wasn't really either of our styles, so for now at least, we were sticking with what we knew.

"It's your song, J, are *you* ready?"

I'd written this song on my own. I was basically singing it alone too – Park was throwing in a few harmonies, but the majority of this one was on me.

That was why I was losing my cool over it.

"Nah." I stood up and sat down my guitar. "I'll be back in a minute."

I could feel Hannah's eyes on me and if I was honest, that was the problem. I wrote this song about her and I was worried as hell that I wouldn't do it justice.

I slipped out of the room, down Park's hallway and onto the back patio. I was reaching for the pack of cigarettes in my pocket when her hand caught mine.

"Look at me," she demanded, her voice soft.

She came around to stand right in front of me.

She had a green knit sweater on and it made her eyes look so unbelievably bright.

"I was just gonna have a smoke."

"I know you were... you're stressed."

It hadn't taken Hannah long to make the connection between my mood and my dirty little habit.

"I can't nail that verse."

She pulled my hand away from my smokes. "You don't need them, you have me."

She was right. Just having her alone had already made me relax a bit. She might have caused me some stressful situations at times, but the woman was my own personal brand of healing balm.

"Alright then, BG, how are you gonna calm me down?"

She had a fuckin' fantastic way of calming me down, but I doubted she was going to suck me off out here in Parker and Charlotte's yard.

She must have been on the same wavelength as I was. "We'll come back to that later." She licked her lips and my dick jumped in my pants.

"Right now, I'm gonna go get your guitar and you're going to sing it to me – just like you intended it to be, okay?"

I nodded, and she stepped around me. She pointed her finger at me. "No smoking."

I saluted her, and she disappeared.

I pushed the pack of smokes back down into my pocket. I'd found these ones hidden in the back of the fridge.

Hannah was forever trying to get rid of them. 'Filthy fuckin' things' she referred to them as. I had to agree with her. I might have looked like a badass, covered in tattoos and puffing on a ciggy, but I didn't want that shit to kill me, I wanted to get old and grey with my woman.

She appeared in front of me again, the Taylor 214ce Deluxe she'd bought me for my birthday in her hands.

"Here we go, Lollipop, it's just me and you now." She pointed to the seat behind me and I sat.

She passed me the guitar and sat in the seat next to me, she leaned back, her face soaking in the sun and closed her eyes.

I sat for a moment, totally mesmerised by her.

She opened one eye to look at me. "Play," she instructed.

I plucked the guitar strings gently, the tune I'd composed coming to life.

A small smile played on the corners of her mouth.

I didn't take my eyes off her as I sang the first verse.

She had a satisfied smile on her lips by the time I reached the chorus.

"That's you, and what you do to me. I'll never recover, you've knocked me to my knees... you own every part I've ever sold...."

Out here, with just her and me, it was perfect.

"You're all I think about when I play this guitar... your smart mouth, your green eyes and your ridiculous pink car."

She laughed. She'd heard this song at least one hundred times, but that part always got a laugh out of her.

I finished the song and strummed the final chord.

"See?" She still hadn't opened her eyes when she spoke. "You've got this, Jasper. That's my favourite song in the world, and I need you to record it so I can listen to it any time I want."

That was all it took for me to know I would do it.

It was scary really. I knew deep inside, that I would do anything she asked of me – that I would do anything to keep her safe.

Nothing was off limits when it came to Hannah, I would stop at nothing short of murder when it came to this woman, and if I was being honest, I'm not even sure I would stop there.

"Thank you, BG." I leaned over and kissed her lips. "Go home if you want, I won't be long."

She smiled at me and I could feel her eyes on me as I walked back towards the house.

"Jasper?" she called.

I stopped and turned to look back at her.

"I love you, so much."

I smiled, my heart warming. "I love you too."

CHAPTER 28

Hannah

WITNESSING that was going to make it so much harder to go through with my plan tomorrow... but I had to do it.

It had to be now.

He could pop the question at any time, and if he did, I would say yes.

Of course.

But then I'd always worry. I'd always be scared that it would all fall apart.

I have to be sure.

He'd gone back into the studio, his earlier uncertainty replaced with the confidence I'd given him.

He'd nail it on the first go now. I knew him well enough to know that about him.

I glanced around Parker and Charlotte's yard and the gate that led through to our house.

I was going to miss this place.

I just hope I'm not gone for long.

———

I needed to pack my bag.

I lugged one of the suitcases out from the cupboard under the stairs and took it up to our room. I couldn't pack everything – he'd notice if all my stuff wasn't where it usually was for the night, but I could pack the bulk of the clothes I was taking.

I contemplated exactly how I was going to get out of here as I threw items into the case.

We were always together.

I was going to have to come up with some bullshit excuse to get out of going with them tomorrow. I need him out of the house, and ideally, he'd be taking Parker and Charlotte too. The last thing I needed was either of them catching me out.

If all three of them were out, then Sammy would go too, and that would be one less bloodhound to give the slip.

I ran my fingers over the cover on the bed and sighed.

I'd slept with Jasper every single night since I'd moved in, all except for two.

The night of Charlotte's hens do and Park's stag, and the night before their wedding...

I didn't even know if I could sleep without him in the bed next to me anymore.

I guess I'm about to find out.

The most important thing I needed to remember to add to the bag tomorrow was my favourite, worn-out old 'Exit Strategy' t-shirt. Jasper had given me one from the first batch they'd ever had printed – cocky shit had even signed it, although that was barely visible now.

I wore it nearly every night. The only time I went without it was when I got behind on laundry and didn't get it washed and dried in time for bed.

I had several backups, but I couldn't sleep anywhere near as well when I didn't have my old trusty on.

Jasper thought I was ridiculous.

Nothing new there...

He'd gotten me a new one after every show they'd done, so I had a drawer full now, but there was just something special about my first.

Exit strategy...

I was going to miss being a part of that for a little while, I'd been there since the very beginning, and I'd supported them every step of the way. They had a concert planned next month and if he hadn't found me by then, I would be missing my first ever show.

Tears welled in my eyes.

Necessary evil, necessary evil...

I chanted the mantra to myself as I put in the last of the things I would need.

I shoved the suitcase in the back of my closet and went downstairs to wait for Jasper.

CHAPTER 29

Hannah
One and a half years earlier

"NO. I'm sorry, but you *have* to come up with a name," I insisted. "You can't be Parker Sloan featuring Jasper Jones forever for God's sake. It's already been months."

Parker shot Charlotte a pleading look.

"Uh uh, rock star, I'm with her. How the hell are we supposed to market the two of you if you can't even choose a damn name?" She sat her hands on her hips.

He threw his head back and groaned.

A shit-eating grin spread across Jasper's face and I knew he was about to pull out some stupid-as-hell suggestion.

"Don't start with me," I warned him, jabbing him in the chest with my finger.

"But it's *so* good." He chuckled.

I rolled my eyes. "I strongly doubt that, but you know what? I'm feeling somewhat patient, so let's hear it."

"Alright, you ready?" He got to his feet like he was conducting some type of friggin' seminar.

Parker grinned and sat up in anticipation.

They were like a couple of little boys when they got like this.

Charlotte tried to cover up a giggle with her hand.

I rolled my eyes for what must have been the one hundredth time this afternoon alone.

"Okay... here it is... 'Well Hung'," he announced, uber proud of himself.

Parker erupted with laughter. He held his fist out to Jasper. "It's funny cos it's true."

Jasper bumped his fist against Parker's.

Charlotte was doing an even more piss-poor attempt at hiding her laughter now than she had been before.

"That's terrible." She cackled. "And also, don't flatter yourselves."

Parker snagged her around her waist and dragged her onto his lap. "You're only lying to yourself... you *know* it's true, Little Red."

She blushed and giggled like a school girl.

Gross.

"Ugh!" I tossed a balled-up sheet of paper at the pair of them. "That's too much information – and there's no way in hell that name is getting approved."

"What about 'Band Name'?" Parker suggested totally unhelpfully in between nipping at Charlotte's neck playfully.

"Or 'One plus one equals sexy as fuck'?" Jasper offered with a wink.

I groaned at my boyfriend's latest suggestion.

"I know! 'Touch my drumstick'."

"Or 'Four balls are better than two."

The two of them carried on like this, back and forth, each name evolving into something dirtier and more stupid than the last, for a solid five minutes before I couldn't take it any longer.

"Oh my god! Enough! This is why we can't leave you two alone for long periods of time!"

Charlotte had been watching them volleying suggestions back and forth with a bewildered expression on her face. "How the hell can you manage to write hit song after hit song, but you can't come up with a fucking band name?" She smacked Parker lightly on the arm, a teasing smile on her lips.

The boys both shrugged innocently.

Good grief.

"I quit," I announced, throwing my hands in the air. "Cutting hair is child's play compared to this."

"You're not wrong," Lotte agreed with me.

"Oh hell, they're mad now," Jasper stage whispered to Parker. "Might be time to use that exit strategy we always had down pat."

Parker laughed loudly, and Jasper joined him, his whole face alight with amusement.

What exit strategy?

"What are you morons talking about now?" Lotte demanded, her thoughts mirroring mine.

Parker winked at her. "All good wingmen have an exit strategy."

"I've seen some crazy birds in my time, Little Red, and a good exit strategy is like a condom, you're fucked without it," Jasper explained.

"That's it!" I interrupted whatever nonsense he was spouting.

"What's *it?*" Parker and Jasper both replied.

"The name." I drummed my hands on the table. "It's the bloody name!"

"Fucked without it?" Jasper answered, nodding his head as though he was tossing the idea around in his brain. "I mean, it's no 'Well hung', but it's not awful."

Oh good grief.

"No, you fool, 'Exit Strategy'... now *that's* a name."

There was silence for a moment as the three of them thought it through.

"Exit Strategy... I like it." Charlotte was the first to speak.

"It's good, Han," Parker agreed.

"It's perfect; my woman's a god damn genius," Jasper bragged, puffing his chest out like a peacock.

He leapt to his feet, dragging me up with him and spun me around in a circle.

He might have just driven me to the brink of insanity with his ridiculous suggestions, but I loved him like this – playful and carefree. He always seemed to know just how far he could push me before doing something ridiculously cute to remind me why I was so in love with him.

He was never one to shy away from affection and he always looked so proud to be at my side. You couldn't be in a room with the two of us and walk away without realising we were together.

Eighty-five percent of the time that we were near each other, he would be touching me in some way. At first I'd thought it was a possessive quality, but after watching the love in his eyes and the way he naturally gravitated towards me, I soon realised it was just the way he was when he was in love... and he sure as hell loved me.

It was one of my favourite things about him.

"Exit Strategy it is." I laughed as the room spun around me.

CHAPTER 30

Jasper
Present day

I HUMMED an upbeat tune as I waited for the coffee machine to fill up Hannah's cup. She was still upstairs sleeping like a baby, and after the night we'd had, I wasn't surprised in the least.

I hadn't had that much sex in a long time. Actually, I wasn't sure I'd had that much sex *ever*.

Hannah had been insatiable, it was as though she couldn't get enough of me, she couldn't get close enough... when we'd finally fallen asleep her body was draped around mine, her hand still gripping my arm tight.

It wasn't out of the ordinary for her to cuddle in

her sleep, or even for us to go at it like rabbits, and I certainly wasn't complaining, but the intensity in her eyes was definitely something to add to the list of weird behaviour Hannah had been displaying lately.

I sat her cup of coffee next to mine and carried it out of the kitchen and back up the stairs.

I pushed the door open with my foot and smiled.

I'd never quite gotten used to the sight of her in my bed.

Our bed.

She was the only woman to ever sleep here and that just made it all the more special to me.

I chuckled at the memory of her when she'd first moved in. I'd found her looking at a bed catalogue, and when I'd asked her what she was doing, she announced that she wasn't making a home in a bed that had had 'a bunch of groupies' in it.

I'd never seen her so ecstatic when she learned that she was the first and only woman that would be taking up residence here.

The only girlfriends I'd ever had were in my younger days, the days before my best friend became a rock star. The celeb life sure brought with it a lot of sex, but one thing it didn't often cater for was finding someone to share your life with.

That had all changed the moment I'd met Hannah.

I took the tray over to her side of the bed and wafted the aroma at her.

She wasn't a morning person, but I'd quickly learned that she could be subdued with a good cup of coffee.

She yawned and rolled over, her eyes opening and closing until they finally opened fully and landed on me. A slow smile spread across her face.

"I brought coffee," I told her as I swept the hair from her face.

"You know me well," she answered, her voice sleepy.

"And I got you a doughnut."

I opened the box that I'd brought up on the tray.

She laughed as I waved them under her nose. "That's not just 'a' doughnut, that's a whole lot of doughnuts."

"I didn't want to be responsible for choosing the wrong flavour."

"You're such a smart man." She pushed up onto her elbow and kissed me on the lips before taking her cup of coffee.

"Where did you get them?"

"I had Creamy Sue's do a delivery."

She frowned at me. "But they don't do deliveries."

I winked at her. "They did today."

She laughed as she bit into a doughnut. "You work that celeb status, sister." She snapped her fingers back and forwards in front of her face. "I don't know how I'm going to thank you for this."

"Trust me, BG; you thanked me enough last night."

She sighed and grinned up at me. "I *really* did, didn't I?"

"Shit yes. I'm hard just thinking about it."

"No you're not." She rolled her eyes and took another bite of her doughnut.

"You're right; I'm not even a little bit hard... I think you broke my dick."

She coughed, almost choking on her mouthful. "Oh god, can you imagine." She cackled.

"I'd really rather not."

I sipped my own coffee as I watched her giggling away to herself.

"What's on the agenda today, boss?"

I plucked a doughnut from the box and bit into it.

She didn't answer me, and when I glanced at her she was looking almost through me, her face pale.

"Hannah?" I reached for her hand, mildly panicked. "Are you okay?"

She shook her head as though I'd startled her.

"Sorry, I'm fine, I just felt sick for a minute."

I deliberately reached for the doughnut she still had gripped tightly. "No more doughnuts for breakfast."

She laughed, but it didn't touch her eyes. "I was just a bit dizzy, I'm fine."

I eyed her carefully. She didn't look fine to me.

"I think you should see a doctor."

She laughed – more genuinely this time. "Don't be ridiculous, there's nothing wrong with me."

"Fine. But I'm giving you the day off, and I expect you to stay in bed and do nothing but watch shitty TV and eat the rest of these doughnuts."

"If you insist."

———

"Where's Han?" Charlotte quizzed as I climbed into the back of the tinted-out car alone.

"I'm forcing her to stay in bed for the day."

"Is she sick?" Charlotte quizzed, looking increasingly worried.

"I'm not sure... she just seems a bit... *off*."

"She's probably on her period," Parker offered helpfully. "They get a little weird during shark week."

Charlotte whacked him on the arm.

"Nope." I shook my head at him. "I can safely say that is *not* the case."

"Too much information," Charlotte groaned as I chuckled.

"She'll be fine, I think she's just tired. I told her we could manage without her today."

"Let's go, Sammy!" Park called out.

Sammy was driving us today, and he'd be acting as our bodyguard. We called him 'our' bodyguard, but in reality, in a situation like this, he was only here for Charlotte most of the time.

Parker and I could usually handle ourselves, but if Park thought Charlotte was at risk then he was a liability.

Just like that first night.

It was just easier to take Sammy or one of the guys with us everywhere these days.

The fans had stepped up the crazy since Exit Strategy had become a thing, and we were rarely able to slide under the radar entirely anymore.

Today we were headed to the most popular radio station in town, for a live-on-air interview and to perform an acoustic version of one of our songs.

We had an entire security team meeting us for this one.

This interview had been advertised on air for about two weeks, letting the fans know that we would be coming in today, so they were going to be out in force.

The studio was providing security too, but they didn't know what they were in for.

It was going to be madness.

I was actually glad that Hannah was giving it a miss. She never dealt particularly well with hoards of female fans throwing themselves at us.

I chuckled to myself at the thought of her shooting daggers at the women calling my name.

"There's a queue right around the corner." Charlotte pointed out the end of the line, nearly a whole block away from the studio.

"It's going to be a long day," Park mumbled as he peered out the window.

"Get those fan smiles ready boys," Sammy called from the front seat.

We pulled up to the front of the building, and the car stopped right as the screaming started.

"Welcome to loopy-ville," I announced as I swung my door open.

———

I yawned as I opened the door and stepped inside.

To say it had been a long day would have been an understatement.

I'd signed things until I couldn't move my fingers and smiled for pictures until my jaw felt like it might have been locked in that position forever.

I still couldn't believe the influence that music could have over people.

So many of those fans were crying – tears of absolute joy streaming down their faces. I'd heard about how our music had changed their lives, got them through a break-up or a death. One woman had even sworn that one of our tracks had stopped her from committing suicide.

As absolutely mental as this life was, moments like that, moments when you felt like you were really touching people's lives, they made it all worth it.

I thought about calling out to Han, but instead

decided that I should just creep up and check on her. If she was sleeping I didn't want to wake her.

I climbed up the stairs and thought about how much I'd wished she was there today after all.

She would have hated eighty-five percent of the women that were there, but the other fifteen percent she would have loved.

I couldn't wait to tell her about the mother and daughter who were the only survivors in an accident that had taken the lives of the rest of their family last year. The VIP passes we'd given them for our show next month in no way made up for what they'd lost, but it had certainly made them smile.

I pushed the door open to our bedroom and peeked inside.

She wasn't in the bed and the TV was switched off.

I strolled into the room, heading for our ensuite bathroom.

She wasn't in there either.

"Hannah?" I called out. "You hiding from me, barbie girl?"

I chuckled as I headed back into the bedroom, looking for the note she was bound to have left me.

I spotted a sheet of paper on her pillow and smirked.

Hide and seek, baby.

My step faltered as my eyes landed on the pink box sitting next to it.

Dread flooded through my system.

Something isn't right.

"Hannah?!" I called again, my voice rising in panic.

The house was eerily silent around me.

I picked up the sheet of paper and my whole world fell out from underneath me.

CHAPTER 31

Hannah
Day One

I FELT LIKE A GUILTY WOMAN.

Maybe I am...

It felt like I was sneaking off to another man –
and technically I was, but it wasn't like that.

I rapped my knuckles on the door yet again and
tapped my foot impatiently. If he didn't open it soon I
was going to lose my nerve and go back home, screw
up the letter and forget about the whole thing.

I knew I had at least a five-hour head start on
Jasper. He, Lotte and Park were in a radio studio
doing an interview and performing, and I knew the
fan situation was going to be out of control. They'd be
out there signing shit for half the day.

I was just about to spin on my heel and stomp away when the door was pulled open in front of me.

"Well, well, princess, if I didn't know better, I'd say you liked getting yourself into these messes." He smirked.

"Tyler," I breathed. "Thank god, I was about to lose it."

Tyler might have started out as nothing more than my best friend's oldest brother, but we were close now. We were friends. He'd always been good to me, and I knew I could count on him not to let me down.

"You? Surely not?" he answered sarcastically as I breezed past him into his house.

"Not funny, Ty, I'm freaking out."

"Again, surely not?" he muttered under his breath.

He caught up to me and snagged the suitcase from my hand. "Sit," he instructed as he pointed to the big leather couch in his living room.

I sat. My brain was overloaded and all I could manage now was to do what I was told.

He sat down opposite me. "Run me through it again... from the top."

"I need your help," I squeaked.

He gave me a cocky grin. "I know... you girls always do."

I rolled my eyes at him. He was such a smug little shit. He had good reason to be, but I wasn't about to tell him that.

The oldest of the Watson boys was a sight that could make even an ice queen melt into a puddle at his feet.

He had deep blue eyes just like Charlotte's, and with them he seemed to be able to look right through you. His dark brown hair was tousled in that sexy way that men had, and it was flecked with red when he was out in the sunlight.

His body was hot if you were into the whole chiselled, broad-shouldered kind of thing.

Who am I kidding, EVERYONE is into that.

He was gorgeous, he really was – and he knew it.

Not only that, but the man was a genius. I'd yet to find something for him to hack that he couldn't make happen.

I could still picture Charlotte's face last year when I'd had him hack into an incredibly well-known and reputable motocross manufacturer's database and upload the information necessary to have a bright pink dirt bike made with a picture of a winking Barbie on the back.

My brand-new bike had turned up a week later – and even though I'd paid for it fair and square, I'd still gotten a lecture from Lotte, and I knew Tyler would have too.

Clearly, we'd heeded that warning loud and clear.

Not.

"What exactly do you need me to do?" he asked, less arrogantly this time.

"I need you to help me disappear."

He nodded. "I can do that."

"I want my last known location to be the airport where I boarded the flight here, but I don't want him to see where I went. Wipe me from everything... flight records, CCTV, *everything*... if he's going to figure out which plane I got on he's going to have to speak to the flight attendants in person. I'll need my next flight wiped too."

I really am crazy...

"I need to be able to see all incoming texts, emails, messages and calls on my phone, but I want them to think I haven't... *shit*, is that even possible?"

He chuckled and gave me a look that made it clear that *anything* was possible.

"Okay then." I cracked my knuckles, starting to get into it now.

"I need a new bank account that's entirely untraceable. I want to be able to see Jasper's internet search history and who he's texting and calling if I can... I want to know if and when he figures out where I am. I need you to swear that you never saw me when they come looking – because they will."

"And *where* exactly is it that you're going?"

"I'm not going to tell you. I want him to be the first to know."

"You know I could track you in about thirty seconds flat, right?" He chuckled.

"Fine then, I want one more thing."

He raised his eyebrow in question.

"I need you to *not* try and find me."

He paused for a moment, staring at me with hard eyes. "No."

The simple word took me by surprise.

"What do you mean, *no*?"

"Either you tell me where you're going... or I'll track you. I'm not having you out there in the world without a single soul knowing where you are, Hannah, you're not only my little sister's best friend, but you're my friend too. I'd never forgive myself if something happened to you. So... I know where you are or the deal's off."

I scrunched up my face in frustration. This wasn't part of my plan, but I knew he meant what he said. It was Tyler's way or the highway.

He'd backed me into a corner and I didn't have a choice.

"Fine," I relented. "Track me if you have to."

He nodded once in agreement.

"Maybe I'll pick up some tips on how to evade you," I grumbled.

He laughed loud and long. "That's cute, princess." He chuckled again. "Real cute."

I narrowed my eyes at him and the bastard winked. He never had been one to give in to my diva antics or outrageous outbursts, in fact, outside of Jasper and Lotte, Ty probably understood me better than anyone else.

"So, can you do it?"

"Seriously, stop insulting me." He sprung to his

feet and swaggered over to the giant computer setup he had going on. It was so massive it took up half of his living room.

"I'll have it done within the hour."

I gaped at him, I was expecting it to take him a couple of days to finalise everything.

I was actually banking on it. I knew the airport info needed to be wiped right away, but the rest of it wasn't so important. I had been planning to stay here with him for at least a few days – I wasn't quite ready to go it alone just yet.

"That quick?"

He chuckled arrogantly. "That quick. And I'll also do you a favour and make sure they can't track the GPS on your cell, or on that smart watch you've got on your wrist."

I glanced at the watch and groaned at my own stupidity.

Of course.

Thank god for Tyler.

"You know, there's really no big hurry, you don't have to rush..."

"I'm not. You seriously have no idea what I'm capable of, do you?"

I shook my head. I was beginning to think I didn't have a clue at all.

"I'm not really prepared to move on today... I was kinda hoping I could crash here for a couple of nights..."

He stopped what he was doing and peered at me over the top of his screen.

"You'll be staying for the week. *At least.* I'm going to do what needs doing and then we're going to have a serious conversation about why you're doing this. So get comfy, princess, we might be here a while."

I breathed a sigh of relief.

I knew I couldn't put off going forever, but I could delay it for a little while at least.

CHAPTER 32

Jasper
Day One

SHE WAS GONE.

"Parker," I croaked into the phone.

"What is it?"

"I need you both over here. *Now.*"

I hung up before he could ask the fifty thousand questions that I knew he would have rattled off. Just the sound of my voice alone would have been enough to put the fear of God in him. He'd have questions.

It wasn't like I could answer them anyway.

I looked at the note once more, wondering suddenly if I'd imagined the whole thing. I hadn't smoked the whacky backy in a long time, but it was still so crazy it was worth a second look.

The words stared at me from the page, taunting me.

My perfect Jasper,

I'm so sorry, but I had to do this.

I had to go.

I want you to know what you've always known, that I love you like nothing else in this world. You are the gin to my tonic, the shampoo to my conditioner... the calm to my crazy.

I love you.

God, I love you like crazy.

I found the ring. I know that you are planning on asking me to be your wife, and I want you to know that the answer would always have been yes.

It still is...

If you can find me, then it's yes.

You'll have to think hard, Jasper Jones, and I'm already so sorry for putting us both through this, but like I said, it's something I have to do – I really hope you can find a way to accept that.

I know it's messed up, but that's me... and if you understand me like I think you do, then you'll figure it out.

Hide and seek, baby...

I love you more than I could ever express,

Han x

I closed the lid of the box that housed the engagement ring I'd had personally designed and made for her.

It would have looked perfect sitting on her long delicate finger.

I shook my head in disgust at myself. Here I was, talking about Hannah in past tense, like I'd never win.

It will *look perfect.*

I'll find her. I have to.

———

"What the actual fuck!" Parker shouted – again.

He'd been pacing the room back and forth for the past thirty or so minutes, doing nothing other than cursing and shouting, and while that was something that I would have normally found entertaining, right now it was just annoying the hell out of me.

"Park," I growled. "Not helping."

I glanced over at Charlotte. She appeared to be re-reading Hannah's letter.

"Little Red," I called softly.

Her face was a mask of disbelief. She looked like she had zoned out to a far away land.

"Little Red," I repeated a little louder.

Her eyes blinked several times as she snapped out of it.

"Huh?"

"What do I do?" I murmured, my eyes locked on her face.

Other than me, she knew Hannah better than anyone. She would know what to do, where to start...

She had to…

"I can't believe she did this to you." Her voice was barely above a whisper.

I could see she was in total shock.

Truthfully, I couldn't believe it either, Hannah had always kept me guessing, and I loved that about her, but this was so far out of left field I didn't even know what had hit me yet.

I was a thirty-year-old man, and my girlfriend had just run away from home.

What the hell…

"What do I do?" I asked again.

She shook her head as tears welled in her eyes. "I have no idea, Jasper. I'm so sorry. She's gone, and I have no idea where you should look."

"Look?" Parker barked. "You're not actually considering trying to find her, are you?"

The disgust in his voice was like a dagger to my heart.

Of course I'm going to try.

Fire raged inside me in a flash, pulling me out of the depths of despair and turning me into the protective lion that only Hannah had the power to create inside of me.

I'd go to the ends of the earth trying to protect that woman, and the sudden realisation that I would go *at least* that far to find her too, nearly put me on my ass.

I'll find her.

She needs me to find her…

This might have been fucked up in so many ways, but it was Hannah's way of making sure she was safe. Of making sure that she could trust me. Of making sure that I was worthy of keeping her forever.

I have to win.

If looks could kill, my best friend would be dead and buried from the death stare I was shooting him.

"I'll... just leave you guys to sort this out..." Charlotte scuttled towards the door, knowing full well that shit was about to go down. "Please don't kill each other," she pleaded as she vanished from sight.

"I'm not 'considering' trying to find her... I'm telling you I *will* find her." I spat the words, not an ounce of uncertainty in my voice.

Parker shot me an exasperated look. "She left you, man. She just up and fucking left you."

"She hasn't left me. Not in that sense."

"And you're just going to run after her like some kind of trained monkey," he carried on, ignoring me – his voice rising with every spoken word.

On any other occasion, I would have also found his inability to keep his shit together something worth laughing about, but not today, not now.

"It's not like that," I ground out, my own anger threatening to bubble over.

I didn't want to go at it with my best friend. Rationally, I knew he was just doing what he thought was right – looking out for me. But this was Hannah we were talking about. This wasn't just some girl. She was my life, and I wasn't always rational where she was concerned.

"Then tell me what it's like," he demanded. "Because if it looks like a duck and it quacks like a duck, then usually, it's a fucking duck!"

I took a deep breath and tried to remind myself that he was just angry.

He'll calm down.

"You know, I knew that girl was fucked up, but this is a new low – even for her."

His words took the last of my resolve with them.

"Don't you *dare* talk about my wife that way!" I roared at him, my whole body shaking with barely restrained rage.

Parker recoiled like I had physically slapped him. I *never* raised my voice like this at him.

"She's not your wife," he replied cautiously.

"She will be," I snapped. "And she is *not* 'fucked up'," I seethed, moving closer towards him with every ragged breath from my lungs.

"You sure about that?"

"I'm fucking sure," I growled.

We were standing face to face now, mere few inches separating us.

"I know this shit isn't *normal. She's* not *normal.* And that's what I fucking love about her. I'm not *normal* either. Do I like that she's gone?" I shook my head, letting myself feel the pain. "Hell no I don't," I choked out.

"Jasp..."

"But in some kind of screwed-up way, I get it. I know it's not a game to her, and I know I shouldn't call it a test, but that's the best way I can describe it to you."

"It's fucked up, J, that's what it is," he muttered quietly.

"Maybe it is," I agreed. "But it's *our* fucked up."

"I just don't wanna see you hurt."

"She's not trying to hurt me. She'd never want that."

"But she has."

I nodded slowly. He was right. But he was also wrong.

He doesn't understand.

I needed to make him understand. "Remember what you said to Lotte on your wedding day, about jumping through hoops?"

I watched as his features softened as he thought about the day that he married the love of his life.

I could remember that day in total crystal clarity.

I could remember every detail as though it was etched into my mind permanently.

It might not have been my own wedding day, but it was one of the most life-altering experiences I'd ever had.

Parker was my best friend had been forever. Lotte was his soul mate.

Seeing the two of them up there, coming together, with me standing at Parker's side as his best man, it made me see what was important in this life.

Looking at Charlotte's beautiful maid of honour at her side had been like looking at an angel.

My Barbie.

Hannah had looked so beautiful in her emerald-green dress, her eyes sparkling with unshed tears as she too witnessed the magic of that day.

That was the exact moment I'd made my decision.

I wanted that for us. Something I thought I'd never find, was now firmly within my grasp.

I decided right then and there that I was going to marry that woman, no matter what it took, no matter the cost.

No matter what it takes…

"I remember." He spoke, dragging my thoughts back to the present. "I vowed to jump through any hoop she needed me to; that I'd do whatever it took to make sure we had a long and happy life together. It's the same thing I told her when she let me back into her life and gave me a second chance."

"Did you mean it?" I asked him. "Would you jump through *any* hoop?"

"Of course I fucking would," he growled, apparently offended by my question.

He would. And so would I.

"Well this is my hoop to jump, man."

He looked into my eyes for a moment before slowly nodding in some kind of understanding.

I breathed a sigh of relief.

"I still think it's fucked up," he muttered.

I stepped away from him, the anger evaporating from me as I collapsed on the couch.

"It is," I acknowledged.

"And I'm not happy with her."

I shrugged, not really caring one way or the other.

"But I'll help you, J. You're the only brother I've ever had... and I'll do whatever I can to help you find her, and not because I agree with it, but because I know you'd do it for me."

I rubbed my temples, trying to fend off the headache I had coming on. "Thanks, man. I think I'm going to need all the help I can get."

———

I could hear their muted voices coming from the kitchen.

I'd fallen asleep on the couch, but it can't have been for long – it still wasn't even dark out.

I'd woken with a start, my whole body breaking out in a sweat.

It was just a dream.

I couldn't shake the vision I'd had of Hannah, standing with her back to me. No matter how fast or hard I ran, every time I looked back up, I wasn't any closer to catching up to her. She was always too far away.

"Find me, Jasper."

Her sweet voice was calling to me.

"She could be anywhere in the world, Parker,

what if he never finds her?" Charlotte's voice sounded like her heart was breaking. For me, for her, or for Han, I wasn't sure, but she was upset – that much was obvious.

This was her best friend – if I didn't find her, Charlotte might never see her again either.

"He'll find her, baby, he'll find her," Parker reassured her in the lovey-dovey voice he used only with Lotte and only when he thought they were alone.

I couldn't make jokes though; I had one for Hannah too.

"Please don't be mad with her," Lotte begged him, "It won't help him if you're hating on her the whole time."

Parker grunted and muttered something I couldn't catch.

"She's my best friend, rock star. I love her even when I think she's making a mistake."

"Doesn't mean I have to like her," he grumbled.

"No, it doesn't. But he *loves* her, Parker. She loves him too. You seem pretty certain that he'll find her – and when he does, he'll marry her. She's his forever and you don't want to stand in the way of that, because if push comes to shove, he'll choose her. He'll choose her *every time* and then you might lose him... and I know that losing him would kill you."

"How do you know that?" he asked her quietly.

"Tell me something... if you were given a choice between me and *anything*, what would you choose?"

"You," he answered without a moment's hesitation. He didn't even need to think about it. And Charlotte was right – neither did I.

Not for a second.

As much as it pained me, if it came down to it, Hannah would win.

She'll always win.

I sat up on the couch and reached for my phone.

I hit the call button and waited for her voicemail to cut in. I knew she wouldn't answer. I'd already tried over a dozen times when I'd first found her letter.

She wasn't going to answer me or anyone else... that much was obvious.

Her voice filled my ears and my breath caught in my throat.

"Hey, you've got Hannah, if you think I'd want to call you back, leave me a line, if I won't – then don't bother."

Her familiar giggle was cut off with a beep.

I cleared my throat awkwardly, still unsure of what I wanted to say. I knew the chances were that she had ditched the phone, but she'd taken her charger with her, so I was still holding on to hope that she'd get my message.

"Hannah..." I whispered. "I'll find you, baby, I swear I'll find you. I'm broken, barbie, you've only been gone a few hours and I miss you like crazy already. I love you... I love you so damn much, and I'll find you, I promise."

I hung up the phone and let my head fall into my hands.

"Jasper?" Lotte called softly from the doorway.

I didn't reply. I couldn't.

A sob wracked my body.

I'd spent the past two years with this woman. This was *our* home. She slept next to me every single night and we were hardly ever apart.

"Oh, Jasper." She rushed over and pulled me into her tiny arms as she sat down next to me. "Shhh, it's okay, we'll find her." She rubbed circles on my back. "*You* will get her back."

Out of the corner of my eye I saw Parker watching from the doorway, a pained look on his face.

"I don't know how to be me without her anymore, Little Red."

She didn't say anything, just hugged me tighter and promised me that it would be okay.

CHAPTER 33

Hannah
Day Four

I MUST HAVE LISTENED to his latest voice message at least twenty times by now.

I paced the room. "Maybe this was a bad idea..."

"Well it's sure-as-shit not a good one," Tyler deadpanned, not even taking his eyes off his computer screen.

"Do you think I should go home?"

This wasn't the first time I'd asked him this question over the past few days and I was surprised he hadn't lost his patience with me yet.

"You've come this far, may as well see it through," he drawled.

I'd spent three nights without him, and I was already struggling.

Hell, I was struggling after one.

I bit down on my lip and looked out the window, looking for some type of sign that I was making the right decision.

I knew this wasn't what people did. But then, I'd never been particularly good at doing what other people did. I'd always followed my own path.

When I was younger I was told that a girl couldn't wear pink princess dresses *and* want to ride a dirt bike. 'You should pick one or the other' they all told me.

Well fuck that...

Here I was at twenty-eight years old – still obsessed with the colour pink, and still riding a bike like a boss.

I was told that if I didn't finish my education I would never amount to anything, yet somehow, I'd managed to drop out of school at sixteen and still make my way into a hugely successful career.

I'd been advised to 'reign in' parts of who I was – 'you'll never keep a man if you show him the real you' my meddling aunty had told me.

Maybe she might have been right about that part...

I'd been called it all... silly, crazy, daft, flaky, insecure, wild, mad...

I've heard them all...

I knew Jasper loved my crazy, I just didn't know how far he was willing to go to prove that to me.

I guess I'll find out.

I needed to get on with my plan. I knew damn well that Jasper wasn't going to be able to find me quickly – Ty was too good, but if he or Charlotte had a brainwave and realised that I might have come here for help, Jasper would be on the first plane out.

I really didn't want him to find me in the home of another man.

"I'm going to hire a car tomorrow."

That halted whatever it was he was doing on that damn computer of his.

"I don't think you should go yet." His words were rushed, hurried, and slightly laced with panic. "Stay a few more days."

I ignored him.

"You know, Ty, that thing," I pointed at his computer, "is probably why you don't have a girl-friend. If you looked at a woman the way you look at that hard drive, you'd be married with kids by now. Why aren't you?"

He shot me a dirty look. "That's not a hard drive," he muttered.

"Whatever. Don't avoid the question."

He shrugged and pushed his chair away from the desk. "What do you want me to tell you? That the right woman has never come along... or that the one time I thought maybe I might have some real feelings, she was so unavailable it may as well have been tattooed across her forehead? Is that what you wanna hear?"

"Brutal."

He nodded. "I'm thirty-six years old and I've got more of a chance of hacking Google than I do of getting myself a girlfriend."

"You done?" I asked, crashing his pity party. "For fuck's sake, Ty, you're not that old, you're smart, gorgeous, kind... you have a hell of a lot to offer a woman if you'd pull your head out of the cyber world for five seconds."

His face crept up into a sly grin. "Gorgeous, huh?"

I rolled my eyes and threw a couch cushion across the room at his head. "Ugh, you already know you're hot, let's not pretend this is news."

He leapt to his feet and did his best impression of Gracie Hart in *Miss Congeniality*, "You think I'm gorgeous... you want to kiss me... you want to date me..."

I tried hard to keep a straight face, I really did, but I failed miserably.

I burst into laughter, tears pooling in my eyes as he pranced around singing the stupid song.

"How many times have you seen that movie?" I cackled.

"More than any grown man should, thanks to my sister."

He went back to his performance and I was in total fits of laughter.

He was such a clown. It was easy to see why Charlotte had turned out so great. Her parents had been virtually non-existent in the process of raising her, but Tyler had always been her fiercest protector – the twins too, until Parker had come along and filled the position.

He's got it covered now.

I missed them. I knew Charlotte would be sad and Parker would be fuming; he would probably never forgive me for this, but I missed him anyway. I didn't know how long I was going to have to go without seeing everyone and the thought made my heart ache.

Ty abandoned his terrible singing and sat down on the edge of the coffee table so he was facing me, our knees nearly touching.

"I have to go tomorrow," I whispered. "I need to go to where I'm supposed to be and then I just have to wait for him."

"What if he doesn't come? Have you thought about that?"

I looked into his blue eyes. "I've thought about that every minute since I left."

He squeezed my knee lightly. "He'll come. He'd have to be crazier than you are to let you get away."

God, I hope he's right.

"Seriously, princess, you're one of a kind."

His hand was still on my leg, and while I felt entirely comfortable with Ty, this seemed a little too intimate.

I laughed it off and got to my feet.

"Wanna get takeout tonight? It'll be like our last supper."

He didn't answer and when I looked back over my shoulder at him, he was still sitting where I'd left him.

His shoulders rose and fell with a deep sigh before he got to his feet and followed after me.

"Beers," he stated. "We need some beers – can't have a last supper without beer." He looked at me with a resigned smile and it made me feel sad for some reason.

Maybe Ty wanted company as much as I did.

Day Five

Tyler had reluctantly agreed to drive me to the car rental place. I was nervous about providing my real drivers license, but he'd assured me that he would wipe me from the database once I returned the car at the airport up the coast.

I had a four-hour drive ahead of me, then a three-hour flight. Once I arrived, I needed to find a taxi to get my stuff up to the house, and then I planned to buy myself a bike.

I had enough money in my account to live off for

a very long time, and I intended to treat myself to a damn nice set of wheels.

I watched as Tyler got smaller and smaller in my rearview mirror before disappearing entirely from view.

One lone tear slipped down my cheek.

Now, I was truly alone.

CHAPTER 34

Jasper
Day Six

"LET'S JUST CALL TYLER. He'll track her, and we'll know where she is within five minutes."

I knew it made sense, and that it was probably our best shot, but the thought of admitting to someone other than Charlotte and Parker that Hannah had walked out on me, made me feel sick.

I rubbed the back of my neck awkwardly. "I'd rather not..."

"Don't be proud, Jasper."

I grabbed the pad of paper I'd made some notes on from the bench.

Wallow in self-pity for days.

Check.

Call Hannah repeatedly.

Check.

Airport.

Airport...

"I'm going to the airport." I grabbed my keys and headed out the door.

I'd called the airport already and there was no record of her ever getting on a flight. It would have been helpful to have Tyler hack into their system and check their security footage, but that would have to wait – I still had my pride... for now anyway.

"Do you want me to come?" Lotte called after me.

Please god, no.

I needed some space right now. Charlotte was a sweetheart and I knew she meant well, she was just scared to leave me on my own... but I could figure this thing out; I just needed some peace and quiet.

"I'm good, Lotte, I'll call you..." I yelled as I made my escape.

———

"Do you remember her?" I held up a photo of Hannah I'd taken about a week ago.

Just looking at it made my heart speed up in my chest.

She looked so damn beautiful. She was lying in bed wearing her favourite 'Exit Strategy' t-shirt, the one with all the holes around the bottom.

I'd given her numerous others, but for some reason, that one was her favourite.

A lump formed in my throat as I relived the time I spent searching for that stupid shirt.

I'd wanted to find it so badly, in the bathroom, under the pillow, in the wash... I just *needed* it to be somewhere, so I could believe she was coming back soon... but like I'd known all along, it was gone, just like she was.

The middle-aged flight attendant I was speaking to shook her head. "I don't think so, I'm sorry I really have to go."

I thanked her and looked around for someone else to ask.

There was a twenty-something-year-old dark-haired girl working at the ticket desk, and while I knew I was running a risk of being recognised, I figured that she was probably my best bet right now.

I waited my turn and when she waved me forward I plastered on my fan smile and did my best to be charming.

"Hello there, sir, how can I help you today?"

I pulled up the photo once again. "I was wondering if you'd seen this woman, she was here about six days ago."

She pulled her eyes from me to glance at the image I was showing her.

Barely.

"I don't think so." She shook her head and batted

her lashes at me. "But you know, I see a lot of people every day."

"Were you working this desk that day?"

She bit down on her lip and counted back on her fingers. "You know what, I was." She pushed her chest forward and pouted her lips.

Subtle.

I held my phone out for her again. "Are you sure you didn't see her?"

She didn't even look at it this time. "Hey, do I know you?" She tipped her head to the side and twirled a strand of hair around her finger in what I assumed was an attempt to flirt with me.

I'd tried all kinds of tactics when it came to fans – young women fans in particular. I'd denied who I was – a stupid option really as my tattoos made it pretty obvious I was lying... especially now that some bored individual had set up an instagram page dedicated purely to each of the marks I wore on my skin.

So that tactic is a fail...

I'd tried bolting the minute I knew I'd been recognised, I'd tried posing for photos and signing all of the shit that got shoved under my nose, hell, I'd even tried being a real angry prick.

Nothing seemed to work quite as effectively as owning up whilst making it abundantly clear that I didn't want to be bothered.

Don't get me wrong, I was happy to give time to the fans... just not *all* of my time.

"That depends," I drawled. "Are you familiar

with music from Exit Strategy?"

Her mouth dropped open a little, but to her credit she kept her cool for the most part.

"Jasper Jones," she cooed. "I thought I recognised you."

She was eye-fucking the shit out of me – it was awkward. I didn't know where to look.

"Congratulations, now could I get you to look at this once more?" I shoved the phone at her again, trying my best to be abrupt.

This time she managed to drag her eyes away from me and actually focus on the picture for more than half a second.

"Actually, I think I did see her... yeah... maybe... is she your sister?"

Seriously, lady?

I resisted the urge to roll my eyes. "My *wife*," I grumbled. "You remember where she went?"

She glanced deliberately at my left hand and ignored my question. "No ring?"

My normally endless patience was wearing thin with this chick. There was no way in hell I was picking up anything she was putting down, but she didn't seem to be getting the memo.

"No ring," I confirmed. She might have been doing my head in, but she had a point... I was going to be getting a damn ring the minute I found Han.

She opened her mouth to speak, her tongue loaded with some stupid fucking pick-up line, no doubt.

"Don't," I warned her. "When a man tells you he's married, that means he's not interested. You understand?"

She nodded quickly, her face a mask of embarrassment like a scolded child might look when they've been told off.

"Now can you help me, or should I just go?"

I felt kinda bad being a prick to her like this – I normally had a lot more tolerance, but Hannah would have hated this girl, and I hadn't exactly been sleeping well, so I couldn't find it within me to care enough to say something nice now.

Her face blushed deep crimson, but she didn't answer me.

"Do you remember what flight she got on? Where she went?"

She shook her head. "I'm sorry, but I have no idea... I'm pretty sure that she bought a ticket. But at least you know she didn't leave the country... not from here anyway." She shrugged.

"How do you know that?" I replied quickly, suddenly interested in the words coming out of her mouth.

"This is the domestic desk... you wanna leave the country then you've come to the wrong place."

Passport... I need to check for her passport...

"Thank you." I turned to leave.

"I'm really sorry, I didn't mean to insult you, or your wife." She seemed somewhat sincere with her comment, so I flashed her a small smile.

"It's fine. Thank you for your help."

"At least you know she didn't leave the country…"

But where the fuck did she go…?

———

Day Twelve

I knew she was getting my messages.

Her inbox would have been full by now if it wasn't being emptied, and if she had indeed ditched her phone, the battery would have been well and truly flat.

I also knew she hadn't left the country. Thanks to the conversation I'd had at the airport, I'd dug around and found her passport in the bottom of a shoe box in the wardrobe.

Maybe she never planned on leaving the country, maybe she knew she was coming back… maybe it was something else entirely…

Whatever it was, it was a relief.

It didn't help me contact her though.

She never answered her phone, her emails and messages never showed up as being read, but I just had a feeling. So I kept sending them. I called her every night and told her that I loved her – that I would be there soon.

I'll find a way.

When I'd finally given in and let Charlotte call Tyler, he'd been convinced that she'd gotten rid of her phone, or that she'd brought herself a burner cell and had the calls transferred so she couldn't be traced back to her current position.

He insisted that her last known location was the airport less than an hour from here; the airport I'd already visited, where she had apparently boarded a flight to nowhere.

I was beginning to think she'd gone there just to confuse me, and hadn't actually got on a plane at all like the girl at the desk thought she had.

No one else in that place could confirm if they'd seen her or not.

That only made me more convinced that she hadn't been there for long – if you saw a woman that looked like Hannah, you'd remember it. She lit up every room she entered.

There was also something off about Tyler. I didn't trust the guy. Not only did he not seem to like me very much, but I could have sworn he knew something he wasn't telling us. I didn't want to suggest that particular idea to Lotte – he was her big brother and she trusted him one hundred percent.

But that didn't mean I had to.

It didn't matter anyway. I'd figure this thing out with or without him. Hannah was trusting me to.

I wasn't giving up.

CHAPTER 35

Hannah
Day Fourteen

"HE'S HOUNDING ME, HAN."

"Jasper?" I breathed.

My heart pounded at the mention of him.

"No, the freakin' pope," he deadpanned. "Yes, Jasper."

"What did he ask you?" I whispered.

"He wanted me to track you; I told him I could only trace you as far as the airport."

"Did he believe you?"

"Not even a little bit."

"Shit," I muttered. "I doubt this will be the last you hear from him."

"He's got quite a temper, huh?"

Jasper? A temper?

"Ummm... are we talking about the same guy?"

"Well, I'm pretty sure from the way that he told me I needed to find his 'fuckin' wife', that it was your man."

He called me his wife?

I cleared my throat, for once in my life I was at a loss for words.

"And since I'm pretty sure you didn't get married without me knowing, I'd say his possessive use of the word meant that he was pretty pissed off."

"He did buy me a ring..."

He was silent for a moment.

"What kind of ring?"

"Engagement," I answered quietly. I couldn't figure out why, but I felt like I was doing something wrong.

"You didn't tell me you were engaged... you weren't wearing a ring."

"I'm not... not yet... I mean if he finds me then I will be... if he still wants me... I dunno... I guess I'll see... I hope..."

"I get it. Stop rambling," he interrupted me.

"I was going to tell you."

"It's not my business, princess," he replied quickly, his voice clipped. "Anyway, I'm pretty sure he and Lotte are both fucked off with me now, but they don't know shit Hannah, they don't even know where to start."

I was torn.

I was so grateful to Ty for not spilling the beans. He might not have cared about lying to Jasper, but he wouldn't have liked having to hide things from his little sister like this. And while I was relieved, I was also disappointed that Jasper was no closer to figuring out where I was.

I knew this would take time, I just hadn't realised how impatient by nature I really was.

"Are you thinking about going back?"

"No. Maybe... I dunno." I sighed.

He chuckled.

"Why am I such a fuck up? Why am I even here?" Tears pricked my eyes.

Now it was his turn to sigh. "You're not a fuck up, Hannah, you're just scared. And as for why you're there? I can't answer that... no one can but you."

He was right... I am scared.

"Thank you for not ratting me out."

"I would never, princess, you can trust me."

CHAPTER 36

Jasper
Day Fifteen

"SAMMY? IT'S JASPER."

"I gathered that from the word 'Jasper' flashing across my screen." He yawned. "What's wrong?" His voice was thick with sleep.

I glanced at the clock.

Shit, 2.00am.

"I've kinda got a situation over here."

"What kind of situation, has the property been breached?" His tone was serious in an instant.

I glanced at the set of green eyes looking back at me. "I guess you could say that."

"You *could* say that? What the fuck? It's a simple yes or no question, Jasper, are you high?"

I could hear him dressing in the background.

Good. This is good. He can come over here and take care of this for me.

"Jasper?!" he snapped. "What the hell is going on?"

I ran my hand through my hair. "There's a cat, man, the damn thing just strolled in from the balcony."

"A cat," he repeated back to me. "You're shittin' me, right?"

I held my hand out cautiously to the thing and it bumped its head against my fingers.

"I don't know where the hell it came from but it's a god damn cat, Sammy."

"I'm gonna ask you this again, are you high?"

"Not even a little bit. I don't know what to do with it."

The cat in question meowed.

"It meowed," I relayed in a hushed tone to our head of security.

"That's great, Jasper."

"Are you here yet? I need you to sort this out."

"It's a fucking cat, Jasper, feed it... chuck it out... I don't give a shit... but don't ring me at two o'clock in the morning again unless someone is threatening to slit your throat."

"You never know, it's probably got sharp claws," I argued as the line went dead. "Head of security my ass," I grumbled as I threw the phone onto the bed.

Clearly, I was going to have to sort this out myself.

I sized up the intruder, trying to plot my next move.

"You're pretty little, huh?" I asked it.

It meowed again.

"Where'd you come from?"

I held my hand out again and it smooched not just its head this time but all the way down its back.

"Huh," I mused. "What am I meant to do with you?"

The small grey animal looked up at me with its big green eyes.

I was no cat expert, but it looked skinny. It was obviously only young, but even so, it looked under-fed.

"You need a pie."

It tilted its head to the side and studied me again before trotting off across the carpet of my bedroom and jumping up onto my bed where it proceeded to prod at the blanket with its feet before curling up.

"Hey!"

It ignored me.

Damn cat.

"Look, cat, if we're gonna do this, I think I better find you some tuna or something, alright?"

I approached it slowly and patted its back softly. It purred.

I smiled.

It's actually pretty cute.

"And we'll have to find out if you're a dude or a chick... can't go calling you 'it' forever."

It lifted its chin and I scratched under its neck.

"You like that, cat?"

It purred louder.

God, I'm a sucker.

"Fine. You can stay... but let's make a deal, if you need to take a shit, meow or something, okay? I'm not cleaning that off my floor."

I paused for a moment, taking stock of the current state of my life. Hannah wasn't here, a stray cat appeared to have taken up residence on my bed and for the first time in two weeks I didn't feel so alone.

Odd.

I went downstairs to find it something to eat.

Damn cat.

———

"Jasper?" Lotte called from the entryway.

"In here," I called back from where me and Cat were watching the baseball game. I hated baseball, but Cat seemed to like it, so I'd left it on.

"Guess the rumours were true."

"What rumours are they?"

"Word on the street was you got yourself a cat."

She came around to get a better look.

"Oh, it's so little," she cried in that voice that people got when they were talking to cute animals or babies.

"She," I corrected her.

"How do you know?" she raised her brow at me.

"Took her to the vet this morning."

"It's a Sunday." She furrowed her brow in confusion.

"Yeah, they weren't too keen, but I tell ya, Little Red, you throw enough money at something and anything is possible."

She snorted a laugh. "What's her name?"

"Cat." I rubbed her behind the ears – it was her favourite spot.

"Seriously? *Cat?* That's the best you could come up with?"

I smirked. "I was going to go with 'pussy' but it seemed a little bit inappropriate.

"Cat it is," Lotte replied quickly.

"Did you hear back from the PI?"

I grunted. "Waste of fucking time that was."

When Tyler had decided to be a difficult little prick, I'd hired a private investigator.

He'd come back with nothing.

The only thing he'd told me that I didn't already know was that Hannah had cashed up some of the money she'd previously had invested.

She'd moved just under eight hundred thousand and nobody seemed to be able to tell me where she'd put it.

Apparently, her investments were doing incredibly well.

Money was something we rarely talked about, we

both knew the other had no shortage of it and we'd left it at that. We each put money into an account that we shared, and we both knew each other's passwords, but I'd never even thought for a second about checking her account. I trusted Hannah and she trusted me.

But desperate times call for desperate measures.

I now knew the exact balance of her account, and holy shit, my future wife was nearly as loaded as I was.

When I found her, I was going to have to have a serious talk to her about the charities she approved of, because there was no way in hell we could spend all this money in a lifetime even if we tried.

"All he found was that she'd transferred some money. He doesn't know where she put it."

"When the hell did she turn into such a sneak?" Charlotte groaned.

"She's just trying to protect herself, Lotte, she's scared."

"I know."

"I just wish she'd talked to me before she made this decision, I doubt there was anything I could have said, but who knows... she's been let down a lot in her life, I know her parents didn't support her leaving school early, they didn't think she could make it as a hairdresser. It's not that they're bad people, I just don't think they realise the power of their words."

"You know her so well."

"I know her better than I know myself."

She reached over and squeezed my hand. "That's how I know you'll find her, J. You're probably the only person in the world that can."

I swallowed deeply. I was feeling the pressure something chronic. I had so much to prove and so much to lose here.

"I hope so, Little Red, this house is empty without her."

"I miss her too."

I squeezed her hand back.

"I'll get her back," I assured her.

"Can you promise me one thing?"

I nodded.

"I just want to be there when you tell her you got a cat." She giggled.

"Deal." I chuckled as I stroked Cat's back.

"You might have to put this search on hold for a bit."

I sighed. "I know. These next two weeks are crazy busy. It's like she's tipping salt in the wound."

"Classic Hannah, causing a ruckus." She smiled sadly.

"I'll call Ty again and see if he can work on anything else, and I promise we'll get back into it right after the show, okay?"

I nodded.

"If we could cancel it, I would, J."

"I don't want to disappoint the fans."

She lightly nudged my arm. "I know... and that's why they all love you so much."

CHAPTER 37

Hannah
Day Twenty-One

I SCROLLED through the mess that was Jasper's search history.

He'd tried searching Google for how to hack into a phone with deactivated GPS, he'd looked up the contact for the FBI and then he'd somehow ended up playing 'where in the world is Carmen Sandiego' for about an hour.

He'd even done a search for 'If your girlfriend runs away, where might she go?'.

I think it's safe to say he's got no idea.

There hadn't been much communication between either Charlotte or Parker to Jasper, or vice versa, but then, they lived next door so it wasn't exactly surprising.

One thing that was interesting was that he'd looked up the number for a private investigator.

I'd watched and waited, but all that had come of it was him logging into my bank account.

I had no problem with him looking – that was why he had the password, but I assumed that meant he knew that I'd withdrawn money.

It was a large sum, I'd gone on the high side because I was worried he'd never come.

I hadn't really thought through what would happen in the future if he didn't come. I would have to go back eventually.

Right now, that was looking like a likely scenario.

At least he's trying.

If he had never even looked I would have been heartbroken, but I would have understood.

This was my crazy train; he was in no way obliged to climb aboard.

Jasper had always been a willing passenger, in fact, if anything, he was more like the excited little kid up the front making tooting motions with his arm than he was the disgruntled older gentleman in the back who looked like he was hating the whole thing.

I hit play on the playlist I had up on my screen and sighed.

I really missed hearing his voice.

Jasper had such a sexy voice.

When he sang I all but burst into flames on the spot.

His voice washed over me now, and I closed my eyes, trying to pretend I was back home, side of stage at one of their shows.

They had a show scheduled for about ten days' time. The build-up to a show was always crazy, and I knew that Jasper wouldn't have time to look for me.

He'd be up at the crack of dawn and falling into bed well after dark.

Charlotte and I had filled their schedules with interviews, appearances for their fans, media conferences and even a VIP intimate show experience the night before the big concert.

I felt kinda bad about it now, they were going to be under the pump without me there to help, but I was glad he was busy.

I'd checked the internet and there was no indication that they were cancelling anything we'd set up.

I was glad about that too – I would have felt even more awful if I'd caused them to let anyone down.

I was enough of a letdown for all of us put together.

I closed the lid of the laptop and massaged my temples. This hide and seek business was proving to be a stressful little game.

I glanced around the small living room and sighed.

I'd been right; it wasn't the same without my grandmother here. I still felt calm and more relaxed than usual, but the place didn't have the same spark to it.

The hum of electricity was gone now.

I needed to get out of the house and get some fresh air.

There was one place I had been putting off going, but I needed to go there now.

Rip it off like a band aid.

I stood up and grabbed my helmet off the couch, heading for the door before I could talk myself out of it.

———

"Hey, Nana," I whispered. "I brought you your favourites."

I sat the bunch of pink carnations in the empty vase.

It didn't look like anyone had been out here for a long time.

I certainly hadn't.

A pang of guilt ripped through me for being such a lousy granddaughter.

I brushed off the stray leaves from the headstone and pulled a few weeds that were growing in the cracks of the concrete.

I'd been here every summer for a time, only then, half of the headstone was empty of writing.

I'd come with my nana to visit her husband – my grandfather.

We'd sometimes bring a picnic, sometimes flowers, and we'd sit here for the longest time, her telling me stories of everything she could remember about him.

I hadn't been back for nearly ten years, since the day we'd laid her to rest.

"I'm sorry I haven't visited."

I knew that avoiding coming here was the wrong thing to do, but I also knew that Nana would have understood why I had.

"I promise I'll come back more often, I'm sorry..."

I sniffed back my tears. Nana had always hated seeing me upset.

I lay down on the springy green grass and looked up at the sky, watching the clouds go by.

There was no one here for me to talk to, but still, I found myself telling stories about my nana out loud.

I vowed to myself that one day, when I was older and had a family, I would bring them here, we'd make a picnic and I'd tell them all about her, just the way Nana had with me.

It was dark by the time I picked myself up off the grass and brushed off my clothes.

I kissed my hand and pressed it to the top of their shared headstone.

"I love you," I whispered as I turned and walked away.

CHAPTER 38

Jasper
Day Thirty-Two

I WAS OFF MY GAME.

No one other than my inner circle would have noticed the slight shift in my stage presence. The crowd were at their usual obsessive, crazy level – they hadn't picked up on a thing... but it still didn't feel right.

We all knew what was playing on my mind.

Hannah.

I'd *never* played a show without her.

I glanced side of stage to the spot she always occupied. It didn't matter which venue, which town, she always had a similar spot.

Not tonight.

Tonight, there was nothing but empty space.

Charlotte even knew to watch from somewhere else this time.

I sucked in a deep breath and sung with Park through the chorus.

He was carrying me, like he had been all night and I'd never been more grateful for my best mate than I was right now.

The crowd went wild, but I just wasn't feeling it.

There was no adrenaline pulsing through my body.

There was no hard-on in my jeans.

There was no excitement running through my veins.

All of this, it was nothing without her.

I looked out into the mass of nameless, faceless bodies that made up the crowd and found myself searching for her. I knew she wasn't there, but dreams were free.

I could picture her smiling face; I could imagine her laughing, her head falling back and her eyes shining bright.

I could see her beaming up at me from in the crowd.

I was hallucinating harder than a thirsty man in a desert.

"Jasper."

I could hear her voice.

I blinked once, twice...

She laughed again and blew me a kiss.

"Jasper."

A hand landed heavily on my shoulder and shook me from my daydream.

"Jasper." This time it was Parker's voice.

I scanned the crowd again, but she wasn't there – she never had been.

"Sorry…" I shook my head. "I zoned out."

"We can flag the encore if you wanna get out of here."

"No." I cleared my throat. "Let's give the people what they want."

"Railroad?" he prompted.

That was what we had planned to close out the night with, but it didn't seem right now.

I shook my head. "Let's do 'Crazy' instead."

He knew as well as I did that playing our previously unheard song was probably not our best idea, but he also knew I was struggling right now.

Somehow playing this song felt like something I needed to do.

"You sure?"

"Yeah, fuck it, man, let's do the damn thing."

"We've got something a bit special for you all tonight." Parker's voice boomed around the stadium.

The crowd screamed back in response.

"Who wants to hear something new?"

The roar was deafening this time.

He chuckled into the mic. "I'm gonna take that as a yes."

I took my spot on my stool and closed my eyes for a moment, picturing Hannah's face.

This song was for her, and I was going to smash it out of the park for my woman.

"You ready, man?" Parker asked as he sat down on the stool next to me.

"Ready as I'll ever be."

He nodded at me and we strummed in time with one another, forming the rhythm of the song.

I dropped into the first verse, the words flowing from me like water in a raging river.

Every emotion I'd been keeping locked down tight, poured out of me now.

I sang about the woman I loved like it was the last chance I'd ever have.

I could hear Park harmonising with me, I could feel the energy of the crowd, but in that moment, it was just her and I.

I didn't even realise the song was over until I stopped playing, my mind might have been a thousand miles away, but my hands were on auto pilot.

The crowd went wild, I could hear them screaming my name over and over, but it was as though I was experiencing the entire thing through a fog.

"Holy shit, J, that was epic."

Because it was for her.

I nodded at him once.

I need to get out of here.

Parker must have sensed that I was done for the day.

"Thank you, beautiful people, and have a good night!" he yelled into the mic.

We went through the usual figurative song and dance that wrapping up a show entailed, before leaving the stage, the deafening roar of our fans ringing in my ears.

Charlotte was the first face we saw, as always, and the pang in my chest from knowing that Hannah wouldn't be next to her came in full force.

"That was amazing." She pushed up onto her tippy toes and kissed Parker on the cheek.

"Seriously, Jasper, you really killed that last song." She smiled up at me with sad, sympathetic eyes.

"Thanks, Little Red," I mumbled as Park tucked his wife into his side.

He glanced backstage and his expression turned hard. He nudged my shoulder.

Shit.

I strode off in the direction of Joe, one of the suits from the record label that produced our albums.

"Go wait in the dressing room, okay, legs?" I heard Parker instructing Lotte.

"Are you two fucking kidding me? What the hell were you thinking going out there and playing your next single? That shit is meant to be under wraps!" he roared.

The dude was fuming. The vein in his neck was enlarged and pulsing.

"Do you not understand the way business works?" he barked the words at us.

He turned back now that we were both following him and stomped off in the direction he'd come from.

This was on me. I was the one that wanted to play that song.

I needed to play it... for her.

"It wasn't about business, Joe, it was just something I needed to do."

"Oh, well, that's okay then," he replied sarcastically. "If you *needed* to do it, Jasper, then it's all fucking fine and dandy."

"What the hell is your problem, man? It's not going to change the success of it, if anything it will *add* to the hype. You heard the crowd, they ate it up." Parker had been walking slightly behind me, and now he moved to go around me – closer to Joe as he spoke.

He was pissed. I knew he had gotten sick of being told what to do a long-ass time ago.

My arm snaked out and landed against his chest.

He caught my eye and I shook my head 'no' at him.

Him going all agro wasn't going to help the situation. This had been brewing for a while now, Joe and I didn't see eye to eye anymore than he and Parker did, but we had to be careful.

Parker knocking him into next week wasn't going to be a great plan.

No matter how good it might have been to watch.

Either something needed to change, or someone was going to have to go.

"It's called building suspense, Sloan. You should take ten minutes to look into it," Joe snapped.

I could almost hear Parker's teeth grinding together.

"If we want to play a song that *we* wrote, we god damn will, Joe," I told him, my voice quiet, but leaving no impression that I was anything other than dead serious.

He stopped in his tracks and we both followed suit.

He turned around slowly, almost as though he was doing it intentionally for dramatic effect.

"Not if it's a song that's going on an album I'm producing you won't," he snarled.

His bald head was covered in a shiny layer of sweat – he was feeling the pressure big time.

We were at a cross roads now. We all knew it. This was the moment things got resolved... or the moment they all turned to shit.

Parker looked at me, his eyes questioning. He didn't even need to ask.

I nodded.

"We're out, Joe," Parker stated. "We're terminating the contract, effective immediately."

Joe's jaw slackened, and a look of regret flashed in his eyes before an arrogant expression replaced it.

"Well, bad luck, boys, you can't just quit."

Maybe he is as stupid as he looks.

But we certainly aren't.

"Actually, we can. You might think we're just thick, tatted-up musicians, but the thing you forgot is that we've got really smart women behind us... there's an out clause, Joe, and we're using it."

His face went a deep shade of purple. "It went through our lawyer," he hissed.

"Yeah, well maybe you should get a new one of those," I drawled.

He was so angry now, his whole body was vibrating with rage.

"Couple of punk-ass little rock stars," he sneered. "You're not even worth my time."

He stormed off, muttering a string of curse words.

"Oh yeah, I'm sure all that money we've been making you was a real god damn inconvenience!" Parker yelled after him.

"Good luck making this look good on your résumé, Joey boy," I added with a smirk.

We both stood watching him walk away – the smoke coming out of his ears nearly visible to the naked eye.

"We've got this... right?" Parker asked me after a few minutes.

Neither of us had moved, we were just standing there motionless, letting reality set in.

I nodded. "Hell yes, we've got this."

CHAPTER 39

Hannah
Day Thirty-Nine

THEY WERE all over the news.

Jasper and Parker had been the talk of the media for days now.

The talk of the town was that they'd thrown in their contract with the label and were going it alone.

I wasn't one to believe everything I read on the internet, but Charlotte had released a statement, saying that they boys and the label were no longer 'a good fit' and they'd be going their separate ways.

This was a storm that had been brewing for over a year now.

There was nothing but drama with that company and Exit Strategy would be better off without them.

The other thing that was all over the net, was clips from their show.

They were almost painful to watch.

Jasper looked so lost, so unsure of himself.

It was ironic really, his confident nature was one of the things that drew me to him so strongly in the first place, and now he seemed to have lost that.

It was heartbreaking to watch.

The only song he'd put any effort into was the one that was threatening to tear me apart now.

It was my song.

He'd played my song.

And if I had to guess, I would say that playing that song had been the final nail in the coffin between Parker and Jasper and the label execs.

There was no way they could have played a previously unreleased song on a whim like that, and not have trouble brew.

I hit the replay key, my eyes fixed entirely on his face as I listened to him sing that song like his life depended on it.

It was the most beautiful and the most heart wrenching thing to watch all at the same time.

"Find me," I whispered at the screen. "Please find me..."

———

Day Fifty-One

I stared at the two pink lines on the stick in front of me.

I shouldn't have been surprised really... it wasn't as though we were exactly careful about it.

Jasper was an 'it is what it is' kinda guy. If something was meant to be – it would be, or so he thought.

I'd told him on more than one occasion that I'd missed a pill or two, but all he did was smile and wink. Once I'd sworn I'd heard him mumble something about getting a baby in my belly one way or another.

I knew he was going to be over the moon.

He would be an amazing dad.

The only problem was that I was here, and he wasn't.

This revelation threw a spanner in the works.

We were on the clock now.

I would have waited as long as it took for him, but now there was a timeframe.

If he didn't find me in the next couple of months, I'd have to go home and pray that he still wanted me... and our baby.

I laid a hand over my belly.

It didn't look any different, but in an instant, I *felt* different.

I wasn't alone anymore. It was me and my little peanut now.

"What am I gonna do now, huh, peanut? Your daddy shouldn't be missing this."

I sighed and took stock of the empty box of pregnancy tests.

I hadn't believed the first one.

I still was having a hard time believing any of them.

How did I miss this?

I hadn't even thought about having a period. Not once since I'd been here had it even crossed my mind; my thoughts were being pulled in a thousand different directions.

It wasn't until I'd heard a guy in the 'women's' section of the supermarket on the phone to who I assumed was his wife. He was complaining in hushed tones about not knowing whether he needed slim fit or regular – heavy flow or light.

It had been entertaining to begin with. I'd strolled past, eavesdropping and smiling to myself when it had hit me that I hadn't put any of those little boxes into my shopping basket since before I'd run away from home.

I'd frozen at the end of the aisle, turned around and put a different kind of box into my shopping basket.

And here I was. A white, pee-covered stick alerting me to the fact that my whole life was about to change.

Can I be a mother?

I grabbed my cell phone and looked up the number for the local doctor's clinic.

First things first.

———

Day Fifty-Six

"Judging by these measurements, I'd say you're around ten weeks."

"There's seriously a baby in there?"

She laughed. "Yes, there is seriously a baby in there."

I laughed and covered my eyes. "I was so worried I'd imagined the whole thing."

She pushed the screen towards me and tilted it so I could see.

"Oh my god," I whispered.

My little peanut was wiggling around.

"And here is the heartbeat." She twisted a dial and a thudding noise filled the room.

"That's incredible," I breathed.

I felt so guilty that Jasper was missing this. He should have been at my side when we had our first ultrasound, but because of me, he wasn't.

"What do I do now?"

She smiled at me. "You just carry on, Hannah. I'll give you some vitamins I want you to take and some information about what things you should avoid, but other than that, just keep doing what you're doing."

I breathed a sigh of relief.

She wiped the gel off my stomach and indicated for me to sit up.

My knowledge of babies and pregnancy was limited, to say the least, but I knew how to Google... I could figure this thing out.

"Is the father in the picture?" she asked. I could tell by her expression that she was nervous about asking, but I could tell by the check box on her computer screen that it was a question she had to ask.

"It's kinda complicated," I admitted. "I'm hoping he'll be here with me soon."

"Does he know about the pregnancy?"

I shook my head. "Not yet."

"How do you think he'll feel about it?" she asked.

I smiled. "I think he'll be absolutely over the moon."

She ran through the rest of the information with me and I got up to leave.

"You're like, really sure there's a baby in there, right?"

She laughed and shook her head at me. "One hundred and fifty percent sure, now go home and look after yourself."

CHAPTER 40

Jasper
Day Sixty-Four

"I'M OVER THIS SHIT, man. You're miserable. *She's* made you miserable. I've had it, just cut this shit off and be done with her."

"Parker!" Charlotte snapped at him.

The expression on her face mirrored the way I felt.

"I'm sorry, legs, but this has gone on long enough. We're not making new music, he's just moping around like a sack of shit all fuckin' day. I've seriously had better conversations with that cat he's got hanging around."

"Stop talking about me like I'm not here," I barked.

Parker dropped his favourite guitar down onto the couch. He never treated that thing with anything other than the utmost respect, so he must have been at the very end of his tether right now.

It wasn't that I couldn't understand his frustration.

I get it.

I was a waste of space right now. Every day was blending into the next and I was passing by in a blur of coffee, takeout and booze.

I was back smoking every day again too, and I hated myself for it.

Lotte despised my dirty little habit too.

Lately she seemed to appear out of thin air every time I went out for a cigarette, and if she wasn't lecturing me about dying young, she was sitting there giving me a death stare in the hopes that I'd put it out.

I watched Parker as he paced the room back and forth – the way he always did when he was frustrated.

I felt bad that he was stressing about me, but there was no way in hell I was giving up on Hannah.

No fuckin' way.

"Park, man, just take a breath."

"I feel like I don't even know you right now. You're a shell of the man you were."

"Maybe I'm not that guy anymore." I shrugged.

"Like hell you're not," he growled. "She's just sucked the life out of you."

I got to my feet. I may have appeared calm, but my emotions were all over the place.

I knew Parker meant well, and he wasn't exactly wrong. I did feel like the life had been sucked out of me.

I did feel sorry for the guy too.

He had it tough right now. He was having to deal with not only me, but Lotte as well. She kept up a strong façade around me, but I knew she was hurting too.

She missed her best friend.

Parker had her to comfort at home, and me to deal with outside of it.

His life probably wasn't exactly enjoyable right now, but that didn't mean I was going to take his criticisms of my girl lying down.

"Enough, Parker."

"No, you know what, J? It's *not* enough. I've stayed quiet for the past six weeks, but it's time you faced facts, both of you," he glanced between Charlotte and me, "she's not coming back, I don't have any fuckin' clue why she left in the first place, but she's clearly not coming back and you two need to start getting on with your lives."

Get on with my life?

Fuck that.

She is my life.

"Rock star, you need to shut up," Lotte snapped at him. "You don't know Hannah like we do. She's... *insecure...* you probably can't even begin to understand that, but we can, and at the very least you need to respect it."

I didn't know what I wanted to do first – knock Park into next week for being such a colossal douche, or grab Lotte in a giant bear hug for being the kind of loyal friend that Hannah needed.

Parker snorted. "Oh, cut the crap... If there's one thing I know about Hannah Montgomery, it's that she is NOT lacking in confidence. This isn't an insecurity issue, legs; this is a 'being stupid as fuck' issue."

Charlotte looked at him like she was genuinely disappointed in him, and my need to punch him evaporated into thin air.

Nothing would cut him as deep as the look his wife was giving him.

"Well, rock star, that's exactly where you'd be wrong. I know insecurity. I've felt it, and I sure as hell know how to spot it in my best friend.... Hannah comes across as being confident and self assured, and in some areas of her life, she really is those things, but most of the time, it's a front."

She was so right.

Hannah put up her walls the same way I did, the only difference was the type of shield we used.

"She's playing games with him, Lotte," Parker replied. His angry, certain voice had morphed into something unsure and hurt.

Charlotte shook her head at him. "She's just a scared little girl under that beautiful face, that smart mouth and that loud voice. She's lacked what she considers to be unconditional love in her life, Parker, so when she does get it, she freaks out. You might not realise how big of a step it was for her to let Jasper into her life in the first place, but *I* know. *He* knows. Other than me, she's never let *anybody* in, not really..."

A lump formed in my throat as I listened to Charlotte speak. She knew Hannah so well.

"So, the only thing that needs to happen right now, is that you need to stop being so judgemental and think about why she's doing this, rock star, because I promise you this is not a game to her."

She turned and hugged me before stomping her way out of the room, right past her husband.

"Charlotte!" Parker called after her.

He winced as he heard the sound of my front door slamming.

"Well, I just got told," he mumbled.

I stared hard at him, not trusting myself to reply just yet.

"Fuck, man, I know this is hard... and I'm sorry." He ran his hand through his dark hair. "I'm trying to be supportive, I really am... but you're my best friend, Jasper. You're my brother and I hate seeing you like this."

I hate seeing me like this too.

He looked down at the ground. "I'm scared for you. I don't know what will happen to you if you never get her back... and I'm mad as hell, because you shouldn't have had to go through this in the first place."

He scrubbed at his face with the back of his hand and I realised he was tearing up.

I breathed in deep and tried to blink back the tears that were forming in my own eyes.

"I'll find her, Park... I have to."

He nodded, his gaze still on the floor.

"Can you do something...? Just do *anything*. I don't care if you don't want to play with me right now, but I need you to do something about it. Get on the bike and go looking... fuck, I don't know, make some calls or whatever... ever since the show you've given up trying, but you haven't let go... you need to make a choice and then do something about it."

He was right. I'd moped around long enough.

I wasn't going to find her sitting around on this couch with my cat.

It was time to stop being a depressed sack of shit and start looking again.

"And for the love of god, stop gambling, you suck at it."

He wasn't wrong there either.

That was just another thing that wasn't the same without Hannah.

CHAPTER 41

Jasper
Two and a half years earlier

"WHAT IS THIS PLACE?" she glanced around the dingy basement and frowned.

I grinned. It was my turn for our 'friends' date and I was getting payback for her making me look stupid in that stupid matchbox car of hers.

"You ever played poker, BG?"

She nodded her head. "Just not particularly well..."

I chuckled.

This will be interesting.

"Did you bring cash with you like I asked?" I raised my brow at her.

She'd been a pretty good sport so far. All I'd told

her was to dress up nice and to bring some money. She'd actually managed to do what she was told for once.

She opened her bag and held it out for me to look. It was stuffed with hundred-dollar bills.

"Holy shit, Han, how much money did you bring?"

"Ten grand..." she replied sheepishly.

I gaped at her.

Oh shit...

"I thought we might have been going to some big super secret Gucci sale or something, I didn't want to risk being under-prepared."

"Gucci? You seriously thought I was taking you shopping?"

She sighed and looked around. "A girl can dream."

I shook my head and laughed at her.

"You see that table over there?" I pointed out one table among the others.

She nodded.

"That's Will, Dave, Craig, Hayden and Kev." I pointed out the five men sitting around it.

"Cool... why is this place so dodgy looking?"

I chuckled. "It's a high stakes poker ring, barbie, we like to keep to ourselves."

Her eyes widened. "Poker ring? No shit..."

"Which one's better again, a flush or a straight?"

"Flush," the guys all replied in unison.

This was the fifth time she'd asked this particular question, and I could have sworn she was doing it on purpose.

At this point, it was collectively agreed by everyone here, that Hannah was either bat-shit crazy or making a damn good show of acting it.

She stared hard at the hand in front of her, like she didn't know what to do.

"Ugh too bad I don't have either of those anyway." She tossed her cards down. "I'm out."

"You *fold*," Dave corrected her.

"Meh, whatever." She waved away his correction.

I laughed into my glass.

She was just taking the piss now.

This was a serious game. Well, it usually was.

Not tonight.

I'd warned Hannah that these guys took this pretty seriously and that they didn't do much in the way of joking around.

She'd shot me a devilish smirk and announced that she would be 'sorting that out, real quick'.

She had.

She had the guys looser than I'd ever seen them. She was joking and laughing, and I was enjoying watching her far more than I was playing the game.

Even if I was up five grand.

"You didn't think to check if she knew how to play before you brought her here?" Kev asked me.

"Hey! Who says I don't know how to play?" she faked outrage.

"Ah, logic, common sense and reason," Will drawled. "That's who."

"Maybe I'm doing that pretending thing... what do you call it again? Bluffing?"

Craig leant across the table in her direction. "Normally when people bluff, they do it to win, not lose." He winked at her.

"Thanks for the tip." She smiled sweetly at him while giving him the middle finger.

I laughed loudly this time.

"There's only one thing for it then," she announced. "Deal us a new hand."

I sipped on my bourbon and watched her with amusement.

We were playing Texas Hold'Em tonight, but I doubt Hannah even had a clue what that meant.

She was down about two grand already, but she didn't seem concerned.

She had the worst poker face I'd ever seen, the one round she'd been dealt a good hand, she'd smiled like the cat that got the cream, so everyone had folded and she'd only managed to take away a couple hundred bucks.

She'd been working on her 'game face' ever since.

"Last round," I announced. "I'm getting her out of here before she either goes bankrupt or one of you lot lose your shit."

Hannah rolled her eyes. "You're such a spoil sport, Lollipop."

"Yeah, Lollipop, stop raining on her parade." Kev smirked.

I gave him a 'shut the hell up' look. These sharks would take her for all she had, given half a chance.

Hayden shuffled the cards and dealt us all two cards each.

I picked up my hand.

A three and a ten.

Terrible hand.

I watched as Hannah slowly picked up her cards, shooting sideways glances at the guys to make sure they couldn't see.

She smuggled them in her hand up to her face so she could look at them.

A pained look crossed her face.

She's got nothing.

I glanced around, everyone was watching her intently, smirks on all their faces.

They knew as well as I did that she was screwed.

"Bets in, ladies," Dave drawled.

I knew I wasn't going to be winning shit with these cards, but that didn't mean I couldn't attempt a bluff.

Kev bet five hundred to start.

"Raise you five hundred." Will tossed in a wad of cash.

"Call." Craig tossed his money in too.

"Raise you another five hundred."

Dave added his money – the bet was at fifteen hundred now.

"Call." I threw my money into the centre of the table.

"Raise you a grand." Hannah smirked.

"Are you sure you wanna do that?" I whispered to her as she added two and a half thousand dollars to the pool.

"Oh, I'm sure." She winked at me. "Go big or go home, right?" she added, her voice cocky.

She really was a terrible actress.

"The lady's sure, Jasper." Hayden smirked before calling and chucking his cash onto the stack.

Hayden dealt the flop.

Queen, nine and a four…

I'm screwed.

We went another round of betting with everyone calling.

If my maths was right, there was twenty-three thousand dollars in the middle of that table right now and I could safely assume that neither Hannah nor I would be leaving with it.

Hayden dealt the turn.

A king.

"Fold." Kev threw his cards down.

"Call."

"Call."

"Call."

"I'm folding, boys." I smacked my cards down on the table.

One of them was bound to have a decent hand and bluffing was getting me nowhere. Most of them were hell bent on staying in, sucking every cent they could out of Hannah now.

We all looked expectantly at her.

"Call," she announced.

I groaned.

There goes a whole shit tonne of money she'll never see again.

Hayden laughed. "Oh, there's no way I'm getting out now, call."

"This was a terrible place to bring you, BG," I grumbled.

She just grinned up at me as though she didn't have a care in the world.

Hayden dealt the fifth and final card – the river.

Another nine.

"I'm out of money," Hannah told the boys. "I've got five hundred bucks to my name, unless I take a loan from Lollipop here..."

"Not happening." I shook my head.

She was going down in a blaze of glory and she was going down alone.

"What do you boys say, you willing to let it ride this round... winner takes all?"

After some bartering back and forth and my refusal to let this evolve into a game of strip poker – Hannah's suggestion, they agreed to a five hundred dollar, last round bet.

"I fold." Craig shrugged. "I'm just here to see what the hell happens next."

He wasn't the only one. I didn't know which one of my poker buddies was going to rob Han blind, but whoever it was; I was never going to hear the end of it.

"You three in?" Hannah asked Will, Dave and Hayden.

"Hell yeah." Hayden smirked.

They all threw their money in the middle.

"This is not how I thought this night would go," I muttered to myself.

"Show me." Hannah lifted her chin at Will.

He laid down a jack and a ten – a straight.

That's that then.

It wasn't the best hand you could get, but it wasn't going to be easy to beat on this draw.

"You..." She motioned to Dave.

He laid down a three and a four – two pairs, he was out.

"Bad luck." She poked her tongue out at him.

"You wanna go next?" She batted her lashes at Hayden.

He sighed and tossed his cards down. "Three of a kind," he grumbled.

He was out too.

It was all down to Hannah now. She might have been doing a fantastic job of building suspense, but I wasn't expecting a lot from the cards in her hand.

She bit down on her lip and glanced around at us.

"Get on with it, barbie girl." I chuckled.

She laid one card down – a queen.

I sat forward in my chair, right now she had two pairs, which if I was being honest, was more than I'd expected her to have.

"I got a bad feeling about this…" Will groaned.

"Boo-ya, bitches!" she cried as she revealed her final card – another queen.

"What's that called again?" she feigned innocence, a huge smile on her face. "A full house or something, right?"

Well I'll be damned.

Will laid his head down on the table and groaned.

"Why do I feel like I just got played?" Dave asked, his eyes blinking in shock.

"Now, I might not 'know how to play', but I'm pretty sure a full house beats a straight, am I right?"

"I did not see this coming." Hayden rubbed his hand over his eyes as though he still couldn't believe what he was seeing.

He's not the only one.

Hannah reached into the middle of the table and made a show of dragging the huge pile of cash she'd fleeced off my buddies towards herself.

"Pleasure doing business with you, boys." She grinned.

I laughed long and loud. She'd fooled us all.

This woman has no idea how incredible she is.

Hannah
Day Seventy-Two

I KILLED the engine and flicked down the kickstand. I yanked the helmet off my head and let my now longer-than-ever hair fall free around my shoulders.

This place was so beautiful at night.

I stopped for a moment to glance out at the moonlight glistening on the ocean.

I yawned loudly, all this sun and salt air was really taking it out of me.

That, and the fact that Jasper had been quiet lately. He didn't text me every day anymore and the messages he did leave made it clear he was drunk.

I'd started reading to fill in the time and to help me sleep. It wasn't any where as good as having the real thing, but book boyfriends had become my new reality.

I had a saucy romance novel waiting on my nightstand, and I grinned thinking about all the filthy things that Hunter 'Lucky' Casarazzi had said to Hope Carter in the pages I'd fallen asleep reading last night.

I was just about to head in and get back to it when I felt eyes on me.

I knew it wasn't rational to think that I could actually *feel* someone's eyes on me – but it was more that maybe all of my senses were coming together to tell me that I wasn't alone.

I *should* have been alone.

Nobody else lived up here.

It couldn't have been Jasper, I would have seen something, *anything*, in his search history if he had figured out where I was... but my heart still raced at the possibility.

He could have figured it out and got on the next plane, not even bothering to search for a single thing...

It could be him...

I spun around and could just make out a silhouette of a figure leaning in the doorway.

It was a male – that was for sure.

"Hello?" I called out, my voice a mixture of terror and hope. "Who's there?"

"You gonna make me wait out here all night or what?" the familiar male voice replied.

I gasped.

———

"Tyler, what the fuck?!" I demanded as I flicked on the light switch and shut the door behind him. "What the hell are you doing out here?"

He picked up a framed photo of me as a little girl at the beach in my swimsuit from the shelf in the living area and smiled. "Cute."

"Ty..." I warned him as I threw my helmet down onto the chair.

He sat the frame down and sighed, but still didn't make eye contact.

"He hasn't found you."

I shrugged. "Not yet."

"It's been two and a half months, Hannah."

"I know." I sat down on the couch and watched him as he wandered around the room, picking up frames as he went, I was aware that the only ones he touched were the ones that contained pictures of me, but what I couldn't figure out was how he could pick me out amongst all my cousins.

He still hadn't made proper eye contact and it was becoming increasingly obvious that he had something he wanted to say to me.

"Ty, why are you here?" I tilted my head to the side in question. "I can tell something's up."

His hand lingered over a photo of me and my

grandmother – the last photo we'd ever had taken together. "I just wanted to check on you."

I knew that wasn't it. He could have just called me if he wanted to check in. There was no need for him to spend hours driving or flying here.

There's something else.

"You look a lot like her. You two have the same nose and the same sparkle in your eye."

I looked across the room and even though I couldn't see the photo from where I sat, I could picture it perfectly in my head.

He was right. I looked a lot like she did when she was my age.

"Thank you," I replied simply.

"Princess, he hasn't found you." He finally turned to face me.

"I'm in no hurry." I shrugged, the lie rolling off my tongue.

He approached me slowly, like he was... nervous...

Scared maybe?

This wasn't the cocky, self-assured Tyler that I was used to bantering with. This was someone else entirely and it gave me a bad feeling in the pit of my stomach.

"I debated long and hard about coming here, I really did..." He sat down next to me on the couch and tilted his body so he was facing me.

I mimicked his position so I could look at him too.

He clearly had something to say and I desperately wanted to know what it was.

"Tyler, what's going on? Is something wrong at home?"

He shook his head quickly.

"Ty—"

"But," he continued, interrupting me, "I figured if I didn't come now then I never would, and then I'd never know what might have been said."

He looked pained. It was the strangest thing to watch – it was almost as though the words he was speaking were causing him hurt... as though he knew they were a bad idea but he was going to make them come out, regardless.

"Tyler, what is it?" I reached for his hand and held it in mine.

His gaze travelled to our joined hands and he sighed. "I already know how this goes, Hannah, and that's the worst fucking part about it, but I still have to say what I came here to say."

"Just say it already, you know me, you know I hate surprises."

"I've got feelings for you," he blurted out. "I have for years. I thought I was over it, but seeing you again, I realised I'm not... I know I should have told you way back when I might have actually had a shot, but I was too chicken-shit, and you were right – I hide behind my keyboard... but I don't want to hide anymore. And I know I'm too late, but I'm here and he's not. You trusted *me* and not him... so I figured it was worth a shot."

Oh my god.

I clasped my chest with my free hand, pain ricocheting through my body as I listened to him pour his heart out.

All for nothing...

My heart was well and truly claimed. It was owned... branded... *possessed* by a rock star with a beard and a mop of blond hair.

There was no coming back from that for me.

I'd read about it in books where a character would declare that they had been ruined for all others to come, and that's how it was for me.

There would be no others. Not now, not ever.

Tyler squeezed my hand lightly as he carried on. "I know you're with Jasper now... if he turns up I guess..." He sighed. "You know, princess, it would have never taken me this long to find you."

I gave him a sad smile. He was right, but it wasn't Jasper's fault that his talents were singing and playing rather than being a cyber genius.

The two couldn't be pitted against each other in that respect – if it weren't for Ty being on board with my plan, I was certain that Jasper would have been able to find me within a week – if not less.

I stared at our hands and tried to breathe deep and long.

"I guess I can't really blame the guy, I've made it near impossible for him..." He rubbed his free hand over his eyes in what appeared to be frustration. "I don't even know where I'm going with this. I just wanted you to know that you had options... you could come home with me now, Hannah. I could make you happy, we could be happy together."

He gripped my hand a little tighter and I looked up at him, his eyes were pleading for me to hear him.

But I couldn't.

I knew there was truth in his words. If I was honest with myself, I too had felt something for my best friend's big brother once.

It had probably been nothing more than a crush, but I could see it...I could see what he had pictured in his head.

If Lotte and I hadn't gone to that club two years ago... if Parker had never set his sights on her, if I'd never met Jasper... *maybe* there could have been something between Tyler and I.

In a different place at a different time.

But I *had* gone to that club that eventful night. I'd met Jasper and my whole world had been tipped on its head.

This wasn't a different place at a different time.

This is here and now.

My life had been irrevocably altered when Jasper had walked his light into it, and there was nothing and no one that could change that for me now.

Only him.

"Tyler..." I choked out.

His face was a mask of pain and disappointment,

and I realised that my expression was telling the story for me.

"I'm so sorry," I whispered. "I hate that you feel this way when I can't return your affection."

He shook his head quickly. "No, please don't feel bad.... I knew coming here, that it wasn't going to go my way, but I still needed to try. I couldn't leave it as a 'what if'. There's too many of those in my life and I didn't want you to be another one."

We sat in silence for a moment.

I squeezed his hand lightly. "I can see it, you know... I know I could have had a good life with you."

He smiled back at me – not in a hopeful way, but as though he was happy that I could share his vision – as unattainable as it may have been.

"You've always been so good to me, Tyler, and I love you – I do. But it wouldn't be enough. I know what love should be like now, how it grows and grows. He's my whole life, Tyler. Every part of me is so intertwined with every part of him now that I can hardly remember what it was like before he came along."

He opened his mouth to speak and I stopped him, already having guessed what he was going to say.

"Don't get me wrong, because I know you're about to lecture me for losing myself in a man, but it's not like that... it's like I've *found* myself through him. He brings out the best in me – or the worst, depending on who's telling the story, but that's the thing... he wants me to be *me*, no matter what that means. No matter if I'm crazy, or wild, or emotional… he wants to see it all – and at the end of it, he not only still loves me, but he loves me even more."

He really is an incredible man.

He sighed in defeat. "I'm really happy you have him."

I snorted. "Are you?"

He thought about it for a moment. "Yeah, I am. I'd never deny you happiness, Hannah. You deserve to be loved for the incredible woman you are." He squeezed my hand before letting it go and getting to his feet.

"You don't have to go…"

"We both know I do."

I'd never felt so horrible in my entire life. I knew it wasn't exactly my fault, but that didn't stop me from feeling like I was crushing someone I loved.

"Ty…"

"I'll be fine, I swear, Han. It's not like I ever had you, ya know? But I guess in a way it still feels like I lost something."

"I never want to lose you from my life, Tyler."

He shot me a cocky grin that didn't quite reach his eyes. "I'm like AIDs; you couldn't get rid of me if you tried, princess."

I knew he was hurting right now, but his smartass comment made me think that everything would eventually be okay between us again.

"I do have one question…"

"Shoot."

"If you feel that way about him, and you know what the two of you have is real... then what are you doing here?"

I opened my mouth to answer, but snapped it shut again when no words came out.

Truth was, I didn't have a good answer for that question.

"I... I guess... I think I just needed to be sure."

His hand turned the handle. "You know, Hannah, you're worth it, you know that? You deserve to be happy... and I think the sooner you stop tiptoeing around like the ground is going to fall out from underneath you, the better."

Long after he'd gone I was still sitting there, thinking about the words he'd spoken, and the words I'd spoken too.

"He wants me to be me, no matter what that means. No matter if I'm crazy, or wild, or emotional... he wants to see it all – and at the end of it, he not only still loves me, but he loves me even more."

I couldn't have been more truthful, but it did beg the question, why was I here?

CHAPTER 43

Jasper
Day Eighty-Eight

I DIDN'T KNOW how much longer I could go on without her.

Parker shrugged me off his shoulder and I fell onto the couch like the sack of shit I was.

I was drunk as hell.

I'd done well these past few weeks, I hadn't touched a drop. I'd searched high and low, following every avenue I could think of... but I was running out of ideas and places to look, and apparently tonight, I'd decided that checking the inside of a bottle was my best bet of finding her.

Hannah was even haunting my dreams. Always

hovering just out of reach. I hadn't slept more than three solid hours in a week.

I was losing.

"I'm not…" My head fell back against the armrest. "Not… win… winning…" I slurred.

"That's a fucking understatement," Parker grunted as he attempted to hoist my legs up onto the couch so I was lying down.

I looked up at the roof and the whole room spun.

"Woah." My head rolled around in circles.

"Put a foot on the ground – it'll help, trust me."

I nodded, but I couldn't seem to figure out how to make my foot move.

I laughed at my pathetic attempt.

"Jesus Christ, J."

"So… cran-cran… ky…" I managed to get the words out.

Parker grabbed my foot and sat it on the ground.

"Be… tter," I mumbled as my eyes began to close again.

"Get some sleep," I heard Parker say, only this time he sounded concerned, not pissed off.

I heard him leave the room, and I dug around in my pocket for my phone, I needed to hear her voice.

As always, the line rang and her voicemail clicked in. I didn't even know what I was saying, but I knew I was hurt. By the time I hung up the phone I had tears streaming down my face.

The pain only lasted a moment before I slipped into a deep sleep.

———

I knew I was dreaming. I knew damn well that I wasn't lying on a beach with Hannah at my side.

"I've always loved the beach," she sighed, *"the ocean air... the crashing of the waves. Hell, I even love the sand."*

Every time I looked around the view disappeared. It was like I was back there, but at the same time I was nowhere.

I was watching myself and Hannah talking... talking about her grandmother and the time she spent with her in the summer.

I could feel myself waking from my dream, but my head was screaming at me to stay – that this was important. I'd dreamt of Hannah every single night since she'd left, but this was different somehow – this wasn't a nightmare. This was a new dream.

"I can still picture every piece of mismatched furniture, every trinket and book..."

I could see light seeping in around the edges of my subconscious as I fought to stay asleep – to stay on the beach with her.

"We could make our own magic."

I felt myself grin at my stupid line.

"... she made me feel like I belonged in this world when other people told me I was crazy..."

The cottage... her safe place... the place where she felt like she could be herself...

"Promise me we'll go there one day."

"One day," the words flew out of my mouth as I sat bolt upright on the couch where I'd fallen asleep in my drunken haze.

My head pounded something chronic at the sudden movement, but I didn't care. I knew where she was.

I did it.

I figured it out.

I win.

CHAPTER 44

Jasper
One and a half years earlier

THE SUN WAS BEATING DOWN on us as we lay, legs intertwined, on a lounger on the sand next to the sea.

Han had complained about the tan lines she was going to get from my legs on top of hers, but she still hadn't bothered to move. She was in her most relaxed state when she was touching me. I'd figured that out pretty quickly. I knew she thought I was a touchy feely kinda guy, and with her I was more than happy to be, but the reason I always had my hands on her was for her benefit.

Mostly anyway.

I glanced over at her and smiled.

She was content. *Happy.*

I'd figured out this past week that the beach was Hannah's happy place. She'd never said as much but I could tell by just looking at her. She was glowing.

We'd spent every morning down here by the ocean, and she was like a little kid at Christmas every single day.

I reached out for her face and gently swept away the lock of blonde hair that was stopping me from seeing her pretty eyes.

"Tell me a story."

She smiled, and her eyes sparkled. "Okay... what kind of story do you want me to tell you?"

"A true one..." I murmured. "About you... and the ocean."

"Okay."

She turned onto her side so she was facing me, our faces only a few inches apart.

"I've *always* loved the beach." She sighed. "The ocean air... the crashing of the waves. Hell, I even love the sand."

I could hear in her voice just how much she treasured it.

"My grandmother would take me for a month every summer since I could walk. My parents would put me on a plane and she would pick me up. From the little airport it was about an hour's drive to the small seaside village. She had a sweet, modest cottage there, up on the cliffs that overlook the sea. It might not have been big in size, but it was so rich in character that place; I can still picture every piece of mismatched furniture, every trinket and book..."

"It sounds incredible."

"It was – I bet it still is."

"How long has it been since you were there?" I asked her gently as I took her hand in mine, sensing there was more to this story that was yet to unfold.

She was quiet for a moment. "She's been gone eight years." Her voice cracked at the end and it damn near broke my heart. "I haven't been back there since."

"That sucks, baby, I'm sorry."

She traced her finger over the shape of my nose, but didn't speak.

"So, who owns it now?" I prompted. "Maybe we could rent it for a while?"

If she was this happy here, I could only imagine how happy she would be there, where her love of the sea started.

"Me," she whispered quietly. "I own it."

"*You* own it?"

She nodded timidly and bit down on her bottom lip.

"Well then let's go." I attempted to push up and off the chair.

Giggling, she grabbed my hand again and dragged me back down.

"I can't. I'm too scared that I'll go there and because she won't be there, the magic will be gone, and it won't be the same."

"We could make our own magic." I winked suggestively, suddenly desperate to get her there.

She laughed and shook her head.

"It's the only place I've ever felt like I was truly home, like I was one hundred percent safe and accepted. I trusted my nana with everything... every secret, every story... she made me feel like I belonged in this world when other people told me I was crazy or a silly little girl. I don't want to lose that security she gave me – even though she's gone."

"She sounds like a real good lady."

"She was. I've always been a runner, Jasper... things get hard or scary and I run. When I was a teenager and I ran, I always went to the same place... to my nana." She sighed. "Don't get me wrong, my parents are great too, but I always shared a special bond with Nana. No one could really explain why – I guess she was just my person. Nobody else had ever understood me like she did."

I reached around and lightly gripped the back of her neck, dragging her slowly towards me. "I'll be your person, if you'll have me."

"You already are," she breathed before pressing her lips to mine. "You get me."

"Promise me we'll go there one day," I murmured against her soft mouth.

"One day," she promised.

I would be holding her to that.

I needed to go there, to see her there. To make

sure she knew that I could give her the security her grandmother had.

I'll make it happen.

———

She emerged from the bathroom wrapped in a towel, her hair wet and her face bare.

This was my favourite version of Hannah.

She looked incredible all dressed up, her hair styled to perfection and her face flawless – that was usually thanks to Charlotte... and I knew that that was how she preferred herself.

But not me...

What you saw was what you got when it came to Hannah's personality, so I loved it when she looked the same way – it just made more sense to me.

She stopped in her tracks when she saw me still sitting where I was when she'd gone into the bathroom. I'd been instructed to 'get dressed in something nice' so we could go out to eat.

I had other plans.

We weren't going out tonight.

We were staying in.

"What the hell happened to getting dressed?" she demanded as she sat her hands on her hips.

I grinned. I loved it when she got all irritated with me. She was so fucking hot when she was pissed off.

I shrugged. "Changed my mind."

"Care to enlighten me?" she asked, her tone thick with attitude.

My grin stretched bigger. She was such a fiery little thing.

"Thought we'd stay in."

"Jasper, you know I wanted to wear that new red dress... and you promised." She stomped one of her feet.

"Did you really just stamp your foot?" I tilted my head sideways.

"Ugh, don't mess with me, Jones, you know damn well you're winding me up."

"If you wanna wear the red dress, wear the red dress."

"But you don't want to go anywhere." She gave me the big puppy-dog eyes and sexy pout.

"Oh, baby, that face is not helping your case." I ran my tongue slowly over my bottom lip and watched her squirm.

"Jas—"

"Put the dress on," I instructed.

"Bu—"

"Put the dress on." I enunciated each word to emphasise how serious I was.

She nodded, with her eyes still fixed on mine and dropped the towel to the floor.

I'd been expecting her naked, not clad in the sexiest fucking fire-engine-red underwear ever known to man.

"Jesus, woman," I growled.

The strapless bra fit her like a glove, and her lace, see-through underwear exposed more of her ass than should have been legal.

Her dress was laid out on the back of the chair next to the bed, but I couldn't just let her walk by.

Not looking like that.

I snagged her hand and tugged her to me.

"Fuck the dress," I growled.

She let herself fall into my lap.

I dropped my mouth to her neck and kissed along her sensitive skin until she shuddered.

"You can wear it tomorrow," I murmured.

"But I'm hungry..." she argued, her voice nothing more than a breathy moan.

"Oh, baby." I chuckled. "By the time I'm done with you, you won't even remember what day it is, let alone be worried about your stomach."

"Don't go making promises you can't keep."

I claimed her mouth with mine in a kiss full of heat and want.

She pulled away first, her lungs gasping for air.

"You know I *never* make a promise I can't keep," I whispered hoarsely against her ear.

She knew *exactly* what I was capable of doing to her; she just liked to poke the beast for fun.

She could poke all she liked... this beast knew how to poke back.

"Prove it."

"Thought you wanted to go out?"

"Tomorrow..." she breathed as I lowered my lips to her collar bone, kissing and nipping as I went.

I chuckled against her skin.

She was so easily persuaded when it came to sex.

I made my way down to the sexy-as-hell bra she had on.

"Matching again," I observed.

"You know me... always after the D."

I smirked as I reached around to undo the clasp. It popped open in my hand and I tugged it from her body before tossing it across the room.

I rolled one of her hard nipples between my fingers and she moaned, throwing her head back with the sensation.

She was rocking in my lap now, grinding herself shamelessly against the hard length in my shorts.

Her hands were threaded in my hair, tugging lightly in rhythm with her movements.

I ducked my head to her chest, sucking her hard nipple into my mouth.

"That's *so* good."

I pulled away and found her mouth again with mine, our lips crashing together in a flurry of passion and need.

Her tongue slipped into my mouth and I heard myself moan.

She was so god damn seductive.

My dick strained against the fabric of my boxer briefs and I shifted, trying to ease the pressure.

Hannah reached for the band of my board shorts

and tugged open the velcro fly, pulling them down as she went.

She freed my hard length and stroked it up and down in her soft grip.

My hips thrust up on their own accord as she worked my dick in the space between us.

I reached around her, cupping her from behind.

There was a sense of urgency in the air as I slipped a finger inside her wet centre.

She let out a cry of pleasure as I worked her the same way she was working me.

"Lose the underwear, BG."

I slipped my fingers out of her as she rose up onto her knees, shimmying her underwear down to her knees.

She giggled as she awkwardly manoeuvred them all the way off.

God damn...

She was waxed bare before me, and I couldn't help myself. I dragged her towards me, burying my face between her thighs.

I licked and sucked as she writhed above me, moaning and gasping.

"Jasper..." she breathed.

I pulled away and lifted my hips, freeing myself from my shorts.

She sank down onto me in one fluid stroke, knocking the breath right out of me.

"Hannah," I choked out as she bounced up and down, her rhythm relentless.

Considering only two minutes ago she looked hell bent on scratching my eyes out, this was an incredible turn of events.

"Slow down, baby, or the closing ceremony will be starting early." I grabbed her hips and gripped them tight, forcing her to slow down.

Her arms wrapped around my neck, pulling my face against her chest.

Her movements changed to a grind as she slowed down, her hips pulsating against mine.

"Oh god," she whimpered.

I knew she was close. Her whole body shuddered every time she hit that sweet spot deep within her.

"I'm... going... I'm..." Her words cut off with a moan as she came, pleasure washing over her.

She leaned into me, her orgasm sucking everything from her.

I held her hips up and pistoned my hips hard and fast, reaching the brink of orgasm within seconds.

"I'm gonna come," I choked out.

She let out a deep breath as I came hard inside her, shooting spurt after spurt of my seed into her.

Our ragged breaths mingled in the space between us, neither of us able to find words.

"You were right," she finally panted, desperately trying to catch her breath. "What day is it again?"

I chuckled and rolled over, dragging her body with mine. "Couldn't tell you..." I puffed. "Think it ends with a 'y'."

CHAPTER 45

Jasper
Day Eight-Nine

"LOTTE, it's me... I know where she is."

I heard a whoosh of breath escape her lungs. "I'll be right there." The words came out in a rush before the line went dead.

I jogged down the stairs to the front door to unlock it for her. She had a key, but this couldn't wait. I was jumpy as hell and I needed to talk to someone.

She burst through the front door only a moment after I sat down at the dining table, Parker was right behind her by the sounds.

"J?" she called out.

"In here."

She came flying into the living area, her red hair a wild mess around her tiny frame.

"You found her?" she asked, her shoulders rising and falling with the exertion of having run over here. Her eyes were wide and brimmed with tears.

This was the first time I'd witnessed just how affected Charlotte was. She was as beside herself as I was.

"I know where she is."

Parker appeared behind her. "Thank fuck for that. Maybe you two can relax now."

Lotte laughed almost hysterically, the tears I'd seen in her eyes now spilling down her cheeks.

"It's not that simple, not yet anyway."

Parker had Lotte in his arms now, wiping away her tears and hugging her close.

God, I miss my girl.

I was dying to have Hannah close and hold her tight.

"I know where she is in theory, I just couldn't tell you where that location is geographically, even if my life depended on it."

Which it does.

"I think you need to start from the start," Lotte replied softly.

I gestured for them to sit.

"I had a dream... it was like I was reliving a conversation we had when we went on vacation a couple of years back. I could *see* us talking. She was talking about her grandmother and the house she inherited when she died."

"Huh," Park mused. "So getting written off actually did help."

"Oh my god," Charlotte whispered. "The beach house... of course..."

"You know about it?" I demanded. "Do you know where it is?"

I was suddenly hopeful. If Charlotte had heard about the house, then she might have known where it was.

Right now, this was the best shot I had.

She shook her head. "I found the letter from the lawyer... it was when we were packing up to move out of our apartment. She told me about her grandmother and that she'd been left the house, but she changed the subject so quick, I've always meant to ask her about it, but you know, life got crazy and I forgot."

"I never asked her anymore about it either." I rubbed my temples in frustration.

"What do we do now?" she whispered.

"I'll go find a map."

"Fuck that, I'll just ring Tyler." Parker reached for his phone. "We'll see if he can narrow it down."

Shit...

I glanced at Lotte. I didn't want to be the one to say it and risk hurting her feelings, but I was backed into a corner.

I was pretty confident that Tyler was in on

Hannah's plan. People didn't just disappear off the face of the earth like this – not of their own free will.

"Don't." I told him at the same time that Charlotte said, "No."

I looked at her in question. I knew why I didn't want to ring Ty, but I had no idea what she had against the plan.

"I think he knows more than he's letting on," she told me, her tone apologetic. "He's been acting really weird anytime I call, and let's face it, Hannah's a lot of things, but tech-savvy is not really one of them... she didn't do all this on her own."

I nodded. "Agreed."

"Maybe someone else helped her?" Parker offered.

"If she'd had someone else help her, then Tyler would have figured it all out within fifteen minutes and made a real show of it too," Lotte told him.

"Exactly."

She was right. Having my thoughts backed up by someone that trusted him implicitly only reinforced my theory.

"Alright then, Starsky and Hutch," Parker drawled, "if Ty is a no go, then what now?"

I smirked. "Ty isn't the only hacker out there, right?"

"You wanna hire a hacker to hack the hacker?" Parker probed.

"Genuis." Charlotte grinned.

I grabbed my cell off the counter.

"Jasper," he answered on the first ring.

"Hey, Sammy, I need a favour."

"If it's about that damn cat, I don't even want to know."

"Oh c'mon, you love her really."

"Get on with it, Jasper."

Fair call.

"You've still got contacts in the FBI, right? I need you to do some digging..."

CHAPTER 46

Hannah
Day Ninety-One

I SAT the phone down on the nightstand and let the tears all come out.

I'd broken him.

Jasper had never sounded more scared or alone.

That wasn't who he was.

This wasn't who I was.

I wasn't the person that should have been making him miserable. That was the last thing I wanted for him.

It was just another black mark next to my name. There were so many there now that I was sure he was never going to come.

I didn't deserve a man like Jasper Jones.

I looked down at my favourite Exit Strategy t-shirt, now wet from my tears and I nearly vomited.

What the hell am I doing?

I'd ruined everything.

Jasper was hurting, I was hurting, and I was still no surer of myself than I had been when I'd left home.

I rubbed my hand over the small bump that had popped out over the last week.

"I'm so sorry, little peanut, Mama's mucked it all up."

I buried my face in my pillow and cried until exhaustion overtook me and I drifted off to sleep.

I was having one of those dreams where you knew you were dreaming, like you perhaps weren't quite fully asleep.

I'm in my bed...

It was the same bed as I was in right now, but it was different. *I* was different.

I'm younger.

I remember this...

I was eighteen years old and crying against my pillow, my first serious boyfriend had broken up with me over text message while I was away for the summer.

Nana...

My nana had come into the room and sat on the end of the bed.

"Oh, baby girl... please don't cry."

She always got upset when I was.

"Tell me what's happened."

"He broke up with me."

I was sobbing my little heart out.

This was the first broken heart I'd ever had, and it hurt.

Nana shuffled up the bed and gathered me into her arms.

"You know what, this hurts like hell right now, I know it does. But I promise you that you'll be okay... that young man doesn't know what he's missed out on, but do you want the good news?"

"What's the good news?" I sobbed.

"Now you're free to wait for him."

"For who?"

"For the right one. You can't find the right man when you're busy wasting your time with the wrong one."

I could feel myself waking up, the light from out the window was bright behind my closed eyelids.

"Nana..." I murmured.

"He was such a good man. So full of love. He was funny and kind and he always knew what to do to make me smile when times got tough. He was a lot of things, and I miss him every day."

She was talking about my grandfather now, but everything she was saying was true for Jasper too.

He was all of those things.

"I found him, Nana," I murmured as I slowly opened my eyes, "I found the right one for me."

Now I just needed to decide if I was the right one for him.

CHAPTER 47

Jasper
Day Ninety-One

I DIALLED the number that Sammy had spent the past twenty-four hours trying to pull for me.

The contacts that I'd discovered he had in incredibly high places blew my mind. I'd known he was more than qualified to be doing the job he did, but I hadn't expected him to be quite so... competent and connected.

I made a mental note not to call him in the middle of the night about a stray animal ever again.

I hit the green phone button and waited for the ring.

I had no idea how this was going to go, but it was worth a shot.

Sammy's contact in the FBI had said that this guy was one of the best in the business.

Apparently, no one knew who he really was, but I didn't care – if he was good enough to get anything from Tyler, then he was hired, no matter the cost.

"Hello?" a voice answered, it was grainy and distorted, and it was clear that whoever he was, he valued his anonymity enough to use some type of voice changing device.

"Hey, this is Jasper Jones, I—"

The voice laughed, interrupting me. "I know who it is."

Right.

Of course... nothing was safe from these hackers.

"So, do you need me to explain what I want, or do you already know that too?"

"Please, carry on."

"It's my girl. She's taken off in what I can only describe as an extreme game of hide and seek. She wants me to find her.... I need to track her so I can find where she is... I mean, I think she's at the beach house, but I need to know exactly where that is."

"Anyone can do a basic track."

"It's not that simple," I argued.

"But it really is," he drawled. "I'm too busy for this..."

Shit, shit, shit...

"Please," I begged. "It's seriously not that easy, I need help... I think Tyler is helping her hide and the guy's a genius, I'm way out of my depth," I blurted out unhelpfully.

I'm screwed.

This guy wasn't going to help me, and I was going to have come up with another way to figure out exactly where she was.

Fuck.

He was silent for a moment. "Tyler who?" he eventually asked.

I ran my hand through my hair. "Tyler Watson... his sister is a good friend of mine... the bastard knows something, I'm sure of it... if he wanted to find her, he could. He's got mad skills."

There was a light laugh through the phone. "You're right about the 'mad' skills..."

There was silence for another moment while I waited hopefully.

"Ya know what? All of a sudden, I'm not so busy after all."

"Seriously?"

"Seriously."

I grinned.

Score.

I could smell the hidden agenda from a mile away, but I was more than willing to roll with it, whatever it was. "What's your beef with Ty?"

"You just let me worry about our friend Tyler, alright?" He dodged the question.

"Whatever you want... what do I call you, man?"

"Armageddon," the voice answered. "And it's *wo*man."

No shit...

"Armageddon, female, got it," I rattled off the list.

"One hour. Wait for my call."

The line went dead.

Well alright then.

———

"First things first, he's been watching your every digital move. I've diverted the system he had onto a loop, so for now at least, he shouldn't notice, but you won't have long if he's paying close attention."

"I won't need long. Did you find her? Is she at the beach like I thought?"

"She is. I'm sending you her exact location as we speak, and I've tracked the GPS on her phone to piece together the last three months for you."

This chick was good. I was seriously impressed.

With only Tyler's name and the information that my girl had gone missing, she'd put all the pieces together.

"Tyler wiped or hid everything for her, airport security footage, rental car information, CCTV cameras, her GPS... *everything...*"

Bastard. I knew it was him.

"That's kinda creepy."

"He's been watching your every move – well I don't actually think he is personally, but he could be if he wanted to... anyway, he's made the information available to Hannah and up until now she's been able to see everything you've typed into Google, she gets notified every time you write an email, send a text or make a phone call."

Holy shit, well played, barbie, well played.

"Will they know we've been talking?"

If they did, that was going to ruin the plan I had forming in my head.

"Don't be ridiculous, this number is totally untraceable. Right now, it appears that nothing is happening with you, it'll show a few texts every now and then, maybe a few calls – all to known numbers, your email will appear business as usual without showing anything that you're receiving from me and I have your search history on loop, so he'd have to be looking pretty hard to even notice that it's all a repeat, but just to be safe I've thrown in a few new key words."

"This is kind of scary."

She laughed. "What do you mean?"

"You know everything about me, don't you? Every single thing that involves a piece of technology is all there for you to see, isn't it?"

"Yeah, you're right, that would be kinda scary for a civilian to contemplate."

I chuckled.

"Anything in there that makes me look bad?"

"You look harmless enough to me, Jasper."

"Damn." I chuckled. "That's not doing any favours for my bad-boy rep now, is it?"

"I can throw in a few speeding tickets if it helps?" she joked.

"Thanks, but I'm good." I smirked to myself.

"So anyway, back to the start... it looks like she got on a flight, went to Tyler's, from there he wiped all traces of her before she moved onto the house she inherited from her grandmother. She's been there since."

"She's okay?"

"You'll have to find that out for yourself I'm afraid. But right now, I can see she's down in the township, walking around, so I would say she's fine."

Relief flooded my body.

Thank god.

"Thanks, look I've got a few things to sort and then I'll call you back, okay, and we can talk about how I want Tyler handled."

She was silent for a beat.

"Well since we're speaking of the devil... there's more."

I had a feeling I wasn't going to like this part. "Give it to me."

"He went there."

He did what?

"What the hell for?" I demanded.

"Well... you're actually lucky that I found that out, I only know because he wrote himself some type of speech...oh god this is awkward... but it seems that

he wanted to offer himself as an option to your girl...
romantically."

I closed my eyes and ground my teeth together.

I was going to kill Tyler.

"When?" I hissed.

"Just over two weeks ago. He arrived at the house, she arrived later on, they both went inside for about ten minutes and then he left. Alone."

That bastard.

There was no way I was letting him get away with this without at least making him shake in his boots for a few minutes.

"Does he know you've gone through all his shit yet?"

She laughed. "Of course not. That boy is cocky, he's not even protecting himself like he should be, he won't know that I've been in there until I want him to."

My thoughts were going a mile a minute.

I had so much to do already if I was going to pull this plan off, but I was going to have to make one more stop on my travels.

It'll be worth it.

"Okay, here's what I want to happen..."

I hashed out my plan to her, bit by bit and she was surprisingly into it. She even threw in suggestions when there were holes or things I hadn't thought of.

Tyler was in for a rude awakening.

———

"Look, I gotta know, you've got something against Tyler, right? You can tell me, I've got something against the prick too."

She laughed. She'd removed the voice changer back on the second phone call we'd had – she'd probably gone through my entire digital footprint and realised that I couldn't have exposed her even if I'd wanted to.

"Let's just say that he's crossed me one too many times. He's actually been off my radar for a while now – I've had bigger fish to fry, but you came knocking and I wasn't going to give up a legitimate opportunity to settle an old score."

I chuckled. This Armageddon chick, whoever she really was, seemed like a real good sort.

"So he's pretty skilled at what he does then, huh? If he managed to cross you, he must be?"

"Oh he's the best, he really is... but he's gotten sloppy. That's where I get him. I'm meticulous where he's careless."

"He's fuckin' careless alright," I growled.

Making a move on my girl was about the most careless thing that bastard could have done.

"Oh, c'mon now, don't go losing that level head you're known for keeping." She laughed. "You can't really blame the guy. That woman of yours might be a teeny tiny bit loony, but she's a beautiful girl."

I didn't even bother asking how she knew about

my personal reputation or the way Hannah looked – I was clearly out of my depth with these hackers; it seemed they could find out anything and everything they wanted to know.

"Beautiful doesn't cut it."

"She's lucky to have someone that cares about her the way you do." There was a pang of sadness in her voice.

I had a feeling that A, as I'd started calling her, might have been lonely.

"Thank you for this, I seriously can't tell you how grateful I am."

"It's no problem, and you'll pay me well anyway."

I chuckled. "Worth every cent."

CHAPTER 48

Hannah
Day Ninety-Three

I CURLED up into a tighter ball.

Tomorrow.

I reasoned with myself. Tomorrow I'd get out of bed.

Every time I closed my eyes I dreamed of Jasper or my nana. Sleep was either my worst nightmare or my greatest fantasy.

So all I did was sleep.

I miss him.

My mind flashed through the experiences I'd shared with Jasper.

All the moments of passion and love.

I could remember the day we'd finally come out

and told Parker and Charlotte that we were an item. It was the first time I'd said the words out loud to anyone. It was the first day the world knew he was mine.

I'd been so nervous.

We'd snuck around behind their backs for such a long time, I was worried they'd be pissed.

We'd actually gone public, in public before we'd even told them.

Charlotte had turned into a hermit after her breakup with Parker, and Park had somehow managed to be even worse.

He'd stopped making music, stopped going out...

That was why we'd held off telling them for so long.

We were blissfully happy together, while both of our closest friends were miserable without each other.

I sighed.

Thank god they'd found a way back to each other.

Parker and Charlotte had got through that, and we would get through this.

We had to.

CHAPTER 49

Hannah
Two years earlier

"I'M FREAKING OUT." I waved my arms around, trying to air out my body. "I'm literally sweating bullets, Jasper... they're gonna be so mad with us for keeping a secret for so long... OMG what if she doesn't want to be my friend anymore? This is a terrible idea! Let's just go home and live in secret forever." I knew I was rambling, but the words wouldn't stop flying out of my mouth.

I tugged on his hand and tried to lead him away from Parker's door.

"Seriously, woman, breathe. We're telling them today. Park first and then Little Red after. I'm putting my foot down, barbie, I can't go on like this. Lotte pretty much caught you the other night, do you really want to have to lie to her again?"

I looked up at him with big wide eyes. "No, but what if she gets mad at me?"

"She's not going to get mad with you. She's your best friend. I know she's having a rough time right now, but she'll be happy for you, okay?"

I nodded. "Okay."

He opened the door without even bothering to knock first.

"Park?" he called out.

"Living room," Parker replied.

I took a deep breath and followed after Jasper.

I needed to brace myself for this. Not only for telling Parker that Jasper and I were together now, but for the state that Parker was bound to be in.

I'd come over last week and he was not in a good way. The place stunk, he hadn't opened the curtains and he really needed a shower.

I'd been tempted to give him a good earful, to try and pull him out of his slump... but I couldn't do it. He just looked so... *sad*.

Lotte didn't look much better.

She got up every day now, she showered and put on makeup and went to work, but she was like a shell of her former self.

She'd spent about a week in a depressed state, and if I was honest, I didn't know which version I preferred. At least when she was crying in bed she was being honest.

I couldn't understand why she'd broken up with him in the first place. I mean sure, it was a hell of a lot to get used to, but she could've handled it if she wanted to.

I was hoping like hell that one of these days, one of them would wake up and realise that it didn't have to be this way – that they could fix what was broken and get back what they had.

I glanced around the living room.

At least he's cleaned up.

He himself didn't look any better though.

His hair was long and scruffy, and he hadn't shaved in at least a week.

He was flicking through channels on the TV, but he didn't seem to be even looking at what was on; it was almost as though he was looking right through it.

"Looking good, Park," Jasper drawled, tousling Parker's hair as he went past.

Parker gave him the middle finger salute.

"Hey," I said quietly as I followed after Jasper.

"Hey, Hannah, how's it going?" he replied without looking at me.

It had been a little over two months since he and Lotte had split, and he still looked like death over it.

"I'd be better if you'd let me give you a haircut."

He chuckled humourlessly. "Maybe another time."

Jasper patted the spot next to him on the couch and indicated that I should sit.

Here goes nothing.

I sat down next to him and he took my hand in his.

Parker stopped flicking though channels and stared at us from the corner of his eye.

"You guys have something to share?"

"Yeah, man," Jasper spoke. "We're together now."

He beamed at me, and I realised just how important it was to him to be able to say those words aloud.

Parker huffed out a laugh. "Yeah, no shit."

I shot Jasper a questioning look.

He shrugged at me before asking. "You knew?"

Parker turned and looked at us, throwing his arm over the back of the couch. "Of course I knew. You two suck at sneaking around."

I didn't know what to say to that. I thought we'd been doing a great job of keeping our shit under wraps.

A smirk spread across Jasper's face.

"Seriously, she's always over there, J. You never shut the curtains, you're up half the night, and you look at her like the light shines out of her, it wasn't exactly hard to figure out."

"We wanted to tell you... it just kinda... took a while. When we finally got together, *officially*, we decided to keep it to ourselves for a little bit and then, well you know what happened... and it just didn't seem fair to say anything," I explained.

"I get it," he answered simply.

He went back to flicking through his channels.

"You're not pissed?" I probed.

He stopped flicking and glanced at me. "Hell no, I'm not pissed. I'm happy for you guys. You'll drive each other fuckin' crazy though, so have fun with that."

He smiled at me, and it was the first genuine smile I'd seen on his face since the day Charlotte left.

"One down, one to go," Jasper whispered in my ear.

———

"Lotte, you here?" It wasn't really a question. If she wasn't working, then she was here. This was our day off, so I knew she would be home.

"In here," she called.

"We've got this," Jasper whispered to me as he gave me a light shove in the direction of the kitchen.

"Have you got a minute? We need to talk to you."

I watched her freeze and slowly turn around to face us.

"Oh, Jasper..." she breathed, her face a mask of relief.

I felt terrible when I realised that she'd been worried I had Parker with me.

"It's just us." I smiled sadly at her.

"Sure... good... what are you guys up to?"

She turned back to the chopping board in front of her.

"We need to talk something through with you," I answered nervously.

"Shoot."

I looked to Jasper and he gave me a 'you can do it' nod.

"So... we've actually been wanting to tell you this for a while now... but it just wasn't the right time..."

"Just spit it out already."

"We're together."

She laughed, but didn't turn around.

"I'm serious, we're in a relationship."

She dropped her knife onto the bench and slowly spun around to face us.

"You're serious?"

I bit down on my lip and nodded.

Jasper wrapped his arms around me. "I'm serious as hell about her, Little Red."

"Please don't hate me, I was just doing what I thought was right," I pleaded.

"*Hate* you? I could never hate you." She flew across the room and enveloped me in a hug. "I'm *so* happy for you."

"You are?" I murmured against her shoulder.

"Of course I am. I don't know why you hid this from me, but it doesn't matter now."

Jasper chuckled. "I told you she'd be cool."

"I'm *always* cool." She laughed.

"I just couldn't tell you earlier, not when you're having such a hard time..."

Charlotte looked at the floor. "I get it... you don't need to explain yourself."

"So, you're okay?"

"I'll be fine." She smiled, but it didn't reach her eyes. "Seriously, I'm so excited for you, you both deserve to be happy, and I can tell by looking at you that you are."

Jasper kissed the side of my head and then moved around me to give Lotte a hug. "I'll give you girls a few minutes."

"I had a feeling about you two, ya know? I probably would have realised what was going on under my nose if I hadn't been so... *distracted...*" She sat down at the table and I joined her.

"I'm sorry... to start with I tried to just keep it light. I tried to keep my distance from him, but it really didn't work." I scrunched up my nose and Lotte giggled.

"I'm so happy that you're happy. I'm jealous, but happy."

"I wish you weren't hurting."

"I'm sorry that my miserable life meant you had to keep secrets."

"Are you really okay?"

She shook her head and her hands shook. "No. But I will be one day I guess... I have to be."

I wrapped my arm around her and let her cry on my shoulder.

CHAPTER 50

Jasper
Day Ninety-Five

I WOULDN'T HAVE BEEN SURPRISED if he knew I was here already. He was bound to have some high-tech security system running in this place, but I didn't care.

I was pretty confident he wasn't going to pull out a gun and shoot me – so it didn't matter if he knew I was waiting for him or not.

I heard him turning the key in his front door lock and I peered down the hallway, only pulling back when I saw the door opening, revealing the man behind it.

It was him. Even if I hadn't already met him in person, I still would have known.

He's just like Charlotte.

It was the weirdest thing, because in terms of height and stature they were physically *nothing* alike, but his features, his overall *vibe* was exactly like Lotte.

I could hear him in the hallway now. He strolled into the living room and sat something down on the floor with a soft thud.

I grinned to myself. It was ironic really, my hundreds of games of hide and seek with Hannah had really sharpened my senses.

I was a master at this point.

I could hear him in the kitchen now; he had the tap running – getting himself a glass of water if I had to guess.

I moved like a ghost into the living room and sank down silently into an armchair directly opposite where he had just been standing.

If he didn't already know I was here – which I was guessing he didn't, he was about to shit himself.

He came out of the kitchen and glanced over at his ridiculously huge setup of computers and technical kinda shit, his eyes skimming over me as though the chair was empty like it should have been.

His body froze as his brain quickly processed the information that he was, in fact, not alone.

I was right about the glass of water; it fell to the ground and smashed against the hard wood floor, liquid splashing everywhere.

I smirked as his eyes slowly made their way to meet mine.

"Tyler," I acknowledged.

The fear in his face evaporated as he recognised me. I couldn't help the chuckle that escaped my lips. I knew Tyler had fucked with some seriously dangerous people over the years, and judging by the look on his face, I'd be willing to bet my last dollar that he had thought someone had finally caught up with him.

"For fuck's sake, Jasper, you scared the shit out of me."

I shrugged unapologetically.

"How the hell did you get in here?"

"Window."

"You make a habit of sneaking into other people's houses?" He bent down to pick up the broken shards of glass.

"If the need arises."

He glanced at me with a frown, and then disappeared to throw out the rubbish in his hands.

The dude was nervous. He might have been untouchable when he was behind his keyboard, but it was obvious that in real life, he wasn't quite as fearless.

I watched him carefully as he entered the living room again. He was a big guy. I was no wimp, but I was glad I hadn't come here with the intention to kick his ass – I'd win, but I wouldn't get out unscathed.

"So... what brings you here?" he asked in an attempt to act casual.

Don't give me that shit.

I narrowed my eyes at him.

"You already know the answer to that, don't you?"

He froze for a moment before composing himself and shrugging. "You might have to be more specific."

"Cut the shit, Ty," I snapped, my cool façade slipping for the first time since this little dance between the two of us had begun.

That got a sly smirk from him.

I put my calm mask firmly back into place. "Wipe that look off your face."

His smirk dropped slightly.

This was the part where I caught him off guard. He didn't know it yet, but he had company in the hacking department, and if I knew anything about him, it was that he wasn't used to having competition.

"You think you're always on top... that you're... *indestructible*... don't you?"

He frowned, but made no move to reply.

Time to drop the bomb.

"Does the name 'Armageddon' mean anything to you, Tyler?"

His face paled, and I smirked and nodded knowingly at him.

That's right.

He growled loudly and threw himself up to his feet before storming over to his computer.

He was smart alright. The moment that name left my lips, he'd known.

He tapped away for what felt like forever, only muttering the occasional curse word under his breath – I could have told him to hurry up, but I didn't mind actually. I was a patient man, and it would be worth it when he realised the full extent of what had gone down.

I closed my eyes and waited.

The abrupt end to the tapping and the word 'fuck', let me know he'd figured it all out.

I opened my eyes and lazily glanced over at him. He sat, at his keyboard, his head hung in his hands, elbows rested on the table.

"So you know everything then?" he asked, his head still hung in shame.

I paused for a moment, deciding whether or not to feed him some bullshit or tell him the truth.

I went with the truth. "I figured out for myself where she was six days ago."

His head snapped up. "But Armageddon was only in here yesterday?"

That's what you think.

I nodded. "You don't know me very well." I stretched my legs out in front of me and crossed my feet at the ankles. "But I'm the kind of man that sees things through – leaves no stone unturned. When I figured it out, I knew she hadn't done it on her own. I had a hunch about you, but I didn't have the... *skills*... to prove it. That's where Armageddon came in."

"Why haven't you gone to her yet?" he asked, disbelief colouring his voice. I could understand his confusion – I'd spent all this time desperately searching for her and it wouldn't make a lot of sense to an outsider that I hadn't rushed to her side immediately.

I smirked. "I had a few things to organise first. You're my last stop."

I could barely contain my excitement knowing that I would see her tomorrow. But I knew it was important that I kept my head on straight – I wasn't done here yet.

Get through this and then I can go to my girl.

"I'll be heading there as soon as I'm done with you."

I didn't mention the fact that I didn't actually find out her location until Armageddon had hacked into Tyler's server.

The house on the clifftop could have been anywhere. The clifftops near the ocean stretched for hundreds of miles along the coast in this city alone. And now I knew that she wasn't even in this city...

So even though I'd known where she was in theory, it was still like finding a needle in a haystack.

I'd remembered that she'd told me she had travelled there every summer when she was younger, but her description of 'about an hour's drive' from some small time airport wasn't exactly helpful information.

That, paired with the fact that she'd moved around a lot as a child, didn't make for easy hunting.

I could have called her parents for the answer, but I didn't really want to involve them in this. I didn't even know if they were aware that Hannah had dropped off the face of the universe or not.

And that wouldn't have helped me sort out Tyler either.

This had been a much better plan.

"Why are you here, Jasper?" Tyler's voice snapped me from my thoughts.

"You know *exactly* why I'm here."

He swallowed deeply, his Adam's apple bobbing up and down.

I got to my feet and approached him slowly. He mimicked my actions until we were face to face.

"If you *ever* go after my woman again, I will end you. No amount of hacking skills could stop me from finding you and making you pay. Do you under-stand?" I ground the words out.

He looked guilty as hell. Not only that, but he looked afraid. I was pleased to know that falling in love hadn't made me any less intimidating.

Actually, it was quite the opposite where Hannah was concerned. She had softened me in a lot of ways, but when it came to protecting her, protecting *us*, I knew I would stop at nothing.

Now he knew that too.

Most men would have given up at the first hurdle, the second perhaps. But I wasn't 'most men'. I was here. Ninety-five fucking days after she walked out that door, I was here... and I was less than twenty-four hours away from holding her in my arms.

I was going to win.

He sighed. "I won't apologise, because I know you won't accept it anyway, and if I'm being honest with you, and I think it's about time I was, I'm not actually sorry for telling her how I feel."

Well shit.

The guy has some balls after all.

"I do regret going to see her behind your back, and I'm sorry for enabling her to put everybody through this – you especially. I know that I can't understand it entirely until it happens to me, but I've been given a glimpse into what the two of you share, and it's pretty incredible. I know I could never compete with that."

"No. You couldn't," I agreed.

I stared hard at him for a few beats, making sure that he understood my message loud and clear. When I was satisfied with what I saw, I turned to leave.

He caught my shoulder mid-turn. "That's it? You're not going to ask me anything else?"

I just laughed and shrugged off his hand.

"A told me everything I needed to know," I called back as I walked away.

"Exactly. You know I went there, to see her... aren't you going to ask me what happened while I was there?"

I paused and looked back at him over my shoulder. "You're here and not there. That's the only answer I need."

I reached for the door handle.

"What if I slept with her while I was there?" he asked.

I knew he hadn't. I could hear it in his voice. And even if he'd sworn black and blue that he had shared Hannah's bed, I wouldn't have believed him for a second.

Hannah was infatuated with me. Totally and utterly besotted.

As I am with her.

She would *never* do that; she would never risk our relationship that way. I doubted she would have even had the thought enter her mind.

I rested my hand on the handle and looked back at him for the last time.

"You know, man, one day you'll meet the right woman and you'll understand why that question isn't even worth answering for me."

I left with one thing on my mind.

The only thing that mattered now.

Hannah.

CHAPTER 51

Hannah
Day Ninety-Six

I TRUDGED up the hill with the paper bag of fruit and vegetables perched on top of my shoulder.

It was so damn hot here; I could feel the sweat trailing down my back.

I should have just taken the damn bike.

I'd been a bit gun shy on my bike the past few days.

I'd nearly come off on an early morning ride. The road was wet, and the corner was sharper than I'd anticipated.

A less experienced rider would have eaten shit.

And eaten it hard.

Thankfully, I'd stayed upright and escaped unscathed, if not a little shaken.

That was the last time I'd ridden.

It wasn't as though I'd never come off a bike before, but I'd never had a tiny little peanut depending on me to keep it safe back then.

My life wasn't just about me now.

I stopped and rummaged through the bag for an apple. Of course, I'd forgotten to bring water – I wasn't exactly doing great with looking after myself right now.

My hand bumped the bottle of pregnancy vitamins that I'd picked up from the little pharmacy on my way back from the farmers market.

The doctor had given me a smaller bottle and I'd been holding off on buying more when I'd run out.

I'd thought I would buy them when I got back home.

I was so sure that Jasper would have turned up by now.

I'd imagined him arriving in a variety of different scenarios... we'd be so excited to see each other, and when I would tell him about the baby, half me and half him, he'd be the proudest dad-to-be in the whole world.

But it had been too long. Ninety-six days was a long time, and I needed to face the harsh reality that he might never find me.

He might never come.

I needed to figure out what that meant for me.

For us.

I munched on my apple as I contemplated my options. My feet were killing me by the time the cottage came into view.

I balanced the bag in one arm as I dug around for the key in my pocket.

I pushed the door open wider with my foot and took a deep breath. This place still smelt the same as it always had, it was calming to me.

It'll all be okay.

The timber had a warmth to it that filled my body with a sense of tranquillity.

I must have been missing Jasper more than usual, because today, I could have sworn *his* scent hung in the air.

My body longed for his, my mind struggled to function without him, and my heart ached so badly I wasn't sure how it was still beating.

I dropped the bag onto the counter and headed for the small bedroom that I'd used as a child.

I dug around in the drawers and pulled out the grey jersey of Jasper's that I had taken with me from our house.

I brought it to my nose and inhaled deeply.

His scent was faded now, but it was still there, if I breathed it in for long enough I could still imagine he was here with his arms around me.

I sat down on the foot of the bed and reached for my cell phone.

I pulled up the number for my voicemail and hit call.

I hadn't heard anything from him for a week and I had a dreadful feeling in the pit of my stomach that I might have gone too far...

That he might have stopped looking...

I listened as the automated voice informed me that I had no new messages. I hit the key for the saved folder and put the phone up to my ear.

The message had been left at two o'clock in the morning. I could tell he hadn't slept. His voice was pained, and he was drunk as a skunk.

"I'm hurting, baby... I'm hurting so bad... I don't know what to do, Hannah, what if I'm not worthy? What if I can't do it? I *need* you, barbie girl... god, I miss you." The line cut off, but not before I heard him let out a sob.

Tears fell down my cheeks. That was one week ago.

He's given up.

How can I do this to him?

What the hell am I doing?

I glanced around the small room – my safe place – and it hit me just how stupid I'd been.

I didn't need him to find me.

He already had. He'd found every piece of me that I'd kept hidden and he'd carefully unwrapped it and made me see that it was okay to be me.

He was my safe place.

He loved me for my quirks. He wanted me exactly how I was.

Tyler was right.

I am worth it.

I grabbed my suitcase out of the closet and hastily emptied the contents of the drawers into it.

I was attempting to squeeze the zip closed when I felt the change in the air.

"You going somewhere, baby?"

I closed my eyes for a moment, trying to decide if this was another dream or if he was really here this time.

He'd come for me so often in my dreams, but whenever I got close enough to touch him, he'd disappear, and I'd wake up in tears.

I dropped the case and turned around, ever so slowly.

There was no one there.

A lone tear rolled down my face.

"Time to wake up," I sobbed to myself.

"No, it's time to come home." He stepped into the doorway and my heart sped up in my chest.

God, he was so gorgeous. He looked different this time. He'd cut his hair; it wasn't super short, but it was nowhere near the length he'd had it when I'd left. And his beard... it was *gone*, in its place, golden, groomed stubble that looked *incredible* on him.

I can smell him.

This was the best dream I'd had yet, even though

it would be over soon, nothing and no one had ever looked this good.

I nodded. "It *is* time to go home."

He stepped towards me.

I held up my hand to stop him. "No, please, just stay a little longer."

He smirked and stepped closer again.

I closed my eyes and waited for the inevitable – the moment I would wake up and be alone again.

"I plan on staying a long time, forever if you'll have me."

He was so close now I could smell the mint on his breath before it disappeared with a whoosh.

I kept my eyes closed tight, trying to hold on to the fantasy for as long as I possibly could.

I shuddered as I felt the warmth of his hands in mine. He was *touching* me, and I hadn't woken up.

"Hannah, open your eyes and look at me," he demanded softly.

I shook my head. "You'll disappear."

He chuckled, and the sound filled my body with heat.

"I'm not going anywhere, baby."

I took a deep breath.

May as well get it over with.

I opened my eyes slowly.

He was still there, in front of me.

Down on one knee.

"Holy shit," I breathed. "Get up, what are you doing?" I tugged his hands. "Oh my god, you're really here. You're actually here, Jesus, you look *so* good. I thought I was dreaming... I can't believe you found me... you shaved your beard..." I was rambling now, but I couldn't make it stop.

"Hannah, can you stop talking for five seconds?" The commanding tone he used caused my mouth to snap shut. "I'm kinda in the middle of something here."

Oh my god...

Is he...?

Holy shit.

"Okay, but you don't have to get on one knee," I blurted out. "Sorry," I mouthed as I realised that I was doing a shitty job of being quiet.

He chuckled and shook his head. "You don't know how happy I am to see that you're still my chatterbox, barbie."

I grinned at him. "I am," I promised. "But I swear to god, if you don't get up off that ground, you'll never hear the end of it."

He slowly got to his feet, a cheeky grin on his face. "I thought I'd better do it the right way."

I snorted. "The right way? What part of any of this has been done the right way?"

"Touché." He chuckled. "Now are you going to shut up long enough to marry me or what?"

My heart thumped in my chest as he wrapped his arms around my middle and pulled me against his firm body.

I sighed and nearly cried in relief at having him here with me.

This wasn't a dream.

This was real.

He's here.

He came for me.

I shrugged. "I guess so. It's not like I have anything else planned."

He laughed, but tipped my head up so he could look into my eyes.

"Seriously though? You'll marry me?"

He looked legitimately worried that I might say no, and my heart broke for him. That was never what I wanted to happen. I never wanted him to second-guess my feelings for him.

"Yes, Jasper Jones. I'll marry you *anywhere, anytime.*"

He laughed gleefully, almost like a child, and I smiled as I imagined our child laughing like that one day.

He rested his forehead against mine. "God, I missed you," he breathed.

"I missed you too, I was coming back... I made a mistake. I'm so sorry I put you through thi—"

He caught my lips in a kiss, cutting off my rambled apology.

My body flooded with warmth at the familiar contact, the smell and the feel of him.

It was everything I'd been missing and everything I'd ever need.

I kissed him back with every pent-up emotion that I'd had these past few months, until we were both left gasping for air.

"I have something for you." He pulled the bright-pink box out of his pocket. "I know it's a bit of a traditional gesture, and I know you've already seen the ring, but I'd really like to be the one to put it on your finger."

I didn't say a word, just held up my left hand to him.

He slid the huge pink stone into place on my long finger, and the victorious look on his face was enough to let me know that he wasn't about to hold a grudge against me for leaving him.

We stayed like that for the longest time, him looking at my hand, me looking at him.

"We need to talk about... something..." I finally broke the silence.

He shook his head in disagreement, his eyes still lingering on his ring on my finger.

"Jasper, we really do."

I was desperate to tell him he was going to be a father, and I needed to apologise to him for causing him to miss the time that he had – not that anything much had happened other than me puking every morning.

"No, we don't," he told me firmly. "I'm not going to lie to you and tell you that I didn't have moments where it hurt like hell."

"I got your messages," I cut in. "I know I hurt

you."

"I knew you were getting them."

"How?" I demanded.

"We'll get to that, baby, I promise."

"You got my messages, so you know I was hurting. And god I missed you, but I understand what you were thinking, I *know* why you left."

"I was wrong," I butted in.

He laughed. "For God's sake, woman, just let me talk."

I scrunched up my nose and did my best to be quiet.

"You needed to make sure you were safe with me, that you could trust me to keep you, am I right? You needed to figure out for yourself that I'll never leave you... that you were worth having, right?"

I nodded, tears filling my eyes. He knew me so well, I'd been so foolish to test him and myself like this.

"This is your safe place, Hannah, you glow here. I can see that. But you glow with me too. I'll *never* hurt you. I swear on my life, I'll never make you feel like you need to be anything other than you. Hell, I promise I'll never *want* you to be anything that you're not... I adore *you*. I love everything about you, baby, even when you're driving me bat-shit crazy, I still wouldn't change a damn thing. I love you, *because* you're you."

"Jasper..." I breathed.

"You can trust me, Hannah Montgomery; I'll

spend the rest of our lives proving that if I need to."

"You don't."

"But I *would*," he promised. "I'd do anything it took, I'd find you anywhere."

"I'll never leave again."

He kissed my forehead, his lips lingering. "I know you won't."

"I was coming home."

"I can see that." He smirked, looking at my stuffed-full suitcase. "But we can't leave just yet."

"I know. I need to tell you something first."

"I know everything, baby, *everything*, it's a long story, but I'll tell you it all."

I smiled at him and wiggled free of his arms. "You don't know this. Nobody does."

He watched me curiously as I went into the bathroom and emerged holding a small cardboard box.

"I got you something." I stood in front of him, nerves fluttering in my stomach.

He reached out and took the box from my outstretched hands.

Ever so slowly he lifted the lid.

I swear I could hear my heart beating as he gazed into the box.

He was silent for so long I was worried he didn't know what he was looking at. I was about to tell him what it was and explain what it meant when he spoke.

"I'm gonna be a dad?" His voice cracked.

I nodded, the tears flowing again.

Damn hormones.

He pulled out one of the sticks that I'd peed on – there were three in there along with one of the pictures I'd been given at the ultrasound.

I had to be certain.

His eyes were wide with wonder as he stared at the two pink lines.

He reached into the box and lifted out the ultrasound image.

"Holy shit, that's a baby."

"You're gonna be a dad," I whispered.

"When?" He shoved the picture back in the box and then dropped the whole box onto the bed before grabbing me and reaching for my stomach.

"There's a little bump," he whispered as he ran his hand tenderly over my sensitive skin.

"I'm about three and a half months along."

"I put that in you."

His words sent shivers though my body. He was so primal, so raw and rugged.

When Jasper gave you something, he gave his everything.

That's what I had, I had *everything*. His whole heart, his mind, his body... and the only time I'd ever have to share him would be with our baby – *babies* if Jasper had his way.

It was the best feeling in the world.

"You put that in me," I confirmed. "Thank you, Jasper. Thank you for finding me, for loving me... for giving me everything, even when I don't deserve it."

CHAPTER 52

Jasper

"PUT THIS ON." I threw the light-pink dress I'd picked out for her onto the bed. It was still in its garment bag and I didn't have a clue if it was the right size, but Charlotte had assured me it would be perfect.

Lucky she's only got a tiny bump.

We certainly hadn't planned for that.

I had to refrain from fist-pumping the air and dancing around like an idiot at the thought of the baby growing in her belly.

I'd never been as proud of myself as I was in this moment.

I found her.

I helped create that.

That's my baby.

"What is it?" she asked me.

"A dress. You'll look fucking incredible in it. If you want to do your hair or makeup, go for it, but not too much." I grinned. "We've got somewhere to be... I'll wait for you out front." I bolted for the door of the room before she could ask too many questions.

"Jasper – what the hell?" she called after me.

I shut the door to the living area behind me and took a deep breath.

I'm gonna be a dad.

I didn't think Hannah would have been able to say anything that could have shocked me after these past few months, but once again, I was wrong.

The fact that she had been packing her bag to come home only made the whole thing that much sweeter. If I hadn't found her, she would have found me.

That's how our relationship, our *marriage*, would work. I'd have her back, and she'd have mine.

Always.

Exactly how it should be.

I ran my hand through my hair and grinned like a loon.

I hadn't even noticed that Charlotte had come inside the house.

"Jasper...."

Our eyes met, and I saw that she had a smile like mine plastered across her face.

"You're having a baby?" she whispered, her eyes glistening with tears.

I held my finger up to my lips in a shush gesture.

"We're having a baby," I whispered back with a nod.

Charlotte did some crazy type of celebration dance that made me laugh louder than I should've.

I pointed at the door. "Out, before she sees you," I hissed.

She grinned huge at me and headed for the door. "You need to put that on," she instructed quietly, pointing at the bag she had draped over the back of the couch.

I shook my head at her retreating frame.

I should have known better than to think that Little Red would let me get married in shorts and a t-shirt.

I walked right into that one.

―――――

The sweat under my collar had nothing to do with the heat of the sun beating down on me as I sat down the end of the small stone path, my guitar in my hand as I waited for my wife.

Parker and Charlotte, and the few other people we were closest to, had travelled here with me and were gathered around to witness this moment.

I'd decided early on that I couldn't do this without Hannah's parents here. I didn't think it would have been a deal breaker for her, but morally, it felt wrong.

I didn't want to be the guy that took away a father's chance to walk his little girl down the aisle.

I could still remember the first time I'd met Hannah's dad. She'd taken me home for the weekend when we'd been together for about eight months. I didn't really blame her parents for the shocked expressions they were wearing. She dropped quite the bomb on them when she brought home a long-haired, tattoo-covered, wannabe rock star. Thankfully I'd managed to win them over by the end of the weekend.

"Jasper?!" Hannah's slightly panicked voice rang out around the garden.

I gave John, Hannah's dad a nod, and he headed off in the direction we'd heard Hannah's voice.

I picked up the guitar and hoped to God that she'd meant what she said when she told me she would marry me anytime and anywhere.

I'd been madly scrambling to pull this together for the past week. The plan had been forming in my head from the moment I'd figured out where she was.

I didn't want to spend another day of this life without her as my wife.

I didn't want her to commit to me anywhere but here.

I strummed the guitar and plucked out the intro to '*Amazed*' by Lonestar. I'd thought about doing one of my own songs, but it kind of felt like a douche move, singing my bride down the aisle to one of my own tunes. I knew she loved this song and it was a classic; it was a win-win.

She came into view, on her father's arm and I had to dig deep to hold myself together to get through the verse.

She was glowing. Her blonde hair was still in loose waves down around her shoulders and the pink dress I'd chosen for her fitted her gorgeous body like a glove. She had bare feet and she could not have looked more perfect.

She must have figured out what was going on because her eyes were filled with tears.

"Jasper..." she whimpered through her tears as she got closer.

I grinned at her; the sound of my name on her lips was something I'd never tire of.

She stood before me now, tears running down her cheeks.

I sung the last line of the song with my eyes glued to hers.

"Don't cry, baby," I whispered as I held out my hand for her to take.

"I can't believe you did all this."

I got to my feet and passed my guitar off to Parker.

She glanced around at everyone. "I can't believe you're all here."

Charlotte stepped forward tentatively before throwing herself at Hannah.

"I'm so sorry, I know this isn't about me, I just wanted to say I love you."

Lotte was crying now too as the two embraced each other tight.

"I love you too," Hannah choked out between her own tears.

"Alright, that's enough of that, c'mon, legs." Park tugged on Charlotte's arm until she released the woman I was about to marry.

Gypsy stepped forward. "Who gives this woman to this man?"

Hannah's dad looked down at her. "I know I'm supposed to say me, but you have always been like a force of nature and I'm not sure I'm qualified to 'give you away', so instead I'll just say that I love you, me and your mother both do, and I'm so happy you're marrying such a wonderful man – tattoos and all."

I chuckled at the last part.

"Dad..." Hannah whispered, overcome with emotion as her father took her hand and placed it in mine.

"I won't let her down, John." I shook his hand.

"Oh, I know." He smiled before kissing his daughter on the cheek and stepping back to stand with his wife.

I took Hannah's other hand in mine as we stood before my sister, facing one another.

"Now, I've never done this before, my brother here didn't exactly give me much of a heads up, but we all know that we're here today to celebrate Jasper and Hannah and the love that they share with one another."

Hannah beamed at me; her face was the picture of happiness.

"I've known Jasper his whole life, and I've never seen him as happy as he is when he's with Hannah. These two bring out the best and the worst," she giggled, "in one another, and I know it might sound like a cliché, but they really do complete each other. I've never experienced a bond that even comes close to the one they share, but seeing the two of them here today, makes me want to keep looking."

Hannah squeezed my hands.

"Charlotte has something she would like to share with Jasper and Hannah."

Gypsy gestured for Lotte to come and stand next to her, in front of our small group.

I had no idea what she was planning to say – this was as much a surprise to me as it was to Hannah.

"I've known Hannah a long time now," she told us all with a smile. "And she's the most fantastic woman I know. She truly is the best friend a girl could ask for and I can't think of anyone that deserves a man like Jasper more. Hannah, this man loves you so hard. He would literally go to the ends of the earth for you, and I can sleep easy at night because I know that your heart is, and always will be, safe with him. A few years ago, we stayed up late drinking wine and talking nonsense – it was just like any other night, but there's one thing I've never forgotten. You found something that struck a chord with you…"

"I remember," Hannah whispered to her, tears pooling in her eyes again.

"I'm going to read that out now, I don't know who wrote this, but they certainly set the bar for Hannah…"

I dropped Hannah's hands and wrapped my arms around her instead.

Charlotte read from a sheet of paper in her hands. "I hope you fall in love with someone who always calls you back, and never lets you fall asleep making you feel unwanted. I hope you fall in love with someone who holds your hand during the scary parts of horror movies, and burns cookies with you while you're both busy dancing around the kitchen… I hope you fall in love with someone who tickles you and makes you smile on hard days and on easy ones."

I kissed the side of Hannah's head.

"But beyond all that, I hope you fall in love with someone who will never leave you behind, and who will never take you for granted. Someone who will stand by you when you're right, and stand by you when you're wrong. Someone who has seen you at your worst and loves you still. I hope you fall in love with someone who kisses you in the rain, and hugs you when you're cold, and wouldn't have it any other way."

"See, you really are my dream man." Hannah sniffed back her tears and looked up at me.

"You really are, Jasper," Lotte replied, her voice full of sincerity. "There isn't a man in this world that could love my best friend better than you, and I'm so grateful you're here."

I felt myself tearing up now.

"Thank you," Hannah whispered to her as she went back to stand next to Park.

I was grateful for Charlotte too. She was not only a great friend to Han, but to me too. She'd supported me over the past three months even when I was acting like a waste of space.

"Let's move on to the vows. If Parker could bring forward the rings, we'll get started."

It was when she called for the rings – *plural*, that I realised my mistake.

I'd picked Hannah a platinum band lined with small white diamonds, but I hadn't thought about the fact that I needed to get one for myself.

"Shit," I muttered under my breath. "I can't get married without a god damn ring."

"You haven't got a ring?" Hannah gaped at me, her eyes wide as saucers.

I shook my head. "This whole thing was about you – I wasn't even thinking about myself."

Hannah's eyes softened. "It'll be fine... we'll think of something."

"I don't suppose there's a high-end jeweller in this little town?"

Hannah just laughed at me in disbelief.

I'll take that as a no.

I really didn't want to get married with a ring that I wasn't keeping forever, but at this point, anything would have been better than nothing.

I was looking around, hoping for a genius idea to strike, when Hannah got in first.

"Oh, I know... it'll be perfect!" Hannah announced.

She turned and ran back towards the house.

"You want me to go with her?" Lotte's voice whispered from off to the side.

I chuckled. "Nah... she'll sort it out."

"She better not take off again," Parker murmured under his breath.

Charlotte turned to face him, her mouth open to tell him off but I got in before she could.

"First and last dig you'll be having, man," I warned him.

Our eyes met, and a moment of understanding passed between us.

He stepped forward and passed me the box housing the ring I'd chosen for Hannah and shook my hand. "I just want you happy, J."

"I've never been happier in my whole life."

He grinned and nodded his head.

I didn't hold a grudge virtually ever, and I certainly wasn't about to start now; with the woman I loved... my wife and the mother of my child.

Hannah appeared around the side of the house again, a giant grin on her face, so I assumed that whatever she had found in there, she was happy with it.

"All sorted, BG?" I whispered in her ear as I took her hand in mine again.

"It was like it was meant to be." She beamed up at me.

God, I missed her.

"Are we ready for the vows now?" Gypsy smiled at us.

"Second-time lucky." I chuckled.

"You're up first, Lollipop," Hannah whispered. "I haven't had time to think."

I looked at her beautiful face and thought about everything I wanted to tell her. "I had notes, ya know? But I'm just going to wing it instead."

She giggled.

"I wrote down that I wanted you to know that I'll always be here for you, and that I'll cherish you forever, but what I really want to tell you is that I would do *anything* for you. There is no limit to my love for you, Hannah. I've always believed that promises were too easy for people to break, so instead of promising you the world, I'll just show you instead. Every single day is an opportunity for me to prove to you how much I love you... how much I want and need you, and I intend to use every single one of those days doing exactly that. There isn't anywhere in the world that I'd rather be than right here with you, barbie girl, and there isn't a thing about you that I'd change if I was given a choice."

I took a deep breath.

"I love you, my beautiful wife, you are the crazy to my calm, the tonic to my gin and the conditioner to my shampoo," I repeated her words back to her.

She laughed, and more tears flowed down her face.

"I've got no doubt that it will be one hell of a crazy life with you, but I'm all in. A life without you wouldn't be a life at all."

"Jasper…" she whispered.

"Will you do me the incredible honour of becoming my wife?"

"Of course."

I slid her ring into position on her finger.

"You don't know how long I've waited to do that, BG."

We stood motionless, smiling for what felt like forever.

"Your turn, Hannah," Gypsy prompted when it became obvious that we weren't in any hurry.

"Oh, right." She giggled. "So, I obviously haven't had a lot of time to rehearse…"

"Just say what you feel," I encouraged.

She took a deep breath.

"I've always felt a little bit lost in my life, like maybe I was incomplete. The moment I opened my heart and my life to you, that changed. I may not have known it right away – but you complete me, Jasper. You make me feel loved, worshipped and treasured. You're it for me; this is the part of the story where we live happily ever after. You keep me sane and drive me crazy all within the space of forty-five seconds, and I wouldn't have it any other way."

I laughed loudly.

"You're the only person I could imagine spending forever with and the only man I'd ever be willing to give my heart to. I want fun-filled days and sleepless nights. I want lazy mornings and passionate afternoons... I want games of hide and seek and late-night takeout dinners... I want to whip your ass on the motocross track and show you up on poker night... I want *you*, every minute of every day. Will you be my husband?"

She held the ring in her hand out to me.

I smiled at her. "Of course I will, but... there's one more thing, before we seal the deal..."

Her face looked panicked as she waited for what I might say.

"What's your status on cats?"

She shrugged, obviously confused by my question. "Umm, I mean I like them just fine?"

"Good, because we've got one."

She laughed. "Should I even ask?"

Sammy chimed in before I could answer. "Nope, you really shouldn't."

Hannah laughed and shrugged. "Well, alright then."

Too easy.

I winked at Lotte and she laughed.

"Okay... carry on," I instructed.

"You can put his ring on him." Gypsy nodded at Hannah.

She slipped the ring onto my finger and I'd never felt more complete in my whole life.

"Where did you get this?" I looked down at the gold ring on my left hand. It had an ornate pattern around the band and it looked like it belonged in another era.

"Do you like it?" she asked nervously.

"It's pretty damn cool, barbie."

"It was my grandfather's. I don't remember him… he died when I was little, but he sounded like a real hard case." Her eyes shone with love. "I think he would have been a lot like you. I think my grandmother would have loved you, J. I think she would have wanted you to have this."

"You're giving it to me?" I choked out around the lump in my throat.

"Only if you promise to keep it forever."

I swallowed deeply. "Easiest promise I've ever made."

We went through the final ritual of committing ourselves to one another, but the only words I really heard were 'I do'.

"Introducing for the first time, Mr. and Mrs. Jasper and Hannah Jones," Gypsy cried. "You may kiss your beautiful bride."

I dipped her back and kissed her senseless until I couldn't breathe.

"Hey, husband." She grinned up at me.

"Hey back at ya, wife."

We were enveloped in hug after hug from everyone around us; they were all so happy and excited.

I'd never felt so surrounded by love in my whole life.

Hannah started crying again and I took the opportunity to share our other news with our friends and family.

"Oh, hey, everyone," I called out as their chatter died down. "Don't go worrying about my wife and all her crying, alright? Pregnancy hormones are *crazy*."

There was a moment of silence as my words sunk in.

"You're pregnant?" Gypsy gasped.

"About three months." Hannah blushed.

Gypsy enveloped her into a giant hug. "Holy shit, I'm going to be an aunty!"

Everyone had tears in their eyes now, even Sammy looked like he was getting emotional.

"You can all remind me how great it is when I'm fat and dying for a beer." Hannah laughed.

Charlotte, Gypsy and Hannah's mum all gathered around, fussing over her and checking to see how big her bump was.

This was my happy place. Hannah was glowing.

Parker mock punched my shoulder and I reluctantly dragged my eyes from my wife.

"A husband and a dad, huh?"

"Crazy right?" I smirked.

His face broke out into a huge smile and he pulled me in for a man hug, clapping me on the back.

"I'm so fuckin' proud of you, man."

"Me?" I quizzed as we let go of each other.

"Yeah, J, *you*... you were right, she was worth it, and I'm sorry that I had moments of doubting your state of mind, but I'm so stoked you got it done and got your woman back. You, her, your family... that's everything."

I glanced over at Hannah and she was looking right back at me.

She smiled at me and my stomach flipped.

"Ain't that the damn truth."

———

I looked out at the sun setting over the ocean, my wife on my lap, and I'd never felt more content.

"I know the perfect place for our honeymoon."

"Oh yeah? And where is that, husband?"

Husband...

That was never going to get old.

"It's a perfect little spot..."

She turned in my lap so she could look at my face.

"Yeah?"

"Yeah." I nodded. "It's peaceful and relaxing, and you know the best bit?"

She ran her fingers through the hair at the back of my head, her arms draped around my neck.

"What's the best bit?"

"We're already here."

Her fingers froze, and she looked at me with a surprised expression.

"Really? Here? You wanna stay?"

I gestured around us. "Hell yeah I do, does it get any better than this?"

Her face broke out in a huge smile. "I'm not sure it does."

"And I figure, and I could be wrong – but I'm guessing that you haven't exactly been relaxing and enjoying everything that this place has to offer."

She nodded. "You know, I thought it was because Nana wasn't around anymore that it didn't feel right out here... I assumed it would never be quite the same again... but as soon as you arrived, the magic came back."

"I told you'd we'd make our own magic."

She threw her head back and laughed. "You did indeed."

"We'll make our own magic forever," I told her, my voice hoarse.

"Can we promise right now that we'll do one thing?"

"Anything," I replied.

"You shouldn't say anything, what if I wanted you to commit murder?"

"Who am I taking out?" I chuckled.

She lightly smacked my arm. "Seriously though, every summer I want to come back here with our kids. I want to tell them stories from when I was little and let my nana's memory live on... I want them to experience everything about this place. Can we do that?"

"That sounds like perfection."

She smiled at me, her eyes twinkling.

It still hadn't entirely sunk in that I was finally here with her – that she was mine to keep.

I tugged on her left hand and pulled it into mine.

I kissed each of her fingers, saving the one that wore my rings for last.

"Do you have any idea how good those look on your hand?"

"I think I just might." She grinned.

"I can't believe you're mine."

"Well you better start believing it, because the second you strolled into my life I was yours, and I always will be, Mr. Jones... forever."

Her hand cupped my jaw as she leaned in and kissed me, gently at first then more deeply and passionately. She moved around, not once breaking our connection until she was straddling me.

I stood up, cradling her against my body and headed off in the direction of the house. "You know what, Mrs. Jones? I can't wait for every moment of this forever."

CHAPTER 53

Hannah
Four months later

WE PULLED up to a huge gate with a giant 'PRIVATE PROPERTY – TRESPASSERS WILL BE DOWNTROUED AND PICTURES WILL BE PUT ON THE INTERNET' sign plastered across the front of it.

Well that's a new one.

Jasper leapt out of the car like an agile cat and strolled towards it – ignoring the sign entirely as he unlatched the gates and proceeded to open them both wide.

I put my window down and stuck my head out. "Hey, babe, I know you like to stick it to the man and all that, but do you really wanna end up with a dick pic on the net?"

He looked at me, then at the sign and chuckled loudly.

"I think I'll risk it."

He jogged back to the car, a bundle of nervous energy and excitement.

I regarded him curiously; whatever he was up to, it was damn important to him, that much I could tell.

My husband didn't get this excited about much, so instantly I felt excited too.

He put the Jeep in drive and drove through the gate without a moment's hesitation.

"Are you sure we won't get in trouble? Isn't this like breaking and entering or something?"

He chuckled. "Nah... trespassing at worst."

I shook my head at his usual blasé attitude.

We weren't on any type of road at all now, and all I could see was bare land all around me as he manoeuvred the four-wheel drive to a destination I didn't have a clue about.

"What is this place?"

He winked at me. "Patience, grasshopper."

"I haven't got a lot of that," I grumbled.

"No shit," he muttered under his breath.

"I heard that."

He grinned at me like a cheeky little boy and my stomach flipped.

I rubbed my swollen stomach and smiled.

I wanted nothing more than for our baby to be just like his daddy.

"Is my girl kicking?" He took one hand off the wheel and slowed down slightly. He rested his big, warm hand across my belly.

"No, our *boy* is behaving just fine."

We still didn't know what we were having. This baby was already giving me grief – crossing its legs so we couldn't see if it was a boy or a girl at our scan.

I was hoping like hell it was a boy. I wasn't sure that I could handle a miniature version of myself. I knew I'd turned out okay in the end, but it had not been plain sailing for a large portion of my life – hell, even now I was doing silly things and making bad decisions more often than not.

Fingers crossed for a boy...

Jasper, however, was certain it was a girl growing inside me.

He chuckled at my insistence.

"Nope, girl... and she's going to have blonde hair and big green eyes like her mama," he replied.

I waved away his comment. "Yeah, yeah, we'll see."

We were still driving, and I was starting to get restless. I'd always hated surprises and that hadn't changed in the least.

"Where the hell are we?" I demanded.

"Put your window down."

"Jasper, I—"

"Just do it, for God's sake," he cut me off with a laugh.

If he didn't look so damn hot when he laughed I would have whacked him. These pregnancy hormones were really making me ragey lately, and he was always provoking me – nothing had changed there.

I put down my window. "Now what?"

"Now breathe it in. Take it *all* in, Hannah."

I did what I was told – for once. His excitement was infectious, and I wanted to know what the hell this was all about.

I rested my head on the frame of the window and gazed out at the long, green grass.

I took a deep breath and then I understood.

"The ocean." I smiled and turned to look at him. "Where?"

He grinned again.

We turned abruptly then and headed off again, faster now.

I heard the faint squawk of seagulls and knew that we were getting close.

"Close your eyes," he commanded.

My eyelids fluttered closed.

The car bumped beneath me. I could smell the ocean air even stronger now.

"Keep them closed," he instructed as we slowed to a stop.

I nodded as he killed the engine and I heard the slam of his door as he got out.

I listened carefully, attempting the near impossible task of hearing Jasper move.

I jumped at the click of the handle as he opened my door for me.

"Can I open them now?" I asked hopefully.

"What do you think?" he murmured sarcastically.

His hand brushed mine as he unbuckled my seatbelt.

I trembled slightly with anticipation.

"C'mon, baby." He took my hands in his and tugged me from the car and to my feet.

The sun warmed my skin instantly and I sighed. There was no place like the beach in summer.

Jasper moved behind my body and clasped his hands over my eyes.

"Just a few steps," he whispered.

I stepped forward three times, he angled me a little to the right and finally we stopped.

"You ready?" he asked quietly. He was nervous by the sounds of it and that made me nervous too. I fed off Jasper's moods and more often than not, I relied on him to keep me calm, but right now he was making me jumpy.

I nodded.

He uncovered my eyes and I blinked a few times.

I glanced around slowly. We were at the beach alright. I was standing right where the grass met the sand.

There was nothing but sand, sea and bare land everywhere I looked.

It was beautiful.

"What is this place?"

"This is a private beach; about three miles of uninterrupted bliss."

"And all this land?"

"There's too much to even count," he replied.

"Do you know the owner? I knelt down to touch the golden sand. "He must be loaded," I thought aloud.

"Oh, he's loaded alright." He chuckled. "More money than sense."

I laughed.

"And there's one thing he's absolutely obsessed with."

I picked up a handful of sand and let it run through my fingers. "Yeah?"

"Keeping his wife out of harm's way."

I let out a very unladylike snort-laugh and got to my feet.

"Sounds like Parker," I joked as I brushed the sand from my hands.

Jasper didn't answer me.

I looked up at him and he was giving me a look that said 'exactly'.

What?

Realisation hit me.

He didn't...

"Parker owns all this, doesn't he?"

"Technically... yes." He leant back against the front of his jeep and crossed his arms across his chest, a victorious smirk playing on his lips.

I narrowed my eyes at him. "What does that mean?"

He beckoned me to him.

I turned when I reached him, leaning my back against his front.

He rested one hand on my belly and pointed down the beach with the other. "You see that red peg way down there, where the sand and grass meet?"

I narrowed my eyes to spot it and nodded when I did.

He turned the other way. "And that one down there?"

I nodded again, spotting it quicker this time.

He pointed out two more red pegs which were out amongst the long grass. The four of them made a square, of which we were currently inside.

"I see it. It's a square."

He turned me in his arms. "This is our block."

Oh my god.

He was giving me a home by the sea. He was giving me my safe place.

"It's ours?" I whispered, desperately hoping I had heard him right.

"Every last blade of grass in that square belongs to us," he confirmed.

I felt tears welling in my eyes – I was so damn hormonal.

He wiped away the moisture from my cheeks. "Don't cry again, baby, please," he murmured. "You are my forever, Hannah Jones, and this is where we'll build our home, where our children will grow and learn... you'll drive me bat-shit crazy right here in this very spot... this is where *our forever* will live."

That did it. The waterworks started up all over again.

"And you know what?"

"What?" I choked out.

"I think Cat is really going to love it out here."

I burst out laughing.

Jasper loved that cat almost as much as he loved me.

And that only made me love him all the more.

EPILOGUE

Jasper

I BURST out into the waiting room where our friends and family were all seated, or in Parker and Charlotte's case, pacing the room anxiously.

I could feel my pulse racing and a fine layer of sweat had broken out over my body. This birthing baby's business was way more of a thrill than performing.

They all looked at me expectantly.

"It's a boy!" I announced, my voice full of pride.

I have a son.

I was instantly enveloped in a bear hug from my best friend.

"Congrats, man, I'm so happy for you." He

clapped me on the back and got out of the way. Charlotte was waiting not so patiently for her turn.

"A boy!" she cried. "How's my girl doing in there?" she asked as she squeezed me with more force than a woman her size should have been able to manage.

"She's incredible," I gushed. "She's just trying to get him to feed and then you can come in."

She beamed at me, her face glowing with her own pregnancy. "I can't wait to meet him."

It was then that I heard my favourite noise in the whole world.

Her laugh.

My mother-in-law appeared in the doorway, holding hands with one of the three most beautiful girls in the world.

"Daddy!" she cried as she came barrelling towards me.

I scooped her up and kissed her chubby cheeks. "How's my big four-year-old?"

Today was her birthday too.

"Good! Grandma got me ice cream." She beamed up at me, her blonde curls bouncing and her green eyes bright and wide.

"That's so nice, baby girl. But listen, I have some news for you."

She shrieked with excitement. "Is the baby *finally* out of Mama's tummy, Daddy?"

I chuckled. Hannah had had an extremely fast

labour – just under two hours, but clearly that was two hours too long for my little girl.

"Sure is, princess, it's a little boy."

She fist-pumped the air, causing the whole waiting room to erupt into laughter.

"Yuss! I wanted a brother!"

Just like that we're a family of five...

"I know you did, and thank god, your mama was finally right." I kissed the tip of her nose. "You wanna meet him?"

She nodded so fast I'd have been willing to bet that she made herself dizzy.

I looked over at Sammy who was cradling my youngest daughter as she slept. "She all good?" I asked him.

"She's fine, J." He smiled down at the little girl that had the ability to soften even the toughest of men. "Uncle Sammy's got this." He chuckled.

"I really appreciate you watching her for me, Olivia." I thanked Hannah's mum.

She pushed up on her tip toes and kissed my cheek. "Anytime, Jasper, you give that to my baby for me, alright? We'll be out here waiting."

I nodded and turned, desperate to be back with the woman I loved and our new baby boy.

"I'll let you know when she's ready for you," I promised Charlotte – I could see she was dying to see my wife, her best friend... her sister.

She shook her head in disbelief. "Irish twins... you two might just be crazy after all." She giggled.

I couldn't argue with that.

Two babies in eleven months. We were mad alright.

Madly in love...

In love with each other, our family, our friends... our *life*.

Every damn crazy bit of it.

ALSO BY

Love like Yours Series

Rushed – Book 1

Pierced – Book 2

Hunted – Book 3

Chased – Book 4

Love like Yours Box Set – Books 1-4

Rock Games Novels

Paper, Scissors, Rock: Vol. 1

Hide and Seek: Vol. 2

My Heart Duet

My Heart Needs

My Heart Wants

Every Last Beat – The Heart Duet Box Set – Books 1 & 2

Calendar Boys

Mr. January

Mr. February

Mr. March

Mr. April

Mr. May

Mr. June

Mr. July

Mr. August

Mr. September

Mr. October

Mr. November

Mr. December

Calendar Boys Box Set – Books 1-4

Calendar Boys Box Set – Books 5-8

Calendar Boys Box Set – Books 9-12

Standalone Novels

Master Manipulator

The First Rule

ACKNOWLEDGMENTS

As always thank you to the readers, without you there wouldn't have been a 'Hide and Seek' and we never would have got to explore Hannah and Jasper and their story.

Huge thank you to Stacey Broadbent, a fellow author and a great friend who puts up with a lot and is always encouraging and supporting me.

Thanks for always being only a message away.

The fantastic editors at Spell Bound – thanks for making it readable!

Bianca, thanks a heap for keeping it real and dropping what you're reading to get stuck into my latest book. I really appreciate having you on my side!

ABOUT THE AUTHOR

NICOLE S. GOODIN is a romance author and mother of two from Taranaki in the North Island of New Zealand.

In mid-2015, she started to write about a group of characters who wouldn't get out of her head. Her first book, Rushed, was published in mid-2016.

Nicole enjoys long walks on the beach, pillow fights and braiding her friends' hair. She dislikes clichés, talking about herself in the third person, and people who don't understand her sense of humour.

Please feel free to contact her either via her website, email, Instagram, Twitter or on her Facebook page, she would love to hear your feedback. If you're feeling really game, you can even sign up for her newsletter.

9 780473 587772